Titles by Dawn Banks

The Spreadsheet Situation
The Boyfriend Setup

THE SPREADSHEET SITUATION

Dawn Banks

First published by

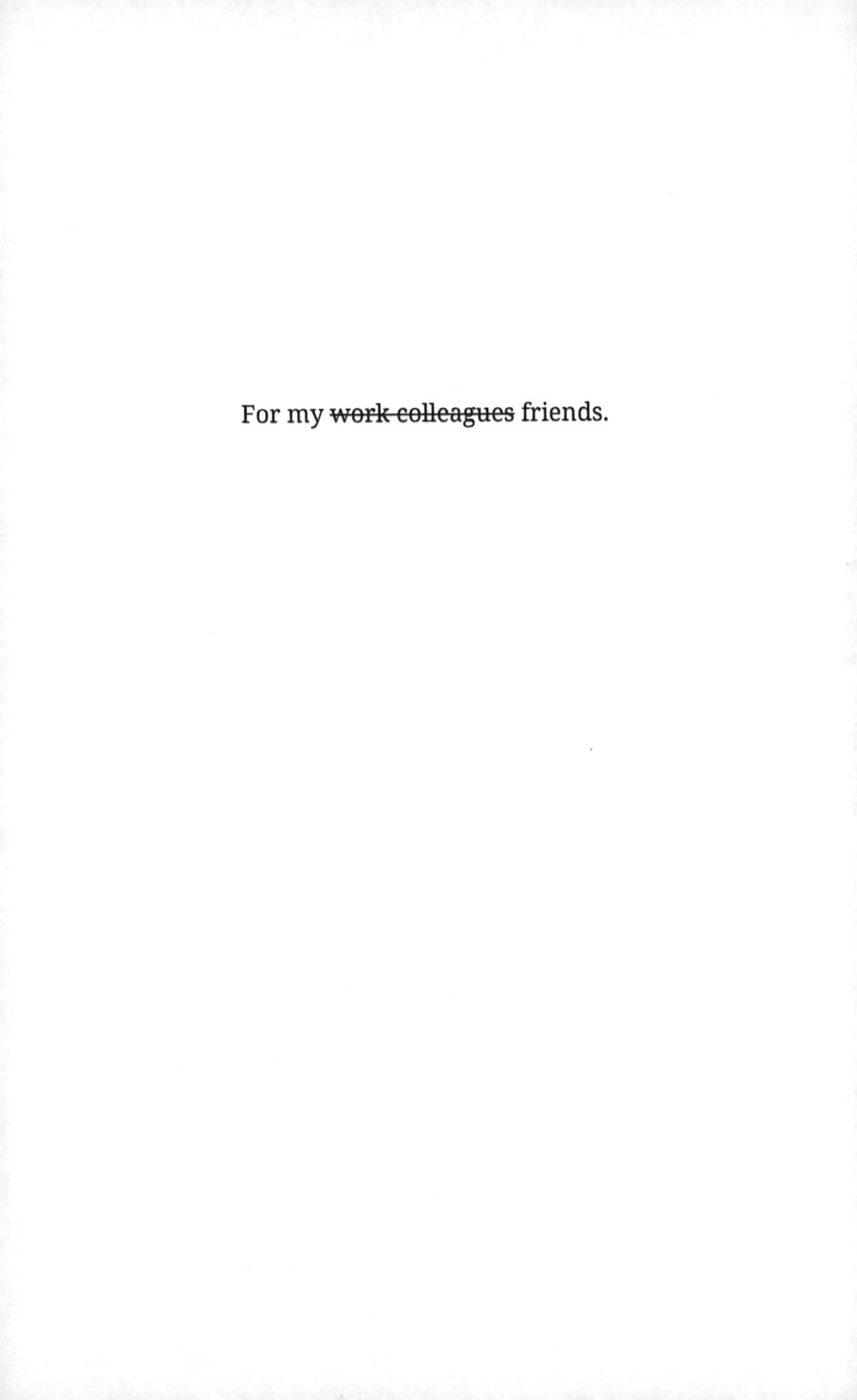

For my ~~work colleagues~~ friends.

Author's Note

This book includes a character struggling with an anxiety disorder and contains scenes with on-page panic attacks. This character's experience of anxiety strongly resembles my own but may not be reflective of others' experiences. There is also a brief description of a character receiving unwanted sexual advances in chapter 16.

CHAPTER 1

"**H**oly shit!" I shout as the timer on my phone blares an alarm and interrupts the intense flow I've been in for the past half hour. My heart thumps from the jarring sound, and I take a moment to breathe deeply and calm myself. I'm the one who set the timer on my phone as a reminder to take a break, so it shouldn't have startled me. But on days like today, when I have the library's end-of-year statistics report to submit to my boss by the end of the week, it's easy to get swept up in the work.

Not that I'm complaining about having such an involved project right now. Summer at a small university library is not the best time of year for a people-person like myself, and throwing myself into projects when my university's campus is mostly empty makes the long days seem less daunting.

I sometimes wonder if I made a mistake taking the job at Cooke University. When I applied for this job, I was charmed by the cute small town and the surrounding mountains, but it's been hard to make close friends here. It doesn't help that I moved to Sapling Grove, Tennessee, without knowing anyone except the people I'd met on my interview. It's not like back home in Pennsylvania where nearly every evening was filled with family dinners with my cousins.

I don't have time right now to ponder the advantages of working somewhere else, though, because I'm supposed to close the library tonight. I scoot my chair back from my desk and hurry out into the study space outside my office, closing the door a little harder than I intend. For a librarian, I'm making a lot of noise, but then, I've never really fit the image of the mousy librarian who only wears her hair in a bun and shushes people while peering over her wire-rimmed glasses. I can't for the life of me pull my hair into anything resembling a successful bun. There's always at least one section of hair that escapes and hangs over my neck like little wisps of scraggly corn silk. I blame the superfine texture of my blonde shoulder-length hair. And forget about being mousy. I laugh too loudly and too often to be accused of anything resembling mousiness.

Even so, shouting obscenities in the library is usually frowned upon. Especially because my office is on the second floor about fifty feet from the balcony that overlooks the main study area. With the tile up here and the vast openness of the first floor, sound carries.

I race through the closing procedure, anxious to get back to my office to wrap up a few things on the statistics report. At least in the summer there aren't usually people hanging around at closing time. Kicking people out of the building makes the process take longer.

After checking the second floor study rooms for stragglers and, unsurprisingly, finding no one, I make my way to the first floor and stop short as I round the corner from the main staircase to the big open study area in the center of the building. Because of course Andrew Brandt, history professor and prodigious flirt, is still here.

I shouldn't be surprised. He's been here every day for the past two weeks, sitting at the table by one of the giant two-story windows with the best view of the campus lake, ever since the air conditioning in his office building went out. My friend Jaclyn has an office down the hall from him and has been texting almost daily to complain about how stuffy it is in there. Summers in Sapling Grove are like living in a 24-hour sauna. It's not that hot here, but the humidity will kill you.

I stop and watch Andrew for a moment. I can't help myself. I'm still not used to seeing him in his summer wardrobe. During the regular academic year, he's always dressed professionally in a buttoned shirt topped with a sweater and nice slacks. But today he's wearing a *Star Wars* t-shirt and a pair of jeans. It makes him look much more boyish than a man in his early thirties should.

The other reason that I can't help myself is that I, Evie Watson, a grown woman, have nothing short of a raging crush on this man. I don't like to admit it, even to myself, but there's really no other way to describe the awkward, heart-thumping feeling I get every time I'm in proximity to Andrew Brandt. I flush, I fluster, and I giggle. It's frankly embarrassing that I'm pushing 30 and am still capable of turning into the same floundering girl I was in high school.

I'll never act on it, though. With everything that happened the last time I attempted to date a colleague, there's no way I would make that mistake again. It's part of why I've kept my distance from Andrew these past three years. Why would I torture myself by spending time with him knowing that even if there were a spark of attraction on his side, it could never happen?

Today, though, he hasn't noticed me yet, so I take the rare opportunity to observe and appreciate the man without risking the usual awkwardness I feel around him. In addition to the casual outfit, it seems like over the summer Andrew must give up on shaving, because he's become scruffier over the past few weeks. Not that the beard he's growing out is a bad thing. It suits him, making him more closely resemble a superhero actor than a history professor. Andrew has sandy brown hair and blue-gray eyes that look like the campus lake after a summer thunderstorm.

Although his usual academia-chic wardrobe hides it well, his summer attire has revealed an even higher level of handsomeness than I thought was possible for this already handsome man. Who knew that under all that cable knit there were arms like *that*? There's no other way to say it. Andrew Brandt is fit.

I shake myself out of my ogling reverie as Andrew leans back slightly from the computer, stretching his arms above his head. His shirt rides up a little, and, yes, my assessment of his fitness was accurate because it's not just his arms that look like he spends at least a little time at the gym. There is a definite tone on that slice of stomach that's revealed.

I have the sudden absurd urge to turn the lights out. Instead, I shout, "You don't have to go!"

Andrew startles, nearly falling out of the chair, but then he looks up at me and grins.

Now *that* is a smile. My breath catches a little as I absorb the full force of it. My face heats, partly because *oh my god* that smile and partly because that's the second time this evening that I've been entirely too loud in the library.

Andrew doesn't seem to notice my distress, though, because he keeps smiling as he shouts back, "Isn't this a library? You're not supposed to shout."

Now he's smirking, and I'm certain he must have heard my loud curse from earlier. That smirk is equally as swoony as his full grin, though, and it must scramble my brain because the next thing out of my mouth is, "I'm in charge tonight. I do what I want."

I have no idea where the extremely confident sounding voice that I'm speaking with has come from, but it's much better than my usual conversational skills when it comes to Andrew. The confidence seems to be paying off, because

Andrew laughs good-naturedly, and suddenly I am walking closer to him with a cheesy grin on my face.

"It will just take a second for me to pack up my things and get out of here," Andrew says as he starts to shuffle the papers on the table.

Before I can think about it too much, I say, "No, that's fine. You can stay. You're a Cooke employee, after all."

Andrew raises an eyebrow. "Are you sure? I don't want to keep you."

I wave a dismissive hand at that. "Seriously, it's fine. I'm not even leaving for a while, anyway."

Andrew smiles again, and my heart skips a beat. "That's good, because I need at least twenty minutes of glaring at this spreadsheet so I can figure out what's wrong with it."

I wonder briefly if he's said that to pique my interest, because solving spreadsheet problems is my superpower, but there's no way he would know that.

"What spreadsheet?" I ask, knowing I sound overly eager.

"Isn't your specialty literature?" Andrew asks with curiosity.

"Sort of. I manage the library's literature collection, but that takes a lot more knowledge of spreadsheets than it does opinions about *Pride and Prejudice*," I say indignantly.

Andrew holds up his hands in a playfully defensive gesture. "Sorry, I wasn't trying to be offensive. I shouldn't have assumed."

He looks sheepish, and I wave away his apology. I've barely spoken more than ten words to him in the three years we've known each other. How would he know that I'm secretly a data nerd?

"Would you like to take a look and see if my spreadsheet is salvageable?" He gestures to the chair beside him, and the look he gives me is so earnest there's no way I could say no. I know he's trying to flatter me, and I'm fine with that.

"Absolutely!"

I suppress a small shiver as I sit because I've never sat this close to Andrew before. I catch a whiff of his cologne, something subtle with a slight spiciness. He turns his laptop toward me then scoots his chair a little closer so we can both see the screen, and I almost perish on the spot. The hairs on my arms tingle with awareness. I take care not to let my leg brush against his as I shift in my seat slightly.

"So tell me what I'm looking at," I say, that confident voice from earlier making another appearance despite my nervously thumping heart.

"You've heard about the General Education Committee's revamping project right?" Andrew asks, and I nod. The committee has been reviewing all the common courses students take during their first two years at Cooke and suggesting revisions to the curriculum.

He continues, "This is the raw data from our pilot study. I'm supposed to get this ready for the committee to review, but...ah...I'm not really a spreadsheet guy."

"May I?" I ask, reaching toward the mouse Andrew's hand is resting on. Our hands brush in the exchange, and I flush at the zap of awareness of how soft his hand feels. I set the mouse down with a thump and scoot my chair a fraction of an inch away from his.

I click through some of the cells in the file and try to hide my increasing horror at the mess before me. This spreadsheet is a nightmare, and it's going to take a lot more than me changing a few formulas to turn this into anything resembling a presentable document.

Andrew nudges me gently with his elbow, and I jump at the unexpected contact.

"Well, Watson? What's the verdict?"

I know my face is doing something unpleasant because Andrew frowns.

"That bad?"

"It's not...the worst spreadsheet I've ever seen."

"But it's almost the worst?"

I hesitate.

"I can take it," he says. There's something genuinely curious in his expression, an openness that scatters all those butterflies I usually encounter with Andrew.

"It's not completely unsalvageable, but it has a lot of problems."

Andrew gestures for me to go on.

"For starters, I don't know what all this is." I select a group of about 50 cells with a mishmash of numbers that don't seem to relate to anything else. "And I don't know what you're trying to do with this set of data, but your formulas all have error messages. Also, have you never heard of pivot tables?"

"Pivot tables?" Andrew gives me a blank look, and I'm worried I've overwhelmed him with my extreme nerdiness.

"Can't say that I have."

"Obviously," I mutter under my breath, but apparently not quietly enough because Andrew laughs, a full bellowing laugh that fills the open study space we're sitting in. I think I might be developing a serious attachment to his laugh because it is doing things to my insides that are not workplace appropriate.

"I had no idea you knew so much about spreadsheets," Andrew says like it's a revelation.

"I really like analyzing data." I shrug.

"Yeah, but..."

"But what?" I furrow my eyebrows at him.

"I don't understand why you like it so much. Give me a good story over a list of numbers any day."

"But that's what data is. It tells a story, and I get to translate it into a narrative that people can understand."

"I'd never thought of it that way." Andrew looks like he's truly rethinking his approach, and I feel a not-insignificant sense of satisfaction for having changed his mind. I have entered Badass Spreadsheet Queen mode, and I like it.

Andrew is quiet for a moment after that, fixing me with a thoughtful look. He rubs his beard and narrows his eyes conspiratorially at me. "You know, this revamp I'm working on could use someone who understands how to find the story behind the data. Would you be interested in working on the project?"

His question catches me off guard. Working closely with Andrew would be, well. Honestly I don't know how it would be. Obviously, I would need to find a way to push aside the silly crush I have on him, but that's not the only thing that gives me pause. There's the email I got this morning for one thing, and the fact that I'm trying not to dive into any unnecessary extra work for at least a year. Plus, I know who's on the committee, and there's one person in particular I would like to avoid. I don't know Andrew well enough to go into details about those things, so I hedge.

"I don't know about that. I've been trying to say no to more things lately because of...well, reasons." I sound less than convincing.

Andrew raises an eyebrow but thankfully doesn't push for more information about my vague "reasons." Instead he asks, "Are you sure? We could certainly use someone with a good eye for statistical analysis. Plus, it's not like you'd be joining the whole committee, just the subcommittee. I think you'd be a great fit for the group."

I almost laugh because my joining the project would mean that more people might find out about my love of data analysis, which would definitely not fit into my year of saying no to extra work. At a small university like Cooke, the better you are at something, the more of it you end up doing, sometimes for little to no extra pay. Cooke is one of those places where everyone wears multiple hats and has about three full time jobs' worth of work to do. It's not that the administration at Cooke takes advantage of workers. It's that the people at Cooke often see the work as something larger than "just a job."

There are good and bad things about that reality. There's a real sense of community here because of it, even if I haven't found my place in it yet. But when you're the kind of person who has a hard time saying no, that "more than a job" mindset can have bad repercussions.

The fact that it's not the whole committee is good, though. I make a noncommittal sound and shrug my shoulders.

"If it changes your mind, the project does come with the sweet benefit of getting to work with me." Andrew winks at me, and my face heats.

Is he flirting with me?

I dismiss the thought almost as soon as it enters my mind. Of course he's flirting. The man has a reputation as the biggest flirt in Sapling Grove. In fact, that's part of what always makes me feel so awkward around him. I can never tell if he's flirting with me because he's flirting with *me* or because flirting is his perpetual state of being.

As much as I want it to be the former, I know it's probably the latter, which is why I try to shake off the ever-rising blush that Andrew brings out in me and instead aim for sarcasm. "Well, how can I possibly say no when faced with such a sweet benefit?"

Andrew looks a little taken aback at my tone. In an earnest voice he says, "No, seriously. You'd be great at it, and I've wanted to work with you on a project for a while."

I know the shock is evident on my face because my jaw drops. I snap it closed, and my mind struggles for traction on the thought that Andrew Brandt wants to work me on a project.

"Ever since you gave that faculty workshop on

collaboration a couple years ago, I've thought it seemed like you would be someone who would be fun to work with on something." The way he says it sounds casual, but sitting this close, I can see a hint of something—nervousness?—in his eyes.

I don't know what to make of this, and I scramble for something to say because those butterflies have come back with a vengeance. What comes out of my mouth is "How much work are we talking about?"

I mentally kick myself because *that was not me saying NO.* But it's too late to take it back because Andrew is filling me in on the details of the committee's goals and the timeline for the project, and I'm nodding because it sounds like exactly the kind of project I like to sink my teeth into.

In an almost trance-like state, I pull out my phone and pretend to check my calendar against the dates for the upcoming committee meetings. I already know I'm going to say yes, though. It's what I do. I don't want to seem too eager, though, so I take my time and scrunch my eyebrow as though there is a question about my availability.

The truth is, despite the looming deadline for that end-of-year report that I've been working on, my summer is looking pretty bland and boring. That is, unless the email I got this morning pans out. I shove the thought aside because I don't want to get my hopes up, especially when I've got an opportunity sitting right here in front of me, being presented by the most attractive man I've ever seen.

"Alright, Andrew. You've convinced me," I say with that weirdly confident voice from earlier in the evening. It feels like we should shake hands or something.

"It's settled, then. I'll talk with the provost and make sure we can bring you on, but I'm sure he won't have a problem with that." Andrew reaches out a hand, and at first, I think we really are going to shake hands, but instead he makes a fist and I realize half a second too late that he's a fist bump kind of guy. We awkwardly fumble through the fist bump, and then my phone shrieks with another alarm. We both jump, and I nearly drop the phone trying to silence it.

When the noise finally dies down, I look at the time and, for the second time tonight, I shout an obscenity into the vast open space of the library. I practically leap out of my chair and start toward the light switches for the first floor study area.

"Sorry, I have to kick you out for real this time!" I shout over my shoulder. "I have somewhere I need to be!"

"No problem," he calls back, and I see that he's already put everything back in his laptop bag. "See you tomorrow!"

Andrew makes his way to the door while I stare after him, a hum of excitement thrumming through me. *I have plans to see Andrew tomorrow.*

I shake my head at the thought and remind myself that it's work related plans.

Glancing at my phone again, I mutter another curse and rush upstairs to close the document I was working on earlier and grab my things. Thankfully I have a few more days before the statistics report is due, since I spent the last thirty minutes of my workday distracted by Andrew.

As I descend the stairs back to the first floor, I take a moment to look back at the table where Andrew and I sat. Even in the evening with the lights out, the library is a beautiful place, with the sun casting a cozy glow around the open study space that takes up most of the first floor. There's a comfortable warmth to the space that reminds me of the way I felt when Andrew smiled at me earlier this evening. That smile that I'm probably going to see a lot more of once I officially join the gen ed project.

I'm hit with a mixture of excitement and nerves as I walk to my car. I hope I know what I'm getting myself into.

CHAPTER 2

I'm late for the movie. I hate being late. It always feels like a moral failure, despite what my therapist says. I had a band director in high school who said that if you were on time you were late, and I internalized the sentiment. Being "right on time" doesn't give me time to catch my breath before an event begins.

So when I say I'm late for the movie, what I mean is that I arrive at the park and make my way to the stretch of grass where Jaclyn and Kylie are sitting on a huge picnic blanket with one minute to the official start time of this week's "Movies on the Lawn." My favorite bar hosts a weekly movie night in the park across the street from them every summer.

This month's theme is "Blast from the Past," and they've

been showing Brendan Fraser movies, which is why Jaclyn, Kylie, and I have been here every Tuesday in May for this run of films. The three of us recently started hanging out more, and when I saw the flyer for the movie series, I talked them in to joining me. It wasn't too hard since we all had crushes on Brendan Fraser when we were growing up. I'll never forget the first time I saw *George of the Jungle*, which is somehow rated PG despite the loincloth.

Tonight's film is *The Mummy*, which I've seen a million times, but I will never pass up an opportunity for a re-watch. I have a special place in my heart for Rachel Weisz's character since we share both a name and a profession.

It seems that most of the people on the lawn tonight have seen this movie before, too, because everyone is quietly chatting as the camera pans across scenes of ancient Egypt and we learn about Imhotep and Anck Su Namun's secret affair. Which is good, because I am practically buzzing with excitement with things to tell my friends this evening.

"Have you heard about the General Education project that Andrew Brandt is working on?" I ask as Imhotep smudges Anck Su Namun's body paint.

"Yeah, a little. What about it?" Kylie asks.

"They're working on the data analysis, and I chatted with Andrew about it this evening." I try to sound nonchalant, even though I'm practically vibrating with excitement.

"Evie, can we not?" Jaclyn cuts me an annoyed look. "I know you love data, but I had an all-afternoon meeting with

Ron. No stats talk. Just mummy fights. Please."

I scrunch my nose at the mention of Ron. Jaclyn is the Associate Dean for the Social Sciences department, and Ron is the Dean. He tends toward pedantry and has a way of "delegating" that seems more like shirking his duties so that Jaclyn has to pick up the slack. Everyone at Cooke cringes when Ron says something in a meeting because it always takes five times as long as it should. If Jaclyn was with him all afternoon, I wouldn't want to cross her tonight.

"I promise this is the only stats talk for the night," I say. She gives me a resigned look, and Kylie gestures for me to go on. "Anyway, like I said, Andrew was still in the library when I was closing tonight, and he needed help fixing some problems on his spreadsheet. I took a look, and it was a mess! So I volunteered to join the project?"

The looks on my friends' faces turn my statement into a question. Kylie frowns with a thunderous expression, and Jaclyn opens her mouth as if to say something and then thinks better of it. They glance at each other, and then turn with alarming synchronization and lock eyes with me.

"How, exactly, does joining this project fit with your year of saying no?" Kylie asks in the way an older sister might. She's older than me by about eight years. Jaclyn is three years older than me. Since Kylie is the oldest of the three of us, she comes across as a bit of a mother hen. I'm pretty sure that's why she and Jaclyn don't get along with each other as well as they each do with me.

"I know, I know. But hear me out. I'm almost finished with the library's stats report, and then I'll have the rest of the summer to work on the General Education project. Besides, he clearly needs the help. He didn't have a single pivot table in the whole workbook!"

"You asked me to hold you accountable with the extra work thing, so that's all I'm trying to do." Kylie pauses, and the look she gives me now borders on pity. "I know helping people is part of being a librarian, but I don't want you to burn out. I worry about you. What if this triggers more attacks?"

I swallow. It's one of the concerns I had when Andrew asked me. Adding extra work like this could send me back into an anxiety spiral like I've been dealing with off and on over the past year. It was Kylie who first recognized what was happening when I started having panic attacks. She and I work closely together because we're both part of the library's User Services Department. I teach library skills in the university's composition courses, and she manages the reference desk and student outreach. I had a panic attack after a class one day, and Kylie witnessed it. She made me visit our campus counselor who got me set up with a local therapist. I don't take Kylie's concern lightly, but I'm not convinced this project will be too much for me.

"I don't think this is going to put me over the edge. A lot of the work has already been done, and Andrew just needs help interpreting the data."

"Besides, why wouldn't you want to work one on one with Andrew Brandt?" Jaclyn wiggles her eyebrows. She knows I have a crush on Andrew and teases me relentlessly about it.

"Jaclyn!" Kylie admonishes her.

"She's not wrong," I say, pinking a little as I picture Andrew's smile for at least the hundredth time since he left the library tonight.

"I'll give you the fact that he is objectively handsome, but that man is trouble," Kylie says with a huff.

I know she's referring to all the rumors about how Andrew takes out a different woman every week. The man certainly flirts like there's no tomorrow. But because I've always been so nervous around him, I haven't had the opportunity to find out for myself if the rumors are true.

"It can't be as bad as that, can it?" I address the question to Jaclyn because she has known Andrew longer than either Kylie or I. They went to high school together right here in Sapling Grove.

"All I can say is that he had a different girlfriend every few months when we were in high school, and his personality hasn't changed much since then. But I also haven't talked to him outside of work in a while, so I don't know. Maybe he's changed." Jaclyn shrugs and then gives me a wicked grin. "He's still hot, though."

I let out a sigh. "Not like any of that really matters. We're working together, not dating, after all. Besides, he wouldn't want to go out with me, anyway."

"Evie Watson! What does that mean?" Kylie demands.

"It means he looks like Chris Evans decided to wear tweed and teach undergrads, and I look like, well, this," I gesture at my hair, which is doing that weird thing it does after a long day at work, poofing out at strange angles from being tucked behind my ears.

"Evie, you are a charming person with a great smile and curves that I'm frankly jealous of, and I wish I had hair as pretty as yours. Don't you dare tell yourself that you're not good-looking enough for someone like Andrew Brandt," Kylie admonishes me.

Kylie may say she wants my hair, but she's convinced her hair is always a mess. She's wrong, of course. Hers is a curly, rich dark brown that's almost black, and she's got a stunning silver streak in the front. I don't balk at her jealousy of my curves, though. I know my assets.

"That's right," Jaclyn chimes in. "Andrew would be lucky to have a girlfriend as sexy as you. You'd make beautiful children."

I roll my eyes at her, although I have to admit that with his blue-gray eyes and my golden blonde hair, our kids would probably be quite adorable.

"Whether or not I want to make children with Andrew Brandt doesn't matter, anyway. You know I don't date colleagues. And...there's something else."

My heart pounds with nerves as I try to drum up the courage to tell Kylie and Jaclyn about the email I got today that could change everything for me. I have no idea how they're going to take the news.

"Well?" Jaclyn asks. In the background, Brendan Fraser runs across the desert, trying to escape a mystical sand storm that takes on the shape of a mummy. My eyes dart briefly to the film, and as the sand mummy screams, I take a deep breath.

"I have an interview for a management position at McDowell University." I say it in a rush, all the words bleeding together.

"Yay!" Jaclyn claps her hands once.

Kylie, on the other hand, looks like I've just dumped a bucket of cold water on her in the middle of January.

"I didn't know you were looking at other jobs," she says quietly.

My stomach swoops, and I feel slightly queasy at Kylie's expression. I should have told her when I applied, but the library is already short staffed, and I didn't want her to worry. We've had a series of people retiring or leaving in the past few years, and now the User Services Department is just the two of us. We make do, but the pressure to do more with less is intense. It's part of why I applied for the job at McDowell. A bigger university means a bigger library staff, and less likelihood I'll burn out because there will be more people to do the work that needs doing.

"It's not a guarantee," I say, trying to take some of the sting out of my announcement, but knowing I sound like I'm apologizing for wanting the job.

Kylie shakes her head. "No. Don't do that. This is really good for you, and I don't want you to ruin your chances by worrying about whether I'll be ok."

I give her a small smile.

"Thank you," I say. "I'm really excited about this job. It's closer to my family, and it's a step up from what I've been doing at Cooke."

"I know you miss being around all those cousins of

yours," Kylie says, leaning over to give me a side hug. "And being closer to them will be nice."

"It would still be hard to leave you all, but it feels like this is the right move for me. It's just an interview, though. I'm not going anywhere yet."

We're quiet for a while, focusing on the movie, occasionally laughing as Rachel Weisz knocks over an entire library's worth of shelving or John Hanna attempts to interpret Egyptian hieroglyphics. But my mind wanders as the images move across the screen.

If things were different at Cooke, if the administration would approve us hiring another librarian, or if my job weren't a never-ending cycle of teaching the same library skills over and over again, I wouldn't have applied. It's not even that I dislike working at Cooke. The people are great, and this new dynamic with Kylie and Jaclyn is making life a little easier. But the inertia of budgets and lack of opportunities to try new things make it hard to want to stay there forever.

"Tell me about the job." Kylie nudges me as one of the American treasure hunters runs away from a hoard of scarab beetles. She's sitting between Jaclyn and me, and leans closer so that we don't disturb Jaclyn who is clearly invested in the movie even though she's seen it before.

I smile, glad that Kylie is at least attempting to be excited for me.

"It's a lot like what I'm doing now, teaching library skills and working closely with students, but it would also involve some management of a group of other instruction librarians." The management side of the job is something that attracted me when I applied. I've always wanted to work in some kind of management or administration in libraries because in addition to my spreadsheet prowess, I like being in charge of things.

"I think you'd be really good at that," Kylie says.

"Thank you," I say quietly, and she gives me a side hug.

"You know," Jaclyn says, startling both Kylie and me. I didn't know she was listening to our conversation. "You could apply for the Director of the Teaching and Learning Center that admin just posted. I know it's not a library job, but it seems like the kind of thing that would be up your alley."

I laugh because I had the same thought about that job. When it was posted, I read the description and for the briefest second thought *This is it. This is what I want to do*. But Jaclyn's right. It's not a library job. Even if I want it, I don't have the qualifications they're advertising. I tell Jaclyn that, and she snorts.

"Evie, this is Cooke University we're talking about. They've hired people with fewer qualifications than you have for higher paying positions than any of us will ever have for years."

I can tell from the look on her face that she's thinking about Ron and his dubious qualifications for his Dean position. I honestly don't know how he got the job. He doesn't have a doctorate, unlike the rest of the Deans, and as far as I know, he's never taught a class in his time at Cooke, which is odd because pretty much *everyone* at Cooke seems to teach at least one class. It's part of that small-school vibe we have going for us. I know Jaclyn would love for Ron to retire so she could step into his role, but the chances of that seem unlikely.

"There's no harm in applying," Kylie says. "Besides, I'd rather you stay at Cooke, even if you're not in the library, than for you to leave."

"Do it," Jaclyn says in a slightly creepy voice, and I let out a loud laugh, which is unfortunate because we're at the scene where Imhotep and Anck Su Namun are finally reunited, and it's not funny at all. A few other moviegoers shoot us a glare, and one person actually shushes us. The three of us devolve into giggles.

It takes us a few minutes, but we get ourselves under control, and while the movie finishes, I mull over the idea of applying for the Teaching and Learning position. The thing that attracted me to the job is that it's a combination of working with faculty and students, which is not unlike what I do now. But instead of teaching library skills in the classroom, the focus is on helping faculty develop new approaches to teaching and connecting students to extracurricular learning opportunities like research fellowships and summer internships. In short, it would mean having reasons to interact with people even over the summer.

I turn my attention back to the last few minutes of the movie, but the thought of the job at Cooke tugs at the back of my mind as the characters literally ride off into the sunset. As the credits start to roll, I come to a conclusion. I turn to my friends and say, "Ok. I'll do it. I'll apply for the job at Cooke, too."

They both erupt in squeals of delight, and Kylie pulls me into a full hug then reaches for Jaclyn and pulls her in, too, even though Jaclyn is not much of a hugger.

"No matter what happens, we've got your back," Jaclyn says, extracting herself from Kylie's grasp.

The warm glow of my friends' support stays with me for the rest of the night, and for the first time since I moved here, Sapling Grove feels a little like home.

CHAPTER 3

The next morning, I get to the library earlier than usual. I tell myself it's not because I'm excited to get started working with Andrew, but it's not a believable lie.

I'm about to go upstairs to my office when I freeze in my tracks, my mouth slightly agape because Andrew is already at his usual table, and it looks like he's been here for a while. It's weird because I don't think I've seen him in here before noon all summer.

"What are you doing here so early?" I ask as I walk over to him. Our interaction yesterday seems to have loosened whatever block I had about talking to him like a normal person, because I'm not feeling jittery the way I used to when he was around. I still reach up to smooth down my hair, just in case it's a mess.

"Evie!" Andrew smiles at me, and I almost stop breathing. I might have made progress on using words around Andrew, but his smile still has the power to make my whole body feel warm.

"I was hoping to catch you when you got here. I stopped by the provost's office first thing this morning to check about having you join the project, and I wanted to tell you the good news. Dobson was thrilled when I said you were interested."

Mike Dobson is the provost. Not to be confused with my boss, Mike Pearce, the Dean of the library. There's also a Mike in the Advancement Office, and another one in Student Success. It's very confusing working here sometimes. Jaclyn, Kylie, and I sometimes joke that administrators at Cooke are contractually obligated to be called Mike, even if it means changing their name.

"That's great! I can't wait to get started," I say.

"Awesome! I thought you and I might be able to work through some more of those spreadsheet pages today so you can work your librarian magic on them. You free this morning?"

I look at my calendar, but I already know that I'm free. I need to do some prep for the video call with the McDowell hiring committee, but the interview isn't until next week. As long as I build in some time to work on it later today, I'll be in good shape to dazzle them. Besides, the way Andrew is beaming at me with excitement is infectious.

"Yes, looks like my calendar is free all day, actually! Let

me run my things up to my office."

A few minutes later, I settle into the chair next to Andrew and open my laptop. Andrew brings up the spreadsheet and turns his laptop toward me so I can see his screen.

"Did you work on this after we talked yesterday?" The spreadsheet looks a little different than I remember it.

"Yeah, I went down the rabbit hole last night and learned how to make a pivot table."

A jolt of happy warmth runs through me, and I grin.

"You learned how to make a pivot table?"

Andrew's face tinges pink, and it is the sweetest thing I've ever seen. I'm sure he didn't look up pivot tables just to impress me, but something in the way he's blushing tells me that was part of it. I don't dwell too much on that and get back to business.

"Tell me more about what you're hoping to find with the data you've collected so far."

Andrew explains that the main goal of the project is to see if any changes need to be made to the general education requirements. These are the classes that every student at Cooke takes, regardless of their major, like composition and algebra classes. Before I came to Cooke, there was a push to increase the humanities courses—art, literature, and history—in the requirements, but right after that changed, the number of students staying at Cooke for their whole college career tanked.

"Dobson wants us to figure out if there's a relationship between the increased humanities requirements and

student retention. I know it looks that way on paper, but..."
Andrew winces.

"But you feel like there's more to the story?"

He looks relieved that he doesn't have to spell it out for me.

"Yes, exactly. I've been cross-referencing the drop in retention with course evaluations from the years since the change, and it's not adding up. Almost all the evaluations for the required humanities courses show high marks and positive qualitative responses."

"That doesn't sound like it supports the retention theory," I say.

"Not at all." He hesitates for a moment, then sighs. "The fear I have is that this data is going to reveal some hard truths about the way some of our professors are performing, so I'm trying to play things carefully. So far, we've only looked at retention for students who had no college credit before starting at Cooke. Dobson's been breathing down my neck about collecting the data on transfer students, though."

I scrunch my nose as I mull over what Andrew's told me. I can probably guess exactly which professors he's referring to. There are a couple of humanities professors who I certainly wouldn't want to take a class from. There's one in particular who doesn't seem to understand why a librarian might need to talk to their students about using our resources, and I do my best to avoid him at all costs.

"I think you're just going to have to collect the data and see what it shows," I say. "Maybe we can spin it so it doesn't sound like we're attacking specific people, though."

"Yeah, you're right. Now that you're on board, I bet we can find a way to make the hard truths a little less hard to swallow." Andrew winks at me. Does he wink at everyone he works with? I'm not sure, but I blush nonetheless.

Andrew clears his throat, and I realize I've been staring at him. I need to stop doing that, but it's hard when he looks at me with those beautiful blue-gray eyes. I turn my attention back to the computer screen.

"Can you share your spreadsheet with me so we can both edit it?"

"Yes, of course," Andrew pauses. "How do I do that again?"

"Seriously, Brandt?" I roll my eyes. "Click the little arrow in the top corner and then type in my name. Now click 'send.'"

"See, this is why I'm glad you're on this project." Andrew looks amused.

"What's so funny?"

"Nothing. You looked so annoyed that I didn't know how to share the file."

Something in the way he says it makes me wonder if he actually knows how to share a file and is trying to get a rise out of me.

"Well now that we've got that lesson out of the way, I'm going to fix some more of your formulas."

Andrew laughs, but turns to his laptop, too.

We work in relative silence for a while. At first, I'm hyper-aware of every minor adjustment he makes in his seat and the accidental elbow grazes as one of us reaches for a pen or a piece of paper. But after a few minutes, the proximity becomes comfortable enough that I relax. I nudge Andrew every now and then to ask about a specific data table, but for the most part, I'm focused on looking through the spreadsheet and familiarizing myself with the data. In fact, I'm so absorbed in the work that when Andrew puts his hand on my shoulder just before noon, I jump.

"Sorry," he says with a small laugh.

His hand is still on my shoulder, and I am fighting to ignore the heat of his palm seeping through my sleeve. If he can hear my heart thumping, I hope he thinks it's because he startled me and not because the direct contact is lighting a fire in me.

"I'm getting hungry. Do you want to go for Indian food? My treat." His tone is calm and cool, like there's nothing unusual about the fact that he's touching me and asking me to lunch.

That flustered feeling he's always given me rushes back, and I take a second too long to answer.

"You do like Indian food, right?" He sounds unsure, his eyes creased with concern.

I force myself to take a breath and clear those damn butterflies that keep taking up residence in my stomach. The lunch I packed today will keep until tomorrow.

"Yes! Of course!" My voice is overly bright as I try to make up for the awkward silence.

"Great," he says, his face instantly brightening as he flashes me another of those heart-stopping smiles. "I'll drive."

I am in Andrew's car, and even though there's a console between us, it feels closer and more intimate than sitting next to him at the library table. It's an automatic transmission, but he keeps his hand on the gear shift between us, and I wonder if he learned to drive with a manual transmission. I watch as his fingers gently flex around the shifter, and my mouth goes dry. I force myself to look away from his hand.

The car is meticulously tidy. There's not a speck of dust on the dashboard or a cache of fast food cups in the passenger side footwell. It smells like him, too. That same clean, spicy scent that I noticed yesterday. There's a languid sexiness to it, which is probably why my brain jumped to images of his hand flexing like that on my thigh.

By the time we get to the restaurant, I am sweating.

I practically leap out of the car, and Andrew gives me a funny look but doesn't say anything.

He holds the door for me as we walk into the restaurant. I am greeted with the scent of cardamom, turmeric, and garlic.

"Hello, Andrew!" The woman behind the host station greets him. She's in her early sixties, and her eyes are rimmed with laugh lines. The way her face lit up when she saw Andrew tells me that he's here all the time.

"Priya! What's good today?"

"Nani's samosas are on the buffet," she says with a wink.

"Excellent!" Andrew rubs his hands together.

Priya glances at me with kind eyes then looks pointedly at Andrew. "And who's your new friend?"

My stomach plummets at the word "new" as I remember my conversation with Kylie and Jaclyn last night.

How many women has he brought here? I want to ask.

"Priya, this is Evie. Evie, Priya."

We shake hands, and she gives me an assessing look.

"Evie. It's nice to meet you."

"Likewise."

There's something in the way she said my name that gives me a chill, but not in a bad way. Like there's more going on here than I'm fully aware of. I don't have time to figure out what it is, though, because Priya is showing us to our table and taking our drink order.

"I've never been here," I say once she's gone.

"Really? It's my favorite restaurant. Priya and my mom have been friends for years, and I practically grew up here. I even did a stint as a waiter in high school."

Andrew's relationship explains that feeling I had when we were introduced. If she's known him since he was a kid, she might be the kind of family friend who keeps tabs on Andrew. Even so, there was something oddly familiar with the way she said my name, almost like she'd heard it before.

"In that case, what's the best thing to order?"

Andrew grins.

"If you want the full experience, get the buffet. It's a samosa day, which means we've hit the jackpot. Those might be all I get." The look of pure joy on this man's face is almost too much to take in. There's a lightness and ease to his demeanor, and it's contagious.

"Good thing I love samosas," I say returning his grin.

After we fill our plates with some of the best looking samosas that I've ever seen, plus tandoori chicken, saag paneer, rice, and naan, we return to the table. I let out a moan of delight as I take my first bite of food. It's an obscene sound, but I don't care. This samosa is one of the most delicious things I've ever tasted.

"That good?" Andrew chuckles, but I think his cheeks look a little pink as he says it.

"It's absolutely heavenly," I say, taking another bite and closing my eyes with a hum of pleasure.

Andrew coughs, and I open my eyes to see his gaze flit to my mouth. I wonder if I have crumbs on my lips, so I gently run my finger along my lower lip to check. He shifts in his seat and quickly looks back to my eyes.

"So, what does Evie Watson do when she's not saving history professors' asses from certain spreadsheet failure?"

"You mean besides my regular job?"

"Exactly. Hobbies, pets, favorite restaurant?" He takes a bite of food.

"Well, this will be a shocker, I'm sure, but I read a lot of books."

"Ha! I never would have guessed that a librarian would do such a thing," he says, setting down his fork.

"Oh, you'd be surprised, actually. A lot of librarians aren't big readers, but I am. I'm also a cat lady."

I pull out my phone and show him a photo of Titania,

my sweet but excitable calico whom I adopted from the local shelter.

"She's very cute."

"Thank you." I preen a little. "I guess that answers your second category, too."

"Indeed it does. Favorite restaurant?"

"Well, my favorite thing to eat is tacos, so I love going to El Charolais down on the parkway."

"A solid choice." Andrew nods.

"What about you? Hobbies, pets? I already know your favorite restaurant." I know this is just friendly conversation, but I'm dying to know more about how Andrew spends his time, especially after the conversation I had with Jaclyn and Kylie about his seemingly active dating life. Not that I'm going to ask him about that.

"I don't have any pets. And maybe this will be a shocker, as well, but I also read a lot."

"A history professor who likes to read? I can't believe it! What do you read for fun?"

"I usually go for books about spaceships and robots," he says.

"I don't think I would have pegged you for a sci-fi guy."

"Spaceships and robots are an important part of literature." Andrew looks incensed, but there's a note of playfulness to it.

"It just doesn't fit with the image of you I had in my head."

"And what image is that?" Andrew raises his eyebrow.

"Oh, I don't know. I figured you probably sit around in

an armchair wearing a blazer with elbow patches and smoking a pipe while reading presidential biographies or historical texts."

"That sounds too much like work to me. I read to unwind after grading terrible sophomore gen ed essays." Andrew lets out an amused chuckle, then pauses and asks, "What about you? What kinds of books does a former English major who loves spreadsheets read?"

I should have known he would ask. It's always awkward talking about my reading preferences with people I don't know well because I never know how they'll react. But if Andrew can own his love of sci-fi, I can own up to my preferred genre.

"I like to read love stories," I say, trying to sound unflappable.

"Love stories? You mean like Shakespeare's comedies and that kind of thing?" Andrew looks intrigued.

"Uh, no...I mean like romance novels." I say it quietly, and my face heats as I meet his gaze.

"Romance. Interesting. Not sure I've ever read any romance books."

I can't tell from his tone if he's judging me, and his expression isn't giving anything away, either. I get a little defensive.

"Not even *Pride and Prejudice*? Or *A Room With a View*?"

"I thought romance novels were all heaving bosoms and sexy men with Fabio hair and no shirts." He gives me a sheepish look.

"Not even close! Austen basically invented modern

romance! And Forster's novel is pretty obviously a love story." My volume increases with my indignation.

"I'm confused. So you *do* like classics?" Andrew looks genuinely intrigued, and I dial back my exasperation.

"Yes, I like classics and adaptations of classics, but my favorite thing to read are...pirate romances." My face flushes at the confession.

"Pirates, like 'Argh matey, swab the deck.' That kind of thing?" Andrew smirks with a hint of mischief in his eye, but it's not mocking. I get the sense he's enjoying this conversation.

"Yes," I admit.

"What do you like about them?"

It's not the question I expected. After his "heaving bosoms" comment, I thought he'd ask me about the salacious details of my latest read or dismiss the entire genre as smut. Instead he's looking at me with that same open, inviting expression that he had last night when I told him his spreadsheet was one of the worst I'd ever seen.

The grip of embarrassment dissipates, and I give him my biggest smile.

"I love the yearning and the conflict resolution. If I could only read one plot for the rest of my life, it would be rival pirates who fall in love despite everything working to keep them apart. As long as it has witty banter, I'm here for it."

"That does sound like fun."

"It *is* fun. And don't get me wrong, the sex is good, too."

The whole restaurant seems to go quiet, and I realize with a start that I've all but shouted that last bit. I cover my face with my hands and peek through my fingers at Andrew.

"Oh my god," I whisper.

"You know, for a librarian, you're not very quiet," he says.

I burst out laughing.

"Do you think anyone heard me?" I ask between laughs.

Andrew snickers and looks around the restaurant. A few people dart their eyes away from our table as he turns.

"No, I think you're good."

He's obviously lying. They probably heard me across the street.

We lock eyes for a beat, both of us struggling to hold back smiles. And then we both lose it, devolving into giggles. In that moment, one thing is clear. Getting to know Andrew is going to be a lot of fun.

After that, we eat lunch together every day.

It's surprising how easily we've gone from practically strangers to fast friends. And friendship with Andrew is better than I could have imagined. Not only is he kind and considerate; he has a way of putting people at ease that makes talking to him feel effortless.

He also seems to know everyone in Sapling Grove. Almost everywhere we go, someone says hello or asks after his grandmother.

On Friday before we leave for the day, he asks to see my phone. I reluctantly hand it over with the home screen unlocked, unsure why he would need it. He taps a few keys, then hands it back.

"Text me this weekend, and we'll plan ahead for lunch next week."

I look at my phone. The messaging app is open, and there's a message from me to a new contact. All it says is "Evie's number," but then my phone vibrates with a notification.

"Andrew Brandt loved your message."

I'm so flustered, I don't say anything, just stare at him with my mouth hanging slightly ajar.

He holds out his hand to fist bump me, and I return the gesture on autopilot.

"Catch you Monday," he says as he turns toward the front door.

I stare after him, wondering again where the line is between friendly and flirty.

CHAPTER 4

I'm still in bed when my phone buzzes the next morning. The cat is curled up next to me, and it's brighter in here than I expect for an early Saturday. I check the time, surprised at how late I've slept. I open the message app and smile as I read Andrew's text.

ANDREW: What are you reading this weekend?

I take a picture of the Lisa Kleypas book that's sitting on my bedside table and send it to him. His response is immediate.

ANDREW: Any pirates in that one?

ME: No, but the male main character says the female main character kisses like a pirate.

ANDREW: How does one kiss like a pirate?

ME: I'll let you know if I ever kiss one.

My hands tremble as I send my response. Within seconds, three dots indicating that he's typing appear on the screen. There's something wild and dangerous-feeling about talking to Andrew about kissing. It's not the kind of conversation I would normally have with a guy friend. Reminding myself not to cross that invisible line beyond friendship I change the subject before he can reply.

ME: What about you? Reading any presidential biographies this weekend?

The dots disappear then reappear. When his message comes through, I let out a relieved breath.

ANDREW: Ha! Not today.

He sends me a selfie. His eyes peer over the top of a book. On the cover there's a robot shooting a laser beam at a building. I hardly register the title and author because my gaze snags on the arresting look in his eyes. I can't see the lower half of his face, but it's clear from what I can see that he's smiling.

I bet he *kisses like a pirate*, I think.

I run my hand down my face, irritated at my impulse to go back to that line of thinking. I deliberately do not analyze the background of his picture. I do not need to know if the pillow behind his head is from his couch or his bed.

I'm still mentally kicking myself when another text notification comes through.

ANDREW: So if I wanted to read a romance novel, where should I start?

ME: Are you serious?

ANDREW: Why wouldn't I be serious?

ME: Because

ANDREW: Because?

ME: I'm thinking.

ANDREW: I'll wait.

I stare at the screen, biting my lip, then send him a truthful message.

ME: I can't think of a good reason.

ANDREW: In that case, which romance novel should I pick up this weekend?

ME: I guess it depends on what kind of story you want.

ANDREW: One of your pirate stories, obviously.

I laugh out loud, my heart warming with more than the flutters of attraction that I already had for this man. I send him a pirate emoji.

ANDREW: The best pirate romance you can think of.

I know exactly which book he should read. I open the app I use to track what books I've read and search for one of my favorite titles. I screenshot the entry and send it to him. A moment later, another message appears.

ANDREW: Purchased on my e-reader. Looking forward to finding out what kissing like a pirate means.

I whimper and throw my phone onto the bed, startling the cat. She darts from the bed, claws skittering on the hardwood floor, as I will my mind to stop dwelling on the thought of Andrew kissing like a pirate.

From somewhere in the tangled blankets, my phone buzzes again.

ANDREW: I think you might like this book. It's about space pirates.

Attached is another picture of a book with a spaceship on the cover.

ANDREW: If you read it, we can compare notes at lunch next week.

ME: Ok. Will do.

I don't hear from Andrew for the rest of the weekend, which is good, because it means I don't think about pirates and kissing and Andrew. Or at least, I don't think about them constantly.

By Monday morning, I've mostly stopped thinking about our conversation. That is, until I leave my office mid-morning for a coffee refill.

The library breakroom is a center of activity. It serves as a buffer between the public areas of the library and the offices for our Dean and the Access Services staff—the people who manage processing library materials before they are put on the shelf. There's a long table in the center of the breakroom that functions as both a work table and a communal lunch space. It's common for there to be two or three people in the room throughout the day, even in the summer. This morning is no exception.

June, the head of Access Services, is unpacking a shipment of books at the table, nodding her head along to whatever music is playing through her earbuds. And Andrew is standing at the coffee pot holding one of the mugs from the library's kitchenette. It's a white mug with a pink flower and the words "Library School Didn't Prepare Me for This" in a fancy script encircling the flower. He smiles when he sees me.

"I finished the book."

I give him a quizzical look.

"The one you told me to read."

"Oh! That was fast," I say.

"The historical accuracy was lacking, but the story was good."

Do not ask him about pirate kissing. Do not ask him about pirate kissing.

"I'm glad you liked it," I say, trying not to let my thoughts show on my face. I step closer to him and grab my own coffee cup—dark blue with a white tree. He slides over so that I can fill the mug, but he doesn't move far. He rests his hip casually against the counter, facing me.

"I'm not sure I figured out how to kiss like a pirate, though." He leans toward me as he says it, dropping his voice so June can't hear him, even though I doubt she can. She didn't even look up when I came in here.

"Guess you'll have to read another pirate romance." My mind blares a warning. *Stop flirting. That way lies disaster.*

"Looking forward to it," he says in a way that has me glancing at his lips.

I deliberately steer the conversation as far away from kissing as I can.

"Anything we need to do before the gen ed meeting this afternoon?"

"Just one thing," he says, and for a split second I think he's going to kiss me, but he reaches past me and grabs a sugar packet and a creamer pod.

He dumps the contents of both in his coffee and swirls

them with a stir stick that he produced from out of nowhere. As he walks toward the door into the rest of the library, he turns back toward me. "You coming?"

"Annnnnd, done." Andrew saves the spreadsheet that we've been working on and closes his laptop. "Ready to head to the meeting?"

I nod, and we gather our things and walk toward the door of the library. Outside, I breath deeply, taking in the summer beauty. It's warm but not too hot, and the sun is bright and cheery. The leaves on the trees are that bright green of early summer, and the sky is a brilliant blue with just a few clouds. A light breeze is blowing, and Andrew takes a deep breath, too, as we walk toward the main classroom building for our meeting.

"I love days like this," he says.

"Me, too. Makes me wish we were meeting outside instead of in a stuffy classroom." I smile at him.

"Ooh, yes. Or having a picnic." Andrew is quiet for a moment. "Actually...did you see that Under the Covers is hosting LeVar Burton this Saturday? He's doing a storytelling tour based on his reading podcast."

"That cute independent bookstore that opened downtown last summer? I didn't know that he was coming, but I've always wanted to hear LeVar Burton speak!"

"Want to go with me? I bought a couple tickets a while ago, but the person who was supposed to go with me can't anymore. But we could go and then grab some lunch and have a picnic. The weather is supposed to still be like this." He gestures around us.

I bite my lip, considering for a moment. Is he asking me on a date? That seems unlikely. If it's a date, my answer is definitely no. But eating lunch together and going to see famous people speak is the kind of thing friends do, right? Plus he said he'd bought the tickets to go with someone else, so I would be doing him the favor of using the ticket for the person who had canceled plans. I really would like to see LeVar Burton in person...

"Sure, that sounds like fun!"

"Awesome. I'll pick you up around 10:00." Andrew grins at me, and I give him my address.

We arrive at the classroom for the meeting, and a few people are already here. I nod hello to them. Cooke is a small enough university that I know everyone in the room. In fact, as I look around, I wonder if this is the whole group. Since it's a subcommittee of the larger general education committee, I wouldn't be surprised. In fact, I would be relieved, since that would mean a certain person isn't involved at all.

There's representation from the different university areas on the subcommittee. Katie Price from Biology is here, and Chris Hensley who works with Jaclyn in Social Sciences. One of the many Mikes—Radford from the Student Success team—is also here. As Andrew and I take our seats, Lauren Carver from the math department joins us.

"We're just missing John," Andrew says. "Once he's here,

we can get started."

I freeze.

John? As in John Vance? Shit.

Suddenly I'm not feeling quite as excited about working with this group. I should have asked who else was on it before I agreed to join. I was so focused on working with Andrew on the data analysis that it didn't occur to me to ask about the other members of the group, and I didn't think to check the rest of the names on the meeting invitation.

John is exactly the person I hoped to avoid. It makes sense that he's on this subcommittee. He's in the English department and teaches composition from time to time, and he's been at Cooke for most of a decade.

He's also the reason I don't date colleagues.

The first thing you notice when you meet John is that he's handsome. Like movie star-handsome, with a suave silver fox vibe. That is, until you get to know him. There's a too shiny quality to him that isn't apparent at first. His teeth are a little too white, and his hair is a little too blonde for a man in his 40s. But it's not until you spend more than a few minutes with him that you see that his jokes are on the wrong side of clever and his compliments are all backhanded.

I know because we went on a few dates when I started working here. I was young and starstruck by the glossy older man who asked me out my first week at my new job. But it didn't take long to realize that we weren't clicking. The dates themselves were fine. It's what happened after that instigated the no dating rule.

I close my eyes and breath through my nose, pushing the memories aside and bracing myself for John's arrival.

He saunters in a moment later, looking like his time is more important than anyone else's. His eyes catch mine as he surveys the room, and he frowns. Well, at least the feeling of antipathy is mutual.

"What's she doing here?" he asks with a glare.

"Evie is joining the subcommittee. Dobson approved it two weeks ago, which I emailed everyone about. She's been working with me on the data analysis, and I'm excited to welcome her to the team," Andrew says in a measured voice. If he noticed the glare, he's managed not to acknowledge it.

John sits down with a "Hmpf."

My back goes rigid. I'd been looking forward to this meeting, but now I'm less than thrilled to be here.

As Andrew starts going over the work we've been doing for the past two weeks, I feel the beginnings of a panic attack settle in. It always starts with a buzzing in my ears. I try to subtly take a deep breath because I don't want Andrew or John or anyone else in the room to notice what's going on. I wonder if I should excuse myself and pretend I need to use the restroom so I can do some grounding exercises, but Andrew is saying my name.

"Evie?"

"I...sorry, I blanked for a moment." I try not to look at John.

"It's ok. I was just saying that you had some ideas about the transfer student data, and I was hoping you could explain them to us." His voice is gentle.

"Oh, right, of course." I clear my throat. There's still a buzzing in my ears, and my fingers are trembling, but I do my best to take a deep breath and explain what Andrew and I had discussed about setting up a pre-assessment for transfer students. I keep clearing my throat as I talk so I can mask the deep breaths I'm still trying to take.

"Anyway, that's the basic idea." My voice is breathy as I finish explaining the pre-assessment. I hope no one has any questions for me.

Andrew gives me a confused look then says, "Thanks, Evie. Katie, would you and Chris plan to start working on the questions for the pre-assessment? I'd really like to get this off the ground by fall. I know that's not a very long timeline, but Dobson really wants this done as soon as possible."

Katie and Chris nod their assent.

Thankfully the rest of the meeting is focused on reports from the other committee members, so I'm able to sit and listen instead of having to contribute. Now that everyone's attention is off of me, I take a few deep breaths as quietly as I can. I feel the buzzing and the trembling start to dissipate, but I still spend the rest of the meeting on edge. I don't know how I'm going to deal with John's presence in these meetings. Maybe I can talk to Andrew about changing my role from being a full member to a consultant so I don't have to participate in person.

As soon as we adjourn, I tell Andrew I need to run to another meeting, and I leave the classroom as quickly as possible. I don't actually have another meeting, but I need to get out of here. I return to the library and go straight to Kylie's office. Kylie will know what to do.

Her office is tucked in a corner of the second floor of the library. It's secluded enough that she doesn't get a lot of visitors, and it's easy to startle her if she's not expecting a visit. I've made Kylie jump enough times that we've developed a system of jingling my keys when I'm stopping by unexpectedly. I give my keys a little shake, then knock quietly on her door.

"Hi, Evie!" Kylie doesn't look away from her computer. "I'm wrapping something up. Just a second."

I pace in the space outside her office. Kylie eventually turns in her chair with a smile, but when she sees me, her smile falls.

"What's wrong?"

My lip quivers, and tears pool in my eyes.

"John's on the project," I manage, my voice cracking.

"Oh, no." Kylie motions for me to sit down in the chair in her office. "And you had your first meeting with them today, right?"

I nod. If I try to talk right now, I'll sob. Kylie puts her arm around me and gives me a squeeze. We sit like that for a few minutes, and slowly my breathing steadies.

"Ok, listen. Don't let John live rent free in your head. I know he's an ass, but you are a badass librarian. You've been working your butt off on that data analysis with Andrew, and from what you've told me, it sounds like they really needed you. We're not going to let one asshole professor ruin this for you." Her words are reassuring, but that's not really what's bothering me.

I let out a breath. "It's not so much that I don't think I can do the work. I...had an attack when he came in to the meeting."

"Oh, honey." Kylie squeezes me again. "I'm so sorry."

"Should I tell Andrew I can't do the work after all?"

Kylie's response is all business, which is exactly what I need right now. "No, absolutely not. We're not going to let John have the satisfaction. Here's what you're going to do. First of all, you're going to go see your therapist. She'll know better than I do how to mentally prepare yourself for those meetings." I start to protest, but Kylie fixes me with a stern look. "Second, you're going to keep being your badass self and do the work so well that he won't have any room to complain about anything."

"Ok. I think I can do both those things." I stand up to go back to my office. Kylie stands, too, and pulls me into a full hug.

"You've got this, friend," she says into my ear.

I thank Kylie and go back to my office, closing the door before I sink into my office chair. I usually leave the door open because it gets too warm in here if I close it, but I don't want anyone to stop by to chat. I lean my head back and close my eyes.

Kylie is right. I should call my therapist to talk about this. I haven't had a panic attack in several weeks, actually, probably because I've been saying "no" to more things.

But then Andrew said he wanted to work with me

specifically. I was so flattered by his attention, and honestly, enamored with his smile and his laugh that I said yes without really thinking things through.

I slowly sit up and pull out my phone to make an appointment with my therapist. If I wait, I know I won't actually make the call. I chat with the receptionist for a few minutes, but there aren't any immediate openings that work with my schedule. I make an appointment for next week, and as I hang up the phone, I let out a long sigh. At least there aren't any more committee meetings between now and my appointment, so hopefully I won't have another panic attack before then.

CHAPTER 5

It's one of those mornings when nothing seems to go the way it should. I wake up an hour late because the sound on my alarm clock is turned down. I curse, startling my cat, Titania, who is the likely culprit. She has a penchant for messing with dials.

The late wake-up puts me in a rush, and I scramble through my morning routine, muttering curses under my breath as I try to do everything at two-times speed. In the shower, I almost forget to rinse the conditioner out of my hair, remembering only after I've turned off the water. Once I rinse my hair, I turn the water off again and towel off. I grab some clothes from my closet, hoping they coordinate with each other.

I get to the kitchen to make breakfast, but when I start

my coffee grinder it makes a horrible whining sound, which can only mean one thing. There are no coffee beans. I open the pantry to get more, but there's no coffee bag in the usual spot. I slap my hand to my forehead as I remember that I ran out yesterday and meant to stop by the coffee shop around the corner after work yesterday.

I gather my purse and work bag and walk to the coffee shop. I'm dreaming of a savory asiago bagel and a latte as I stand in the long line of people waiting for their morning caffeine fix. When I get to the counter to order, the barista gives me a sympathetic look and says he just sold the last of the bagels. I grumble internally and opt for a biscuit sandwich instead, even though I know that any time I get a biscuit here it takes an extra ten minutes. I've never been able to figure out if they bake the biscuits fresh when they're ordered, but they taste like they're straight from the oven.

Fifteen minutes later, with my coffee and biscuit in hand, I'm finally in my car about to head to work, but the refuel light comes on. I bang my head once on the steering wheel, wishing I could go back in time and start this morning over. I estimate how much gas I likely have, and while I could probably wait until after work to refuel, with my luck this morning I'd end up having to call roadside assistance. The nearest gas station is in the opposite direction of the university, but it can't be avoided. I drive the extra five minutes out of the way and fill up the tank.

I hate starting my workday frazzled, but it's extra frustrating today because I have my video call with the

McDowell hiring committee this morning. I arrive at the library with barely enough time to find my copy of the job ad and my notebook. I straighten the things on my desk and click the link to the video call, hoping that the interviewers won't notice my harried state this morning.

It turns out I didn't need to worry about being late because ten minutes later, I'm still in the call's waiting room. I wonder if I mixed up the days, so I check my email for the hundredth time. There's nothing new from anyone at McDowell, and today's date is clearly marked more than once on the invitation. I debate whether I should call the library director's office to see what's going on. I don't want to appear unprofessional, but this seems like an excessive amount of time to sit in the waiting room.

When another minute ticks by, I dial the number at the bottom of the invitation email. The phone rings and rings, then goes to voicemail. I leave a quick message for the director and let her know I'm in the waiting room.

Out of nervous desperation, I try calling again almost immediately. After two rings, there's a beep, and I think I'm getting routed to voicemail again. But then, thankfully, someone answers.

"McDowell University Libraries, Michelle speaking."

"Hi, this is Evie Watson. I'm supposed to be in a video call with the hiring committee for the Research Services position, but I've been in the waiting room for almost... fifteen minutes. I wanted to see if there had been a mix-up?"

"I'll have to check. Do you mind if I put you on hold?"

"That's fine," I say, although sitting on hold after I've

been in video call limbo sounds like the least fine thing right now.

There's a click, and then my ear is assaulted with some of the worst high-pitched hold music I've ever heard. If I get this job, I might have to campaign to get this changed because it is excruciating.

After a couple minutes, a voice comes over the line, and I think at first it's Michelle back to let me know what's going on, but it's an ad for McDowell's undergraduate admissions.

"At McDowell University, you matter. That's why we offer fully customizable degrees. Can't decide where to focus your studies? No problem. With McDowell's Bachelor of General Studies, you can take courses on anything from 19th Century French Literature to Kinesiology. And with our generous federal student aid package..."

The ad cuts off as Michelle comes back on the line, and I'm grateful to be out of hold music hell.

"Ms. Watson? I'm going to transfer you to Katherine's phone if that's ok."

I tell her yes and brace myself to endure the screechy hold music a little longer while the transfer goes through.

"This is Katherine," a voice says.

"Hi Katherine, it's Evie."

Almost before I stop speaking, she launches into an apology.

"I am so sorry about this. The link you received was the wrong one, so we thought you were a no-show. I'm so glad you reached out, though. If I send you the correct link, could you join the other video call?"

At this point, I've been waiting almost twenty-five minutes, more than half the amount of time the hiring committee told me to expect the interview to take. It feels a little wrong to take more time away from my current job to interview for another one. But since I cleared my scheduled for the afternoon, it's not like I have another appointment to get to.

"Yes, of course," I say.

Katherine sends me the link, and I confirm that I've received it before we hang up. I take a moment to check my hair and makeup, then relax my shoulders and smile as I click the link. Almost immediately, I'm let into the video call room and greeted by the faces of six people in little tiles.

The rest of the interview goes off without a hitch. They ask the standard questions. *Why did you apply for this job? Where do you see yourself in five years? What are your strengths and weaknesses?* And I answer as enthusiastically as possible.

The longer we talk, the more relaxed I am, and by the end I'm excited about the position in a way I wasn't before.

For the rest of the week, I get a surge of hopefulness every time a new email comes to my inbox. But by the end of the day on Friday, I haven't received anything from them. As I head home, I try not to obsess about hearing back from the hiring committee. After all, I don't want it to ruin tomorrow's excursion to see LeVar Burton.

CHAPTER 6

It's still dark outside, and when I glance at the clock, I groan. It's 5:45. On a Saturday. And I am wide awake. I'm not really surprised. I haven't been sleeping well between the committee meeting and the anticipation of hearing from McDowell, but I hoped I would be able to sleep in today so I'd be well rested for my date with Andrew.

No, not a date, I remind myself.

My friendly visit to a bookstore to hear one of my favorite actors speak. With my work colleague who I definitely have not been having steamy dreams about. And then a picnic afterward.

I groan again. I probably shouldn't have agreed to go with him, but apparently I'm finding it really hard to say no to Andrew Brandt. Curse his adorable smile and glorious forearms and blue-gray eyes that make my heart melt when he looks at me. And curse the fact that he's kind and funny and keeps showing up at the library and asking me to join him at his table so we can work together.

I close my eyes again and will my body to go back to sleep, but after a few minutes, it's obvious that being awake is a foregone conclusion. With a grumble, I throw off the covers, startling the cat, who was curled up by my feet. I roll out of bed and go to the kitchen to make some coffee.

If I'm honest with myself, I'm nervous about spending time with Andrew today, but not because of my undeniable attraction to him. I've been avoiding him the past few days because even though I tried to hide my panic attack during that meeting, I'm pretty sure he noticed that I wasn't acting like myself after John arrived.

I eat some breakfast—coffee and a microwavable breakfast burrito—but it's almost three hours until Andrew is supposed to pick me up for the author event. I need something to do, or I'm going to start pacing around the house.

I try to read a book, but I can't concentrate on the words. I think about pulling out the paint set I bought after my first therapy session. My therapist had suggested that I paint my emotions. I initially rolled my eyes at the idea, but I ended up giving it a try and actually do find it calming. But painting is too messy for this morning, and it involves too much set up to be a useful outlet for this nervous energy I have.

I look around the kitchen. There's a stack of pasta boxes

on the counter that wouldn't fit in the pantry, and several spice jars from last night's dinner are lining the space by the oven. Not to mention the dirty cutting board and knife, and the crusty skillet sitting on the stove. I know I should clean as I go when I cook, but I'm always so focused on getting things to the table that I never seem to have time to move the dirty dishes to the sink. And once I finish eating, I just want to get to whatever book I happen to be reading.

It's clear, though, that part of the problem with this morning is that my kitchen needs to be reorganized. At least, that's what I tell myself as I attack the mess with a sense of determination.

Two and a half hours later, I survey the kitchen again. I did, in fact, clean out the pantry. I also rearranged most of the cabinets and washed all of the dishes. I'm sweaty and dirty, but I feel better. I haven't thought about John Vance or the general education project all morning, and now I have a very clean kitchen. I resolve that I'm going to keep it that way the next time I cook.

I check the time, and it's just over half an hour until Andrew's arrival. I have time to take a shower and get dressed, and as I'm putting the finishing touches on my makeup, the doorbell rings.

I take a deep breath before I open the door. This is going to be a fun day, I tell myself. I open the door, and there's Andrew with that devastating smile aimed right at me.

"You look great," he says, his eyes moving up and down my body.

Something about the look he's giving me makes me

blush, and I know he can tell because I'm wearing a green sleeveless vee-neck shirt, and I'm sure the top of my chest is blotchy.

"You, too," I say, my voice croaking a little. He's wearing a snug looking t-shirt and a pair of jeans that are leaving very little to my imagination about the musculature of his thighs. I swallow and push aside a mental image of how those thighs might flex in certain positions.

"Ready to go meet LeVar Burton?" he asks as if everything is normal.

"Mmm-hmm." I'm not capable of speech at the moment. Those jeans are quite distracting.

Andrew walks me to the car and opens the door for me. As we pull away from my driveway, he glances at me. "So, what's your favorite LeVar Burton role?"

His question diverts me from my lascivious thoughts, which is good, because they had no place on this friendly outing. Emphasis on *friendly*.

"It's probably going to make me sound like a cliché, but I'm partial to *Reading Rainbow*. How about you?" I'm thankful I've found my voice again and that it doesn't sound like I was just picturing my friend in much less clothing.

"I've always been a fan of his stint on *Star Trek*," he says with a grin.

I can't help but return his grin, and suddenly, the nervousness about my panic attack and the awkwardness at the sight of Andrew in those jeans dissipate. We're back to that comfortable back and forth that we've developed these past few weeks.

"I've never actually watched any of *Star Trek*," I say, then quickly add, "Oh, except for the one movie with Chris Pine."

"Somehow, I'm not at all surprised to hear that, Watson." Andrew laughs.

"Really, the biggest reason I consider myself a fan is actually his library advocacy. He's always speaking out about censorship, and he even served as the honorary chair of Banned Books Week."

"That's really cool."

"Yeah, it is. I love a man who stands up for the right to read." I smile.

Talking about books and libraries with Andrew is easily one of my favorite things to do these days. I should have known there was nothing to be nervous about. All that stressing out I've been doing since the meeting seems silly now that we're hanging out.

The venue is in the downtown area of Sapling Grove, which isn't too far away from my house, so we arrive a few minutes later. There's already a line down the street of people waiting to go in.

Once we're inside, it doesn't take long to find our seats. The chairs are crammed close together, and there's a huge crowd. The person in the seat to my right is sitting practically on top of me, so I scoot a little closer to Andrew. I'm suddenly very aware that our thighs are touching, and my mind flashes back to that mental image of Andrew's thighs flexing. I shake my head to clear it. It has no place at LeVar Burton's storytelling hour.

Instead, I apologize to Andrew for sitting so close to him. He shrugs. "It's ok. I don't mind."

Someone from the bookstore stands at the podium in the front of the meeting space and calls for everyone's attention. They introduce Burton, who takes the stage a moment later. As he begins to read a story—an Amal El-Mohtar piece about a woman who keeps pulling increasingly bizarre things out of her pockets—I relax a little. I'm having fun, and I'm glad Andrew invited me, after all.

At some point during the reading, Andrew puts his arm around the back of my chair. Because of the lack of space between me and the person on my right, I have no choice but to lean closer to Andrew as the story goes on.

Andrew isn't faring much better. The woman on his left keeps fidgeting, so he keeps scooting closer to me. Burton reads to us for about an hour, then does a short Q&A about the story with the person from the bookstore. By the end of the Q&A, we've shifted so much that I'm fully snuggled up against Andrew's side.

At the end of the talk, the bookstore representative announces that there will be a table set up for a book and memorabilia signing at the back of the venue. They're dismissing the audience in zones, but give anyone who isn't staying for the signing a chance to leave first. The woman next to Andrew leaves, but Andrew doesn't move away from me. Instead, he turns to me, and his hand slides to the space between my shoulders. My skin prickles with excitement at his touch.

"Do you want to get in the signing line?" Andrew asks.

"Do you really have to ask?" I laugh. I pull out my *Reading Rainbow* tote bag and the library's copy of *The Rhino Who Swallowed a Storm*, the children's book LeVar Burton wrote.

"I should have expected as much," he says quietly as his eyes meet mine. He still hasn't moved his hand from my shoulders, and our legs are still touching. The air around us feels heavy, and for a moment, it seems like it's just the two of us in the room instead of hundreds of people waiting to meet a famous actor.

The bookstore representative announces it's time for our seating zone to join the book signing line. Andrew's hand leaves my shoulders, and I shiver slightly at the lost contact as we stand.

***

Half an hour later, I have a newly signed book and tote bag, plus a picture of myself with LeVar Burton. He even high-fived me when I told him I'm a librarian.

As Andrew and I walk back to the car, my stomach rumbles. "Sounds like we need to get on to the next part of our adventure today. I believe I promised you a picnic," Andrew says with laughter in his voice.

"I can't believe you heard that," I mumble.

Andrew laughs again, but not in a mean way. He pulls out his phone and scrolls for a minute.

"Bingo!"

I raise an eyebrow at him.

"You're in for a treat," he says, but doesn't elaborate on what he saw on his phone.

We drive to a park nearby, and there's a food truck stationed by the parking area. They serve Thai and Laotian dishes, and it happens to be one of my favorite places to get take out in Sapling Grove. It's also a lot of other people's favorite, as evidenced by the mass of people waiting to order.

"Looks like we're doing a lot of standing in line today," I laugh.

"I can think of worse things than standing in line with you all day," Andrew murmurs, and my eyes widen.

"I mean, because I'm enjoying your company," he adds quickly.

"I'm enjoying yours, too." I smile as we move forward a few steps.

"Yeah?" Andrew smiles back. I notice what looks like a pink tinge to his face, and I wonder if he's getting a sunburn.

The line moves more quickly than I expect, and within minutes we've placed our order and have our takeout boxes. We walk toward a picnic table that has just been vacated and sit down across from each other. The table isn't very wide, so our knees bump. I move my leg away from Andrew's, trying to maintain some distance and my own sanity after being practically in his lap during the bookstore event.

I open my container of stir fry noodles, and Andrew

unwraps the Thai tacos he ordered. The food smells delicious, and I realize I'm starting to associate the best meals with Andrew. Every time he picks where we eat for lunch during work, I find myself discovering a new favorite dish.

"So..." Andrew looks uncomfortable.

"So?" I ask.

"There's something I wanted to ask you about."

My heart races. With nervousness or excitement? Both maybe.

Is he about to ask me on a real date? I banish the thought because it's so silly. We're just friends. Work colleagues, really.

I look at Andrew, and he's hesitating.

"Go on," I say in a breathy voice.

"I feel like you've been avoiding me, and I wanted to make sure everything is ok." He says it quickly, in a single breath, like he's ripping off a bandage.

I frown. So he noticed.

"Everything's fine. I haven't been avoiding you," I lie.

"Are you sure? You seemed...off...at the committee meeting."

I frown again. Dammit. Seems he noticed the panic attack, too.

"I don't know what you're talking about," I say, trying to avoid his eyes.

"You barely said anything during the meeting. You're usually so passionate about the work we've been doing, but you seemed... timid, I guess."

"Oh, that? Well, I had that other meeting I had to rush to, so I guess I was just distracted." I laugh nervously. He raises a skeptical eyebrow, and it's clear he's not buying my explanation.

"Ok." Andrew runs his hand through his hair. "I just...I want to make sure you're not feeling pressured to be part of the project. You had mentioned something about saying no to more things, and I don't want you to feel forced to work on this."

I sigh because the clear concern on his face is breaking down the wall I'm desperately trying to put around this.

"No, it's ok. I have been turning a lot of things down, but I promise this isn't something I can't handle. I was having an off day, that's all."

He doesn't look convinced, but he lets it drop. Instead, he asks me what my favorite part of the LeVar Burton talk was. We talk and enjoy the sunshine and the Thai food for what seems like no time at all but turns out to be a couple of hours. Long after our takeout containers are empty, we gather up our things, and Andrew takes me home.

I stand on my porch and wave to him as he leaves. I feel bad for lying to him about the panic attack, but I don't know what else to do. I don't want him to think of me as some sort of weakling who can't handle being around an asshole faculty member. Plus I want to keep working with him on the general education project. But it feels disingenuous to keep that part of me from him. As his car turns the corner at the end of my street, I'm left feeling uneasy about the whole thing.

CHAPTER 7

ndrew and I haven't talked about my anxiety at the committee meeting since the LeVar Burton event. A few times, he's looked like he wants to bring it up, but then thinks better of it. I'm relieved he's left it alone because I'm not sure I'm ready to let him in to that part of my life. The friendship we're building is too new.

Although I haven't been avoiding Andrew like I was last week, I've spent more time working by myself this week. My boss, Mike Pearce, has me busy with another statistics report, this time for a regulatory audit for the U.S. Department of Education. It is as thrilling as it sounds.

My mind is going to turn to mush if I have to write one more sentence for this report. Needing a break from staring at my computer, I stand up from my chair and stretch. I reach my arms out and try to touch both walls on the short side of my office. The room is tiny, only an eight foot by six foot rectangle, and I can almost touch the walls on either side if I stand in the middle of the space.

I decide to walk around and loosen up my joints a little, and I start toward the main floor of the library to see if Andrew is in the building. I take a longer route than usual, heading toward a second staircase on the far side of the second floor. As I round the corner by the literature section of the bookshelves, I stop short. The floor is wet, which is never a good sign, especially in a library. Books plus water equals disaster.

I look around for the source of the water, but there's so much I can't tell where it's coming from. And then I hear it. I don't know how I missed it before, because there is unmistakably the sound of rushing water coming from somewhere a few rows down from where I'm standing.

I sprint toward the sound, and dread sinks into me as I see it. There is So. Much. Water.

It gushes from the ceiling, drenching the books directly below and seeping under the shelving units for at least three rows. There are pieces of ceiling debris all over the floor, and books have fallen into the vast puddle that's growing as I stare in mute horror.

I freeze, unsure at first what to do. Or at least, I think I freeze, but I must actually scream because Kylie, June, and Andrew all come running from different directions. The three of them stare blankly at the mess, the shock of the scene almost incomprehensible at first. I've had enough time to recover my wits, though, and I launch into crisis management mode.

"Kylie, go get Mike and let him know what's going on. And call Facilities while you're at it." That confident voice I've been using lately is back.

"On it," Kylie says as she rushes toward the stairs.

"June, we're going to need some book carts and towels, and probably some gloves." I don't wait to see which direction she goes.

"What can I do?" Andrew asks.

"Help me get as many books out of the water as you can."

We grab books by the armful and run them to the tables nearby. For now, the goal is to get them out of the direct line of the water. I dump the books in my arms into a soggy pile and rush back to get more. Andrew and I nearly collide as we zoom back and forth between the shelves and the tables. A few times, I almost slip on the slick tiles. The floor is drenched, and my clothes are already soaked through.

It feels like hours before Kylie shows up with Mike and Ted, the head of Facilities, but I know it must only be a few minutes.

"I need you two to get out of the way," Ted barks at Andrew and me. "My crew is shutting off the water, but we need to get in the area to see what's going on with the pipes."

June arrives with a book cart and a bunch of rolls of paper towels.

Kylie and June unroll the towels and lay them out on the

tables to dry the books. Mike rolls up his sleeves and starts arranging things on carts.

"Here, let me help," I say, reaching for a roll of paper towels.

Mike stops me.

"I think you might want to go dry off a bit first."

"I'm f-fine." My teeth are chattering, and I wrap my arms around myself. The air conditioning is blasting, and I only now realize how soaking wet I am. At least I wore a dark blue shirt today, so I only look like a drowned rat, not a drowned rat whose bra is visible.

"I've got a towel in my car. Be right back," Andrew says, and he runs down the stairs.

Andrew comes back with the towel a few minutes later, and I don't mean to stare as he walks toward me, but *oh god*. He's completely soaked, too, and unlike me, he is wearing a light colored shirt. Ever since that day when he asked me to join the gen ed project, I have been trying not to imagine what the rest of his stomach must look like, but I do not need to imagine any longer because I can see everything where his shirt clings to him.

He hands me the towel, which is warm from sitting in the car in the sunshine. I wrap it around myself.

"Th-thank you." My voice is trembling, and it's not just because I'm cold.

"Of course."

"I th-think I need to go w-warm up. I've got a h-heater in my office."

"Do you mind if I come with you? I'm a bit cold myself."

He gestures at his wet clothes, and I try not to look.

"That's fine. Mike? Kylie? Do you need anything?"

"No, you go on," Mike says. "Get warmed up, and then come back so we can triage this mess."

As we make our way to my office, I feel the adrenaline rush dissipate. I glance back over my shoulder before we turn the corner. It hits me how bad everything looks. There are hundreds of books in that pile, and it's going to take a lot of time to sort through everything and salvage what we can. Worse than that, with the cuts to the library's budget for the upcoming year, I don't know how we're going to manage replacing all the things we have to throw away.

The problem is that once a book is water damaged, it's almost impossible to salvage it, especially with the level of water most of these books took on. And most of the damage happened in the literature section, which means there are a lot of older items that might be out of print and hard to replace.

I'm worrying over all the work and money that this flood is going to cost us as we arrive at my office. I take out my keys to unlock the door, but my hands shake, and my ears buzz. My lungs feel tight, like I can't catch my breath, and my heart squeezes uncomfortably in my chest. It feels like I'm having a heart attack, and the thought makes my stomach swoop.

Everything sounds far away, and I'm only vaguely aware that Andrew is saying my name. The world feels like it's spinning, and my legs give out from under me. Before I hit the ground, strong arms reach around me and ease me into a sitting position.

"Evie! Are you having chest pains? Should I call 911?" Andrew's eyes look stricken.

"Panic...attack...can't...breathe..." I gasp for air, but my breaths are shallow.

The terrified expression on Andrew's face shifts into relief tinged with resolve. "Panic attacks I can help with. I need you to breathe with me, Evie."

"I can't. I can't. I can't." I shake my head, but he catches my face between his hands, making me look into his eyes, even though I resist.

"Yes, you can, Evie. Breathe with me." His voice is gentle. "Look at me, Evie."

"I can't." I try shaking my head, but his grip is steady, although not painful. "I can't. I can't."

"You can. We're going to breathe together. I'll count four, and you'll breathe in while I count, and then I'll count again, and you're going to hold it, and then I'll count one more time, and you'll breathe out. Got it?"

I swallow, then give a slight nod, finally giving in to Andrew's gentle commands.

"Ok, one...two...three...four." As Andrew counts, I do my best to take a deep breath in.

He counts again. I hold my breath, but my hands are still trembling.

"One...two...three...four," he counts one last time, and I breathe out. I still have that hollow feeling I get after a panic attack, but the worst of it is over.

Andrew lets go of my face and takes my hands in his. I

keep my gaze on him.

"Ok, that was good. Let's do it again." He's calm but determined as we breathe together again, twice. My ears stop ringing, and my hands steady.

"How did you know to do that?" I smile weakly at Andrew.

"My mom had panic attacks while I was in high school after my dad died. I used to help her breathe through them." His voice breaks a little, and he clears his throat, pushing the emotion aside.

"Thank you," I say, shivering again. Right, my clothes are still cold and wet.

"Do you think we could get that heater in your office going?"

I nod and hand him the keys. I'm not ready to stand up yet. He unlocks the door, then helps me up off the floor. Once I'm standing, he pulls me into a hug. He's never hugged me before, and I have a weird cocktail of emotions swirling within me. I'm exhausted from the adrenaline and the panic attack, but I'm also extremely aware of every point at which our bodies touch. The top of my head fits perfectly tucked below his chin, and at this close range, the smell of his cologne hits me with full force. It wraps around me like a blanket, and I can't help but breathe deeply.

I never want this hug to end, but I know we're approaching the line between a friendly hug and extremely awkward. I pull away, but Andrew holds on for a second longer than I expect. As I look up at him, though, I can see that we didn't cross that extremely awkward line after all.

Concern still lines his face, and I get the sense that if I let him, he would keep holding me until the end of time.

We step away from each other and walk into my office, where I turn on the heater. An instant feeling of relief settles over me once the blast of warm air hits me.

Since my office is so small, we sit inches apart on the floor so we can both feel the warmth from the space heater. I hand him the towel, realizing that this whole time I've been wrapped in it, and he hasn't had a chance to dry off yet.

"Do you mind if I ask how long you've been having panic attacks?" As soon as he opened his mouth, I knew he would ask. I decide that there's no use keeping it from him now.

"No, that's fine. They started about a year ago."

"What happened a year ago?"

I hesitate. I don't really like talking about that awful day, but I have a lot of trust in Andrew.

"It's ok if you don't want to tell me," he says. He doesn't look hurt or judgmental, just like someone who's willing to listen.

"No, actually, my therapist said it's better to talk about it because it takes away some of the power of the moment." I take a deep breath. "About a year ago, I was walking into the dining hall at the same time as John Vance, and I made the mistake of asking him when he was going to schedule my visit to his class."

John was teaching composition that semester, and I was supposed to visit all the composition classes to introduce library services to the students.

"John and I have never really seen eye to eye on the need for a librarian visit, though, so when I asked him, he screamed at me and asked me what gave me the right to think I could come to his class."

My voice catches, and I take another deep breath. I close my eyes, and the memory of John's outraged shouts floods my mind. The vein in his neck that pulsed, the spit that flung from his mouth onto my sunglasses. I count my breaths again, then open my eyes. Andrew doesn't say anything, but his jaw is clenched and he looks angry.

"I tried to explain that it's my job to teach about library services, but that just made it worse. He kept saying something about me infringing on his academic freedom. I don't really remember the specifics. By the time he stopped, I was shaking and trying to keep him from seeing me cry." I can feel fresh tears forming at the memory, but I blink them away.

"That asshole," Andrew growls. His brow is furrowed in anger, but then he smacks his forehead. "That's why you were so uncomfortable at the meeting the other day."

"It's not a big deal," I try to wave it off. I debate whether I should tell him the part about how John and I went out in my first year at Cooke and how when I broke things off, his true nature became apparent.

"Yes, it is. What he did to you is unacceptable. Did you talk to anyone about it?"

"I...didn't. At the time, I was so stunned and embarrassed that I didn't know how to respond. The panic attacks started not long after that. The chair of the composition department told John he had to schedule me for a library day, but he was so demeaning during the class that I..."

A lump of emotion forms in my throat, and I pause.

"Kylie figured it out, though, and made me go to the counseling center."

"Evie, you should have told someone in the provost's office." Andrew's expression is thunderous, and I'm surprised by how upset he seems.

"I appreciate your concern, but at this point, it's too late to say anything. It's been too long, and I'm managing ok."

Andrew looks like he wants to argue with me over that, but Kylie appears at the door and knocks lightly on the frame.

"Are you two warmed up?" If she notices the weird tension in the room, she doesn't acknowledge it.

I give her a wan smile.

"Yeah, all better. Still a little damp, though."

"Mike wants everyone to gather by what we're now apparently calling the triage station so we can work on salvaging what we can."

"Ok. Did facilities figure out what happened?"

"Yeah, burst pipe in the attic."

"Really? I thought that was something that only happened in winter."

"Apparently summer is actually prime time for bursting pipes, according to Ted. Plus this building is so old that the pipe was in bad shape. We'll probably be without water in the library for a few days while they repair it, so we're supposed to go over to the Faculty Office Building when we need water."

I turn to Andrew.

"I guess you'll have to move back to your office for a few days."

"Yeah, maybe." Andrew seems like he isn't really listening. Is he still thinking about John Vance?

"Ready to go see how bad the damage is?" Kylie asks. I nod, bracing myself for what we're about to go do, and the three of us leave my office.

———

"This looks really bad," Andrew says. The sight of the water damage seems to have pushed his frustration with the John situation out of his mind.

"I think the word you're looking for is 'catastrophe,'" I offer. My nerves are still shaky, but I do my best to focus on the task at hand.

By now the rest of the library staff has gathered in the area where we piled the books. A few people are already working on wrapping books in paper towels.

"We need to work quickly if we want to save as many books as possible," Mike says. "June is already downstairs making sure the freezer is empty so we can put as many books in there as will fit. And Ted is talking with dining services to see if they have space in their walk-in freezer. Fortunately, with the summer schedule, dining services aren't as busy, so there's a good chance they'll have plenty of space."

Andrew looks confused at the mention of the freezers.

I lean over and whisper, "When books get this much water damage, they have to be dried out, but with so many books to dry, there's no way to do it quickly enough. Freezing them stops mold growth and buys us some time to get drying stations set up."

"Evie, Kylie, I'd like the two of you to coordinate with June to start figuring out which books are a total loss that we'll have to reorder. I'm going to talk to administration and make sure someone contacts the insurance company."

As Mike steps away, I see him pull out his phone, probably to call Ted and get an update on the freezer situation. A few of the facilities staff are still on site working on cleaning up the water. Andrew is getting a lesson from one of the Access Services staff on how to properly wrap a book for freezing.

I motion for Kylie to join me, and we go downstairs to talk to June.

"I hope you don't mind my jumping in on this," I say to June, "but I went to a workshop on disaster planning for libraries a couple months ago, and I have some ideas."

"Not at all! Honestly, I'm glad Mike put the three of us together on this, because I was worried he was going to stick me with the whole thing myself," June replies.

Kylie and I chuckle at that. Mike isn't a bad boss, but he has a tendency not to realize the extent of some of the projects that he assigns to people. Usually, collaborations and partnerships end up coming together naturally. Whether that's by Mike's design or just how we've all learned to adapt, I wish he would be a little more tuned in on the day-to-day.

The three of us talk through my ideas, and we decide on a plan for the next few days. I'm going to investigate companies that do book preservation full time and see if there's an affordable option for outsourcing any of the work. Given the budget situation, we agree that seems unlikely, but it's worth a shot. In the meantime, Kylie and June are going to focus on getting as many books dried out as they can so that the dining hall can have their freezer back as soon as possible.

"Evie, I'm nominating you to lead this effort," Kylie says with a grin. "You're really rocking the ideas today."

"Me, too," says June. "I don't mind taking a back seat on this one."

"Thanks for your confidence. I'll do my best."

The library staff works for hours to get the books prepared for freezing. Andrew stays and helps until his phone starts ringing nonstop. He answers the call and then makes his apologies as he rushes out of the library.

Ted and a few more facilities workers eventually come back with wheelbarrows, carts, and plastic tubs to help move the books to the dining hall freezer.

After all the books are stored safely in the freezers, Kylie looks at me and sighs. "You should go home. No offense, but you look frightful. We should have sent you home to get clean clothes after you got soaked earlier."

Kylie gives me a hug, and we wish each other goodnight. It's not as good a hug as the one Andrew and I shared earlier, but it still lifts my spirits. As I leave the building, I've never been more happy to be going home than I am tonight.

CHAPTER 8

As soon as I'm home, I take the longest, hottest shower of my life then change into my comfiest sweatpants and a soft t-shirt. After the day I've had, all I want to do is sit on the couch and watch a 90s rom-com.

I decide to go old school and get out the DVD of *Clueless* that I've had since high school. It's one of those early 2000s DVDs with the interactive menu screen and the cheesy animations, and it is an instant comfort, pulling me right back to movie nights with all my cousins piled onto my parents' couch.

The memory of those movie nights makes my stomach rumble. We would always have popcorn, and my mom would make cookies and bring them to us on a plate, the cookies still warm and slightly crispy.

I realize I haven't eaten anything since this morning except for a granola bar Kylie handed me after a couple of hours working on the books this afternoon. I know I should make myself a real dinner, but I'm exhausted, so I check the freezer and find a pint of Ben and Jerry's. I'm about to dig a spoon directly into the container when my phone dings with a message.

ANDREW: Hey, sorry I disappeared this afternoon. I wanted to check on you and make sure you're doing ok.

A wave of fizzy warmth washes over me as I read Andrew's message. I quickly send back a reply.

ME: I'm doing much better. Thanks.

ANDREW: Have you had dinner yet? Could I bring you something?

I bite my lip as I read the message and then look at my ice cream. Andrew was an immense help this afternoon, and I probably ought to thank him in person. Plus I've learned by now that when Andrew Brandt offers to bring you food, it's going to be good. Ben and Jerry can wait.

ME: Sure. I haven't eaten yet.

My text is far more nonchalant sounding than I feel.

ANDREW: Ok. Be there in about 20 minutes.

I put the ice cream back in the freezer and look around my living area. The house I rent has one of those open-plan living areas with a kitchen that flows into the dining room and living room. My gaze snags on a pile of books from the public library that looks a bit messy, and there are definitely a few socks that haven't made their way to the laundry hamper. Even though I went on a cleaning spree on

Saturday, it needs a quick tidying.

After fifteen minutes of me fussing over every detail of my living space, the few bits of clutter are cleared away, but I still have this weird energy buzzing inside me. I don't want to admit it, but I'm nervous to have Andrew inside my house. He picked me up for the author talk on Saturday, but he didn't come inside.

If he doesn't show up soon, though, I might rearrange the furniture in the living room. It's something I do when I'm stressed because it gives me a sense of calm and newness after I'm finished. And honestly, that's exactly what I need today.

I'm about to move the couch when the doorbell rings. I take a deep breath and answer the door. Andrew is standing on my porch with a bag of something that smells suspiciously like Indian food.

His face lights up when I open the door, and he flashes me a smile that makes my insides wobbly.

"I brought samosas."

"That sounds wonderful," I say, sounding a touch more breathy than I intend.

"I remembered how much you liked them when we went for Indian food, so I thought they'd be the perfect comfort food."

I lead him into the house, and he sets the food on the dining table while I get plates and silverware from the kitchen. I clank the plates together when I get them out because my hands are shaking a little. I hope he can't tell how nervous I am that he's here.

We sit across from each other at my little round dining table, and Andrew opens the boxes of food. We each scoop some rice and saag paneer onto our plates, then divide up the samosas.

I want to dig into the food, but there's this awkward silence settling over us, and I can tell Andrew is waiting for me to break it. He's giving me space to open up about this afternoon, but I'm not ready to dive right in to talking about it yet.

Instead, I point the conversation at him.

"Do you mind if I ask where you ran off to earlier?" I ask as I gather a forkful of rice.

"Not at all. I've been helping my mom move my grandmother into an apartment at a nursing home."

"Oh. That sounds...tough."

"Yeah, it was a hard decision for my mom and her sisters, but I think Gran will be in a better situation now." He looks sad, and I want to hug him. It's an urge I quickly tamp down. Even though he hugged me this afternoon after my panic attack, I don't know if we're the kind of friends who do that.

"My grandmother died when I was in high school, but I remember my parents having to deal with the logistics of nursing homes and care. If you want to talk about it, I'm here," I offer.

"Thanks. That means a lot. My Gran is one of my favorite people."

"Tell me about her?"

The look he gives me almost breaks my heart in two.

There's a mixture of joy and sadness in his eyes and the upward tilt of his lips.

"She had retired by the time I was born, so she looked after me while my mom was at work when I was a baby. When I started school, I would walk to her house after and spend the afternoon with her. She taught me how to cook."

"I didn't know you could cook." I'm not surprised, given Andrew's love of food.

He grins. "My specialty is Gran's chicken and noodles. It's this savory, comforting pile of carbs and herbs. I could eat it every week."

"That sounds amazing!"

"I'll make it for you some time."

"I'd like that." I blush at the thought of Andrew cooking for me. I can't think of a time a man I'm not related to has cooked for me.

He launches into a story about the homemade strawberry jam his grandmother always kept in the fridge for afternoon snacks of toast and jam. He tells me about growing up as the only grandchild on his mom's side. His dad's side of the family lived across the country, so he never saw his cousins.

"I can't imagine what it would have been like to be the only grandkid," I say. "My aunts and uncles all lived within walking distance of each other, and my cousins, siblings, and I were all stair-stepped in age."

"How many cousins did you have close by?"

"Seven, plus my brother and me."

"That's...so many."

"We always had someone to play with." I shrug.

"I wish I'd had that. Not that I was some loner who was never around other kids. Just that it sounds like it would have been nice."

"Most of the time it was nice, but we fought sometimes. It does mean my mom expects to have a lot of grandkids herself someday, though."

"Is that something you want?"

"Maybe? But I'd have to find someone like you who'd be willing to help me make grandkids first."

Andrew nearly chokes on the samosa he's eating and my eyes widen with embarrassment.

"Oh my god. That wasn't...I mean...I didn't...Oh. My. God." I bury my head in my hands, peeking through my fingers at him. He looks like he's trying really hard not to laugh. "I just meant a man. Not, like, you specifically."

Good save, I think ironically.

"I should stop talking. Go ahead and laugh. I can tell you're dying to."

Andrew struggles to regain his composure.

"No. Nope. Not gonna laugh." His lips quirk, and it's clear he's about to lose it. And frankly, I'm about to lose it, too. We look each other dead in the eye, and we both burst into laughter.

"Oh my god, Evie. The look on your face!" He says between giggles.

We laugh for a long time, and each time it seems like we're about to stop, one of us makes a face and sets the other one off. By the time we finally get ourselves under control, we both have tears streaming down our faces, and my whole body feels light. I sigh contentedly.

"I'm so glad you came over, Andrew."

Andrew's expression shifts slightly. There's still a trace of the humor of a few moments ago, but it's joined by a twinge of concern.

"I was worried about you after what happened today. I wanted to make sure you were ok."

"I really appreciate that. And thanks for all the help with the books. You're basically a librarian now."

Andrew looks pleased.

"I couldn't ask for a better compliment." He winks at me.

What is it with this man and the winking? And why do I feel tingly every time he does it?

We're quiet for a beat, and then Andrew is back to his serious face.

"And as far as the panic attack? Everything ok on that front?" The question is quiet, and there's a softness in his eyes that burrows its way into my heart and sets me aglow.

"Yeah. Thanks again for helping me through that. I would have gotten there eventually, but it's easier when there's someone else to ground me." I give him a small smile, and he reaches for my hand in a comforting gesture.

"No problem. I know they can be scary in the moment. You can call or text me anytime you need someone to help you through one."

"Thanks. That's incredibly kind of you." I pull my hand away from his, worried he'll feel my rapid pulse.

"It's the least I can do for my favorite librarian."

I know I'm blushing again at the compliment. I clear my throat, trying to dislodge the emotion that's taken up residence there. Before I turn into a puddle of grateful tears for this man's kindness, I change the subject.

"So, when you texted, I was about to eat most of a pint of Cherry Garcia ice cream. I know we ate a lot of samosas, but would you like some?"

"That's my favorite kind of ice cream."

"Mine, too." I grin.

Andrew gathers the plates and takeout containers, and I get the ice cream from the freezer. I fix us each a bowl.

"I usually eat this straight out of the container with a spoon," I say over my shoulder as I finish scooping.

"Ha! Me, too." Andrew laughs.

I hand him his bowl, and we sit on the couch.

"So, tell me more about your plans for—how did you put it?—finding someone to help you make babies?"

I nearly drop the spoonful of ice cream that's en route to my mouth. I shake my head.

"You do not want to hear about my sad dating history."

"Oh, I'm sorry. I upset you." Andrew looks remorseful, and I rush to reassure him.

"No, no! It's ok. I'm not upset about it. I haven't had much luck with dating since grad school, and since the incident with John, I've been dealing with a lot of things. Things that make dating hard."

"Right. Of course. I can see how something like what that asshole did would put a damper on wanting to date." Andrew's eyes are alight with something fiery. He still seems to be angry about what John did to me. I don't want to ruin our evening by talking about John anymore, though.

"Anyway, I went on a few dates when I first moved here, but then I got busy with work, and then the panic attacks started. So I just...haven't dated in a while. But enough about my sad dating history. How about you?"

"You want to hear about my sad dating history?" Andrew seems surprised.

"Only if you want to share." I feel the tips of my ears burn. The truth is I'm dying to know, especially after what Kylie and Jaclyn have told me about all the text messages from all the different women on his phone.

"What do you want to know?"

"I guess what I want to know is if the rumors are true." I bite my lip, not sure if I'm ready for this moment of truth.

"Which rumors?" Andrew cocks his eyebrow.

I swallow. He's going to make me say it.

"You know. The rumors...about how you take out a different woman every week." Now it's not only my ears that are pink, my cheeks are there, too.

"Oh, those rumors." Andrew sighs and rolls his eyes. "I wish people would stop spreading that around."

"Is it...not true?"

"Like all rumors, there's an element of truth to it. I grew up around here, and I dated a lot in high school. I had sort of a reputation as a bad boy heartbreaker, although a lot of that was overblown high school bravado. So when I started working at Cooke, some of that followed me. That's the downside of being a local."

"So, you're not currently a bad boy heartbreaker leaving a trail of women behind you?"

"Not to my knowledge, no."

"Well, that's...good."

Andrew looks amused, a sly smile barely evident on his lips.

"Wait! What about all the women who text you? Kylie and Jaclyn both said that you had a bunch of different women constantly messaging you."

Andrew laughs.

"I do have a lot of women who message me, but it's not what you think. It's my aunts. They are constantly texting me with requests for help with Gran or moving furniture or you name it. It's a pain in the ass sometimes."

"Aww, I think it's sweet."

Andrew waves my comment off, but I can tell he's pleased.

We talk for a little longer, Andrew telling me more about his relationship with his mom and aunts, and me telling stories of the shenanigans my cousins and I would get up to when we were kids. I'm having such a good time, that I don't notice how long we've been talking until I let out a huge yawn. I glance at the clock and am surprised to see it's after 10:00. Andrew has been here for hours, but it feels like he just got here.

"It's later than I thought," I say as I yawn again.

"Yeah, I probably ought to head home," Andrew says as we both stand up.

"I should go to bed. I'm sure tomorrow will be a long

day." I stretch again, lifting my arms over my head and arching my back. When I straighten back up, Andrew has a funny, almost flustered look on his face.

"Goodnight, Andrew?" I say, more like a question than a statement.

"Goodnight, Evie," he says, clearing his throat. He pulls me into a hug.

Huh. Maybe we are the hugging kind of friends now.

"Let me know when you want me to come back over to make chicken and noodles," he says as we walk toward the door.

I stand by the window to watch him drive away. Titania the cat comes up and rubs against my legs, and I let out a breath.

I'm glad I've got Andrew as a friend. Yes, he's incredibly attractive, but finding the kind of friend who will jump right into a disaster and then bring you dinner is hard to do as an adult. It's his kindness and humor that keep me wanting to spend time with him, and those seem like the things he's most willing to give.

I wave to him one last time as he pulls out of my driveway, then turn back to my living room with an unexpected feeling of contentment.

CHAPTER 9

Kylie, June, and I have a meeting first thing this morning to make a plan for deciding which books can be saved and which need to be discarded and replaced, so I get to work earlier than usual.

I expected to sleep poorly last night after the stress of discovering the flooding and the subsequent panic attack, but I woke up feeling refreshed and relaxed. Maybe something about surprise samosas made a difference in the way I sleep.

As I walk toward the library, I stop short because who's standing there but Andrew, holding a box that looks suspiciously like it came from Hole-In-One, the local donut shop that is inexplicably golf-themed but makes the best donuts fresh every morning. He's also got one of those boxes of coffee and a bag that I'm guessing is full of sugar and creamer packets.

"What's all this?" I ask as I walk closer to where he's standing looking like he's trying to figure out how to open the door without dropping anything.

Andrew hits me with one of those smiles that makes my insides turn to goo.

"I thought the library staff could use a little fuel to get through the day of flood clean up."

"That's so thoughtful of you! Thank you, Andrew," I say, blinking back a sudden prickle of tears in my eyes. The utter kindness of Andrew Brandt will never cease to amaze me.

I unlock the door—the library doesn't open for another hour—and wave Andrew inside. After yesterday, I don't think anyone will have a problem with him being in here before opening time. I lock the door behind us and walk with him into the workroom.

He follows me to the small kitchenette—literally just a fridge, a microwave, and a coffee pot—and sets the box that is most definitely from Hole-In-One on the conference table in the center of the room. I peek under the lid and confirm that it's donuts, and my mouth waters because these look like fresh ones, probably still warm.

Andrew opens the drawer where we keep the mugs and puts them next to the box of coffee. Since he's been spending so much time in the library, we gave him his own space in the staff mailbox area, and he regularly uses our dishes. He even added himself to our kitchen cleaning rotation.

I send a message to our library staff chat so that everyone else knows about the treats and tell them who to thank for the donut delivery.

Andrew is about to leave the workroom when I stop him.

"Thanks again for last night. I really appreciated the check in."

"You're welcome. And I'm serious about the chicken and noodles. Let's find a time soon to do that."

I promise him we will, and he leaves, I assume heading for his usual table.

I get myself a cup of coffee and a donut (maple glazed topped with bacon) and open my laptop to get ready for the meeting with Kylie and June.

June walks in a few minutes later, obviously excited about the unexpected breakfast treat, because the first thing she says is, "Yes! Donuts!"

"I know, right? Best way to start the day after what happened yesterday."

I've always liked June. She's a bit older than me, closer to Kylie's age. We don't have a lot of overlap in our usual work, so I'm excited to have the chance to collaborate with her, even if the reason for it is unfortunate.

June and I chat while we wait for Kylie. We've mostly been talking about our favorite kinds of donuts, when June suddenly says, "So, tell me about you and Andrew. How long have you been dating?"

I nearly choke.

"What? We're not dating."

"Oh, sorry. I figured since you're together all the time and the way he looks at you that you must be."

"No, no. Just friends. Nothing going on there, for sure." *And I plan to keep it that way.*

June raises an eyebrow but doesn't push the conversation any further, and I'm left wondering what she means about the way he looks at me.

"What'd I miss?" Kylie asks as she joins us a moment later.

"Nothing!" I say quickly, worried that June is going to bring up Andrew.

Kylie glances between June and me with a skeptical look.

"Ok? Ready to talk about trashing some books?"

"Yes, please!" I'm definitely ready to talk about the books and not about Andrew.

"Are you still interested in being the lead on this, Evie?" June asks.

"I can if that's what you and Kylie want."

"That's what we want!" Kylie beams at me.

"Well, in that case, I'll do it. I was thinking the first thing we probably ought to do is figure out which books, exactly, we're going to have to review."

"That should be easy enough," June says. "I can pull a list out of the online catalog for all the books in that row."

"Excellent. Once we have the list, Kylie and I can probably start looking through it and see if there are any books that we can go ahead and withdraw without spending time and resources on trying to dry them out."

"That works for me," Kylie says. "We'll have to figure out where each book is in the freezer, though. We weren't exactly careful about where things went when we were pulling them off the shelves."

"Yeah, sorry about that. Andrew and I were trying to get as many books out of the deluge as possible."

"It's ok. I don't think there was any way to salvage as much as we did if we'd tried to take things off the shelves in an orderly fashion." Kylie gives me a warm smile.

As we continue talking through the logistics of dealing with the books, a plan comes together quickly. June is going to coordinate with the other Access Services staff to prioritize the physical work of defrosting and drying the books.

We're about to wrap up the conversation when Mike Pearce comes in. "How's the planning going?"

"Actually, pretty well," I say, feeling good after our productive meeting. "We've got at least an idea of how we're going to approach things. I might need to look at budget information with you, though. We're hoping to be able to outsource some of the preservation."

"Sure, sounds good. I'm sure we'll hear a decision from the insurance company in the next few days, too."

"Evie's got some brilliant ideas about how to approach this," Kylie interjects, and I blush a little at the blatant compliment in front of the boss.

"Wonderful! Keep up the good work, Evie. I know you're up to it." Mike smiles and gives us a small wave as he goes back to his office.

As Kylie, June, and I stand to leave the breakroom, I realize I really need a restroom. It's not my fault that the coffee was sitting on the table during the whole meeting smelling delicious, but I shouldn't have drunk three cups of it. I thank the women for their time and start toward the staff bathroom, but Kylie calls out to me, "Don't forget they haven't turned the water back on yet!"

"Oh right! I guess I'll go over to the Fob. Thanks for the reminder!"

I leave the library and walk quickly to the building next door. The Faculty Office Building, affectionately known as the "Fob," is the oldest building on campus. It was originally a dorm when it was built some time in the 1910s, but was converted to offices in the 1980s. It's somewhat awkward as an office building, but I like the charm of the old woodwork and quirky office spaces. Each office has something a little unique, like a fireplace in one and built-in bookshelves in another. But because it's such an old building, it's hard to keep it maintained. Last fall, I heard that one of the Deans had bees living in the walls of his office, and the air conditioning is notoriously difficult to keep running, which is what drove Andrew to seek an alternate office space this summer.

It's for exactly that reason that I'm expecting it to be miserably hot in the Fob, but it's surprisingly cool. In fact, it's almost chilly.

I make my way to the bathroom, use the facilities, then walk upstairs to Jaclyn's office. She's not on campus much over the summer, but she texted me last night to say she'd be here today and wants to go to lunch together.

"Hi, friend," I say as I knock on the door frame to her office.

Jaclyn looks up from her computer screen and smiles. "Hi, Evie. What brings you to the Fob?"

"The water's still out in the library." I shrug.

"Oh, right."

"When did they fix the air conditioning over here?" I figure it must have happened in the last few days since Andrew hasn't moved back to his office yet.

"Maybe a month ago. Not long after we went to see *The Mummy*, in fact."

I can't believe my ears. A month ago? Andrew has been coming to the library even though he didn't have to this whole time! If it's not the air conditioner keeping him in the library, it must be something else. Something else I'm not sure I can let myself think about.

"You ok? You look shocked."

"What? Oh. No, I'm fine. Just..." I trail off.

"Just what?" Jaclyn cocks an eyebrow.

"Hmm? Nothing. Sorry, I need to get back to the library."

"You sure you're ok? Not worrying over a particular history professor who's been spending his time in your building instead of his?" Jaclyn smirks.

Of course she's figured it out. Jaclyn is probably the smartest person on the Cooke campus, or at least the most observant.

"Dammit. Jaclyn. How do you do that?" I know there's no use trying to pretend she hasn't figured me out.

"I'm just that good." Jaclyn gives me a devious grin.

I shouldn't be surprised. Jaclyn is incredibly perceptive.

"Now, am I right or am I right? I never see Andrew in his actual office anymore, and I think we both know who he's been spending all his time with." She fixes me with a pointed look.

"Yep. You hit the nail right on the head." I heave a defeated sigh.

"And you're trying to figure out if it means anything."

I nod.

"I can't tell you for sure if it means anything. The man loves attention, after all, and you hanging out with him all day is definitely giving him attention."

"That makes sense. Plus, I feel like we're becoming pretty good friends."

"I bet you do. He's really good at making people feel like the most important person in the world."

I frown, and Jaclyn quickly adds, "I'm not saying it doesn't mean something. It very well could. It's hard to tell with him sometimes because he's the kind of person who makes everyone feel like the center of the universe. I mean, most people. I don't believe in feelings, so not me specifically."

"Right, of course, no feelings ever at all," I say with a wink.

Jaclyn shrugs. "What can I say? I'm a stone cold ice queen."

I laugh. I know Jaclyn's not as icy as she likes to pretend, and she knows I know even if we don't acknowledge it. We finalize our plans for lunch before I head back over to the library.

As I walk back to my building, I brood over the conversation with Jaclyn. She's not wrong that Andrew's been making me feel like I'm important to him, and his habit of intently listening to new people when we've been out together is something I've witnessed firsthand. But the amount of time we spend together has to count for something, even if it's only friendship. Right?

I'm lost in my thoughts as I return to the library and quite literally bump into Kylie as I walk in the door.

"Oof, sorry!" I say as we collide.

"No problem. I wish these doors had windows," Kylie says.

The library was built in the middle of the last century and still has the original solid wood doors. For reasons unfathomable by the current Cooke librarians, the original design did not include windows in the doors, which makes for a lot of bumpy encounters in the doorway.

"Maybe we could get new doors if we didn't have to pay for things like new pipes." I pause. "Hey, did you know that the air conditioner in the Fob was fixed a month ago?"

"No, but that's great!"

"Yeah, great." I glance toward where Andrew is sitting by the window.

Kylie looks over her shoulder to see what I'm looking at.

"Oh, I see."

Before Kylie can launch into one of her cautionary speeches about getting too close to Andrew, I say, "We're just friends. It's fine."

Kylie raises an eyebrow.

"If you say so."

"What's that supposed to mean?" I scrunch up my nose.

"Sorry, I shouldn't have said anything." She looks contrite, but I push her on it.

"Kylie. Tell me what you were thinking."

"He's flaky. He's a nice enough person, but I've seen him do this before. It's easy for relationships with him to become one-sided."

I lift my eyebrows.

"He told me the heartbreaker thing was a rumor and that he's not like that."

Kylie frowns.

"That doesn't surprise me. I don't think he does it maliciously. It's more that he can't seem to commit. I doubt he realizes he's doing it." She pauses, but before I can defend Andrew, she adds, "Remember how Jaclyn said she hadn't hung out with him in a while? They used to be together all the time. This was before you started working here, and she doesn't talk about it much."

"I had no idea. I thought she just knew him from high school. What happened?"

"They were best friends for years, but then he basically ghosted her for a month and started hanging out with Veronica from the Medieval Studies department. Jaclyn was pretty broken up about it for a while."

I'm not sure what to make of that. Jaclyn isn't the kind of person to be upset about something like that, and Andrew doesn't strike me as actually being that flighty.

"Thanks for the warning," I say, even though I don't feel particularly thankful.

"I'm not trying to throw a wet blanket on your friendship with him. I just don't want you to get hurt when he doesn't meet your expectations." Kylie gives me a look that is very close to pitying.

She's so much like an older sister sometimes, and I love her for it. But sometimes older sisters are well-meaning and frustrating. I sigh.

"I really do appreciate it. I know you're looking out for me."

Kylie gives me a quick squeeze on the arm and says goodbye as she leaves for a meeting. I don't stop at Andrew's table, although he looks up and waves at me as I walk by. I don't want to talk him after that conversation with Kylie. Not that it's his fault.

I stay in my office until lunch, and when it's time to meet up with Jaclyn, I don't invite Andrew to join us. Jaclyn and I talk about other things, and I keep the internal battle I'm having over the Andrew situation to myself.

After lunch, I notice that Andrew's not at the table anymore, and it looks like he's packed up all his things. It's unusual for him to leave this early in the day, and it makes me wonder if my friends are right after all. If he's really as flighty as they say, how can I possibly maintain a friendship with him once the summer ends? I tend to be an all-in kind of person when it comes to friendships, and the thought of my friendship with Andrew turning one-sided unsettles me.

I've been staring at my computer screen but not doing any real work for the past fifteen minutes, so I push the thoughts of Andrew aside and sigh as I go back to investigating book preservation companies.

CHAPTER 10

The flood clean up efforts have been taking up most of my time these days, pushing the general education project to the back burner. On the one hand, it's been a good distraction from worrying about the status of my application with McDowell. I haven't heard from them since my phone interview two weeks ago. On the other hand, despite my conversations with Jaclyn and Kylie about Andrew's flakiness, I miss our time working together.

While we haven't spent entire days working at the same table since the pipe burst, he's been here every day. We've been to lunch a few times, too. He doesn't ask about my panic attacks, but I know he's checking on me, making sure I'm coping well with the flood. But something about our relationship now is different, and I can't decide if it's that

I've been pulling away or if he has.

Today, though, we have a meeting with the provost.

"Are you ok? You look anxious." Andrew reaches out and gives my shoulder a squeeze.

"I'm fine," I say. "Just pre-meeting jitters. I don't have a lot of meetings with Dobson, so I'm not sure what to expect."

What I don't tell him is that part of me is waiting for him to ghost me like he did Jaclyn.

"You don't need to worry. I'll do most of the talking if you want, but you are so good at translating the data. I know you'll do well in the meeting."

"Thanks. I appreciate the pep talk. Do you think he'll be mad about our recommendation?"

While I've been working on flood clean up, Andrew has been drafting a proposal to assess a larger sample of course evaluations, but it's a big ask, because it would mean looking more closely at students' perceptions of specific faculty. While it has the potential to help with our retention problem, it also has the potential to tick off some long-time faculty.

"I don't think he'll be mad. The data backs up the need for the deeper assessment, so it will be ok. Plus, if you feel like you're going to have a panic attack, I'll be there." The look he gives me is so sincere I feel like I could cry, and suddenly all my worry about our friendship dissipates.

I take a deep breath because I definitely do not need to start crying right now, then I give Andrew a shaky smile.

"Ok, let's do this."

We walk over to the Fob and check in with Dobson's

administrative assistant, Amber. A few minutes later, Dobson comes out to greet us. He shows us into his office and gestures for us to sit in the two chairs across from his desk. And that is when I realize the huge mistake I've made.

I'm wearing a blue and yellow color block dress that I borrowed from Kylie. I like it because it makes me feel confident and professional. The hem hits slightly above my knees when I'm standing, but as soon as I sit down, it rides up to the middle of my thigh, revealing a lot of skin. Kylie and I wear similar sizes, but my hips are just enough wider than hers that I should have realized the skirt would fit me differently than it does her. It wouldn't be so bad except the chair is completely exposed with no table to hide my legs under.

I am suddenly aware that if I'm not careful with how I position my legs, I'm going to give Mike Dobson a perfect view of what's under my skirt. What's actually under my skirt is a pair of nylon shorts that I wear under dresses to prevent accidental flashing, but still. Giving Dobson an eyeful is not going to make this meeting go smoothly.

I do my best to cross my ankles so my knees will stay together while Andrew and Dobson exchange a bit of small talk. The small talk doesn't last long, though, and Dobson's attention is on me sooner than I would like.

"Tell me about how the data analysis is going so far," Dobson launches straight to the point, which is unusual. He's famous for going down rabbit trails during meetings. It's well-known among the faculty that he's easily distracted by whatever shiny idea has recently popped into his head. I once sat in on a meeting with him that was supposed to be about curriculum development when he turned to the registrar and asked for an update on the academic calendar revision she was working on.

I'm still marveling at Dobson's directness and am vaguely aware that I should be responding when Andrew clears his throat and says, "Well, as you know, since Evie has come on the project, we've been looking more closely at the data as it relates to our transfer students. Evie had this great idea for a pre-assessment that transfer students could take in their first semester. We've been working on developing the questions for it with the hope to launch it for the fall semester."

"That's great news. I knew when you suggested adding Evie to the team that she would be a good fit. I've also been hearing good things from Mike Pearce about the work you're doing on the clean up efforts from that god awful flood."

I am floored. I had no idea that Dobson had such a high opinion of me, and the compliment relaxes me a little.

"Thank you, Dr. Dobson!"

"Now then, Evie, tell me a bit more about this pre-assessment."

I remember to breathe before saying, "Like Andrew said, we're curious to look at transfer students' understanding of humanities topics when they're in their first semester at Cooke. That way we have a touch point that gives us not only transfer students' baseline knowledge but also a way we can compare the transfer students' knowledge with students who came to us in their first year without any prior college courses."

I shift in my seat a bit, but then I remember that my skirt is still too short for a meeting with the provost, so I shift right back to the way I was sitting before.

"Excellent. And tell me more about this proposal to look at the course evaluations."

I hesitate. I knew Dobson was going to ask for more details on the proposal, but I wasn't expecting him to direct the question at me.

"We're hoping that the further analysis will show strong evidence for continuing the current teaching practices among the humanities faculty," Andrew jumps in. I'm glad he does because while I was trying to figure out how to reply, I forgot to focus on keeping my knees together, and I snap them back together now. Andrew gives me an odd side look and I shrug a little, but Dobson doesn't seem to have noticed any of our strange little exchange because he's turned around looking out the window.

"It sounds like there's a 'but' at the end of that statement." Dobson is frowning as he whips his swivel chair back around to face us again.

Andrew grimaces.

"We're not done going through all the data, but the initial data analysis is indicating that there might be a problem, at least with a few...ah...specific professors."

Dobson's frown deepens. "Hmm, that is concerning."

"We won't really know for sure until we have the data from the second set of course evaluations, though," Andrew adds quickly.

"Right, right." Dobson pauses like he's about to say something else, but then the silence stretches long enough that Andrew and I glance at each other with twin questioning looks. Suddenly, whatever thoughts Dobson got lost in, he shakes off and says, "Well, keep working on the data and let me know what you find as you get through more of the analysis. Tell Amber I said to give you access to whatever you need."

I start to stand, thinking we've been dismissed, but Dobson tilts his head to the side with an eyebrow raised. I quickly retake my seat, pretending I was adjusting my skirt.

"Now for the real reason I wanted you to come in today," Dobson says as I settle back into my awkward posture.

I glance at Andrew again, and he looks as confused as I am by Dobson's statement.

"The ReGENerate Conference is coming up, and I want to send the two of you. It's a conference on general education assessment in Washington, D.C. I've already told Amber to help you register. I think the conference will be helpful for the work you're doing."

"Sounds great!" Andrew says, sounding far more enthusiastic than seems necessary.

"Yes, looking forward to it," I agree, and am a little mortified to hear myself matching Andrew's enthusiasm. "When is it?"

"Amber will have all the details. Stop and talk with her on the way out." With that, Dobson walks us to the door and wishes us a good afternoon.

The conference, it turns out, is in two weeks. It's short notice, but thankfully, both Andrew and I are available to attend. Amber registers us and makes our hotel reservations, and I text Kylie to ask her to feed Titania for me while we're gone.

Once we're out of the building and walking back across campus to the library, I breathe a sigh of relief.

"I thought we'd never get out of there!"

"What do you mean? I thought it went fine!" Andrew laughs.

"Easy for you to say! I spent the whole meeting trying not to flash Dobson!" I flush as I say it.

Andrew's eyes widen in shock. "What!?"

I gesture toward my legs.

"My skirt. It's too short. I didn't realize until I sat down, and it rode up."

Andrew glances down at my thighs, and my ears turn pink. He takes a long time observing the length of my skirt, then he slowly looks up. As his eyes move over my body, I feel practically naked at his attention. I fight a shiver as he finally makes eye contact with me.

He clears his throat, but his voice is a little hoarse as he says, "I don't see anything wrong with your skirt."

I swallow, but it feels like I can't catch my breath. I try breathing deeply, but it's making my chest heave slightly as I look at Andrew. He licks his lips, pulling my attention away from his eyes, and it's all I can do not to stare at his mouth. It takes effort for me to meet his eyes again.

When did we move so close together?

A breeze blows past us, loosening a strand of my hair and whipping it into my face. Andrew reaches for the strand of hair and tucks it behind my ear. His fingers trail along my jaw and send goosebumps down my arms. My mouth goes dry as Andrew seems to lean toward me, just slightly.

"EVIE!" someone is yelling my name across the campus green. I tear my gaze away from Andrew and look to see who it is. Kylie is half jogging toward us, and I can't decide if I'm glad or annoyed to see her.

"Evie! Oh hi, Andrew! Am I interrupting?" She's a little out of breath as she comes up to us.

Yes, you are interrupting, I think, although I'm not sure that the electric feeling from a moment ago was mutual.

"No, we were on our way back to the library," I say, but my voice sounds squeaky, like I still can't get enough air.

Kylie glances between us and cocks an eyebrow.

"Ok. Well, I'm glad I caught you. I need to run an errand, but Mike's in a meeting, and the Access Services folks are all in that workshop with the book preservation folks. I'll be back in about an hour."

"Ok, thanks for letting me know. I'll wait to have lunch until you're back."

"I can pick up some lunch for you," Andrew offers.

"What? No, you don't have to do that." I'm still a little flustered from whatever was happening between us before

Kylie showed up.

"I don't mind at all." Andrew grins. "Tacos?"

At the suggestion of tacos, I relent.

"You know I'll never turn down tacos. Thanks, friend." It's deliberate, calling him "friend." Not for him. For me. Because apparently I need the reminder that that's all this is.

"Alright, since your lunch needs are taken care of, I'll see you later." Kylie gives me a quick hug.

We say goodbye to Kylie and walk back to the library together. Andrew writes down my taco order, then I settle in at the service desk and look up the ReGENerate conference.

The conference website looks overproduced, and the words "ReGENerate: Reimagining General Education Best Practices in the 21st Century" appear in huge letters at the top of the screen.

While I'm looking through the schedule, which includes some surprisingly intriguing-sounding sessions, my phone rings. I don't recognize the number, but it's a D.C. area code. My heartbeat picks up a little.

I really shouldn't answer at the service desk, but I'm nervous and excited that this might be an invitation for a second interview, so I glance around the library to see if anyone is within earshot. When I see no one, I frown, then remember that it's summer and all the students are gone. And since it's summer, no one is likely to wander in unexpectedly, and Kylie already told me everyone else is occupied for at least the next hour. I answer the phone before I can talk myself out of it.

"Hi, is this Evie Watson?" the voice on the phone asks.

"Yes, this is she."

"Hi, Evie! This is Katherine Miller at McDowell University Libraries. How are you this afternoon?"

My hands tremble with excitement, and I try to keep the quaver out of my voice as I answer, "I'm doing well. What can I do for you?"

"Well, Evie, I'm calling because I would like to invite you for an in-person interview for the Research Services Team Lead position that you applied for. Are you still interested in the position?"

I open my mouth to say yes, but then I hesitate for a moment. I think about all the reasons I applied in the first place, the bigger staff, the budget stability, the proximity to my family. Even though the staffing and spending limitations making it hard to work here sometimes, I still love my job at Cooke. And while being closer to my family would be nice, I've built good relationships here. Kylie and Jaclyn both come to mind, and Andrew isn't far behind them. I know our friendship is still new and that it might fizzle out, but there's the potential for it to become a deep friendship.

"Are you still there?" Katherine asks, and I realize I've taken longer than a few seconds to reply.

"Oh, sorry, I wasn't expecting to hear from you today!" I shake my head at myself. It's not like taking an interview means leaving is set in stone. I don't have to decide until they offer me the job and hand me the paperwork. "Yes, I'm still interested. I'd be glad to come for an interview."

"Wonderful! Let me pull up the list of potential dates for you." Katherine gives me three options, and I bring up my calendar. All the dates are around the same time as the conference, which causes me a brief panic. But then I realize I only have to travel to D.C. once. I ask for the day before the conference so I can get through the interview out of the way and not spend the whole conference worrying about preparing for it.

Katherine and I go over a few more details about the interview, and she promises to follow up with me via email. As I hang up the phone, Andrew walks in with a to go bag from one of the taco places near campus.

When he gets to the desk he asks, "What's got you smiling so big?"

I grin even bigger, then frown. I have to tell Andrew about the interview because we're supposed to drive to D.C. together, and I doubt Cooke will pay for Andrew to stay at my hotel for the interview. Maybe I can convince McDowell University to pay for the extra room.

"Hey, what's wrong?" Andrew looks concerned, probably because I went from grinning like I'd won the lottery to wrinkling my nose.

"Sorry, it's not you. I...I haven't told anyone except for Kylie and Jaclyn about this." I bite my bottom lip and hesitate before I blurt out in a single breath, "I have a job interview! It's in D.C. right before the conference!"

Now it's Andrew's turn to frown. I don't know why this news would make him so disappointed.

"I didn't know you were thinking about leaving," he says, furrowing his brow.

"I'm not, really. I applied because it looks like a step up from here. I didn't really expect anything to come of it. But now I'm in the running, and I want to see how far I get."

Andrew doesn't say anything, and the silence between us stretches for an uncomfortable amount of time, so I add, "I applied for the Teaching and Learning job here, too."

That knocks the stony expression off his face, and the smile is back in his eyes.

"Well, if we need to drive up early for the conference, I'm down for that. I don't mind doing a bit of sightseeing while you interview."

"I didn't think Cooke would pay for an extra hotel night for you."

Andrew waves a hand at that. "Don't worry about it. I can get a room at whatever hotel they put you up in, and then we can switch to the conference hotel. Now, let's eat these tacos before they get cold, and you can tell me all about the job."

I follow him to his table by the windows. He pulls the tacos and a side of guacamole out of the bag, then surprises me by also setting a box with a slice of très leches cake on the table. It's things like this—his thoughtfulness in getting lunch for a friend—that make me question the things Kylie has told me about him. I don't see how he could ever be a heartbreaker.

We eat our tacos and talk about the parts of the McDowell job ad that convinced me to apply. Andrew listens attentively, but I can't help feeling like he looks a little sad whenever I get excited about the position.

Later, after we part ways for the day, I keep thinking about Andrew's half-smile. It bothers me that he wasn't more excited for me, and I can't ignore the nagging feeling that if I take the job at McDowell, my friendship with Andrew would be over.

CHAPTER 11

It is a well-known fact in the library world that if a book is misshelved, it may as well not exist. Librarians spend a lot of time cataloging and assigning call numbers to the books and other materials in our collections, but the second a student worker accidentally shelves PS3573.A425635 V37 2020 in the PR section, it's like it was never there to begin with. Why? Because between PR3753 (English Literature of the 17th and 18th Centuries) and PS3573 (American Literature, 1961-2000) there are hundreds, if not thousands, of places it could be hiding on the shelf.

Add in the fact that it's roughly that range of books that were waterlogged when the pipe burst a few weeks ago, and the likelihood of finding John Vance's dissertation on narrative structure in *Infinite Jest* goes from zero to negative never.

This morning, June handed me a list of the still-unaccounted for titles from the flooded area. When I saw that John's book was on the list, I nearly lost my breakfast. I've been running around, checking every possible place it could have been misshelved. It's not looking good, though, and I have the sinking feeling that it was one of the books that took on the initial deluge and was tossed as unsalvageable. If John finds out that we've lost our copy of his book, he'll be livid, and I don't want to give him any reason to take that out on me.

I check the time and curse under my breath. The gen ed committee is getting together again this morning to talk about Dobson's feedback on the project status.

I'm running a few minutes later than I'd like to be, thanks to John's missing book, but I get to the room where the others are gathered just as Andrew is calling the meeting to order.

"Sorry I'm late!" I say as I take my seat.

"It's no problem. We hadn't started yet." Andrew smiles at me.

From across the room, I hear John let out an annoyed sigh. I tense, but concentrate on what Andrew is saying, trying not to give John the satisfaction of seeing that his presence—and the fact that I can't find his book—rattle me.

"Before we get into the data," Andrew is saying, "I wanted to let you all know that Dobson asked Evie and me to go to the ReGENerate conference in Washington, D.C. at the end of this month.”

Someone scoffs.

“Something wrong?” Andrew looks at John.

“Why’s she the one who gets to go to the conference? She just joined this group. The rest of us have been working our asses off for months!” John says with a sneer.

Andrew gives John a tight smile. “Yes, and we kept running into problems with the data analysis that Evie fixed in a matter of days.”

“So? She obviously doesn’t need to go to the conference, then, if she already knows everything about data analysis.”

I frown but take a deep breath. If this were any other meeting with any other faculty member, I would jump in to defend myself, but John sets me so on edge after everything that’s happened between us that I’m afraid I’ll burst into angry tears. I’m already agitated enough from being late, and I’m worried it won’t take much to push me into a full-on panic attack. No, better to let Andrew handle this.

Andrew glances at me out of the corner of his eye, and I give him a small nod to let him know I’m ok. He must get the message because he turns back to John and says, “I don’t know exactly why Dobson wanted to send Evie and not you or anyone else on the committee. If it’s really that big a deal, I suggest you go talk to him yourself. Meanwhile, the rest of us are going to talk about the latest work we’ve been doing. Is that ok with you?”

John sets his mouth into a grim line, then crosses his arms and huffs, “Fine.”

“Good. Now, back to what I was saying. Evie and I are

going to the conference in D.C., but I'd like everyone to take a look at the conference program and help us figure out which sessions look the most useful for one of us to attend so that we can divide and conquer when we get there."

The rest of the meeting goes smoothly, although John continues to grumble any time I start to say something. I'm thankful when the meeting finally ends.

"I've got another meeting over lunch, but I'll see you in the library this afternoon," Andrew says as we walk out of the classroom together.

"Sounds good. Same table as usual?"

"Like there are any other tables I would use." Andrew laughs.

I smile at him, and Andrew reaches out to fist bump me. I'm still grinning as I walk out of the building, but John is standing on the porch talking on his phone as I exit. He glares at me as I walk by, causing my smile to falter a little. But he doesn't engage with me beyond that, and I forget about him soon after I get back to my office.

Later that afternoon, Andrew and I are sitting at our usual table. We've been working diligently for most of the afternoon, but my leg is bouncing under the table.

"You can't seem to keep still over there," Andrew says. "Everything ok?"

He doesn't ask about how I'm doing after the meeting with John, but the question is implied.

"It's not about the meeting." I glance around the room to see if anyone can hear our conversation. "I've been working on my presentation for my interview. I need to practice it in front of an audience, but Kylie and Jaclyn are both busy this weekend.”

The corners of Andrew's mouth turn slightly down, but only for a moment.

“I could help with that.”

“Are you sure? I was hoping you would, but I can find someone else if you don't want to.”

“Yeah, I can help.” Andrew doesn't look enthusiastic, but then he's been a little reserved every time we've talked about my interview.

“Wonderful! How about Saturday evening? We can eat dinner at my place first.”

He smiles, and the lack of enthusiasm seems to disappear.

“Sounds perfect. But I'm in charge of the food.” He winks at me.

“I can deal with that.”

———

On Saturday afternoon, I answer a knock at the door and find Andrew on my porch with a couple of bags of groceries and a stock pot.

“I wasn't sure what kinds of pots you had, so I brought my own,” he says when I raise an eyebrow at him.

“I was expecting takeout tonight. What's all this?”

“I promised you a batch of Gran's chicken and noodles. It will take a while to make, so I also brought snacks.”

“Mmm. You're speaking my language.”

Andrew sets the groceries on the counter and looks around the kitchen.

"Where can I find a cutting board?" he asks as he opens a cabinet.

"In the cabinet on the…" I point toward the cabinet near the sink, but then I remember. "Oh wait, I rearranged the cabinets a few weeks ago. Hold on, I'll have to look with you."

I join Andrew in the kitchen and start opening cabinets. I don't do a lot of cooking, so I honestly can't remember where the cutting boards are because I haven't made anything except boxed mac and cheese since I rearranged everything.

It's not a very big kitchen, so we keep scooting around each other. After trying most of the lower cabinets, I open one in the corner and find the cutting boards. Andrew is standing next to me, where he's been looking in one of the upper cabinets. When I stand up and turn to face him, we're standing so close I can almost feel the heat radiating off his body. I try to back up, but because I'm in the corner, I sort of bounce forward when I bump into the counter. Instead of giving Andrew more space, now we're standing even closer than we were before.

"I found the cutting boards," I say with a shaky voice. Andrew is standing there so tall and solid, and if I breathe a little too hard, we'll be chest to chest.

"I can see that." Andrew's voice is thick as he stares down at me. "I'll just…" He leans toward the open cabinet, and I take a step to the side so he can reach a cutting board.

As he straightens back up, I clear my throat. "I'll get out of your way."

I move to leave the kitchen, but Andrew catches my hand, and I am suddenly very aware of all the nerve endings in my palm.

"I was hoping to show you how to make the chicken and noodles." Andrew's voice is quiet. His hand is smooth and warm against mine, and his thumb is pressed hard into the soft spot between my thumb and index finger, like he's resisting something.

"I'd like that."

He gently tugs and guides me to the counter where he sets the cutting board he's been holding. He lets my hand go, and starts pulling groceries out of the canvas bags. A whole chicken, potatoes, celery, onions, carrots, and rosemary line the counter. There's also a bag of flour and a small carton of eggs.

"I'll need a mixing bowl for the noodles. We'll do them first because they have to dry out for a little while."

I find a bowl, and Andrew opens the bag of flour. He dumps an indeterminate amount of flour into the bowl.

"Gran never measures how much flour she uses. She does it by sight and feel. I've made this with her enough that I know about how much looks right."

"That's some high-level kitchen savvy," I say, and Andrew grins at the compliment.

He adds salt to the flour, then makes a well in the center of the flour and cracks an egg into it.

I am not prepared for what comes next. He rolls up his

sleeves, revealing the corded muscles of his forearms, and slowly mixes the dough with his hands. He's using his fingers to rake through the mixture with gentle strokes, slowly incorporating the dry flour into the wet dough.

I try not to gape at the movement of his hands through the dough, but the sight is sending my imagination running in all kinds of directions. Andrew's fingers stroking other places, kneading, caressing. My entire body is on fire.

I force myself to step away from watching him continue to work with the dough and get a glass from one of the cabinets. I pour myself some water and drink it in one big gulp. Then I pour myself another glass.

As I sip on the water, Andrew finishes forming the dough into a ball and covers it with a towel which he must have found in a random drawer while I was having a premature hot flash.

"I need to let the dough rest for a bit," he says as he washes his hands. "While that happens, we're going to assemble the stock."

I nod. I've cooled down some, so I think I can stand a bit closer to Andrew while he works on the chicken. There's nothing sexy about watching a man wrestle a dead chicken into a stock pot, thank goodness.

"Will you slice the onions and celery while I spatchcock the chicken?"

My eyes go big. "While you...what?"

Andrew bursts into laughter. "Spatchcock. You know, cutting it up and removing the spine? It makes it easier to break down the bird so that it cooks faster."

"I...did not know that word." I shake my head, laughing.

The laughter seems to clear the air of the weird tension from a moment ago. I work on slicing the vegetables while Andrew finishes...whatever it is he's doing to the chicken. We fill the stock pot, and Andrew covers everything with water, then seasons it with salt, pepper, and rosemary.

"While that's coming to a boil, I'll go ahead and roll out the noodles. We also need to wash and peel the potatoes so we can make mashed potatoes." Andrew looks through the drawers for a rolling pin and clears a space on the counter.

As we work on the various parts of the meal, I smile to myself. Cooking with Andrew is a lot of fun. At some point, I hand Andrew my phone and ask him to pick some music to play on the kitchen speaker. He picks Taylor Swift's *1989*, "because it makes me feel things." He makes sure I know that he always listens to Taylor's Version.

"You know she bought her masters back, right?"

"Yeah, but I remember. Oh I remember!"

I laugh as he sings the last bit, a goofy grin on his face and his hand raised as though he's holding a microphone. His joy is infectious, and I start singing along. We dance around the kitchen being completely silly as we chop and stir and season the food. As much as I love Jaclyn and Kylie, this isn't the kind of thing I would ever do with them, and it strikes me as so refreshing to have a friend who will sing along to "Wildest Dreams" at the top of his lungs with me.

The chicken and noodles take a long time to finish cooking. After the stock comes to a boil, we turn it down to simmer for an hour. While we wait, we go to the couch to talk through my presentation.

I'm presenting on cross-department collaborations in libraries since Kylie and I have been working so closely with June and the Access Services librarians on the flood clean up project. I'm using the fallout from the flood as my primary example, but I want Andrew's take on whether I should include the work we've been doing for the general education project.

"Is it too far from library work to really make sense with what I'm talking about?" I bite my lip.

"No, I don't think so. I think it demonstrates that librarians and teaching faculty can have mutually beneficial impacts on each other's work. Besides, you can brag about how teaching faculty don't understand spreadsheets and need a librarian to fix things." Andrew's eyes sparkle with mischief as he teases me.

I roll my eyes. "Where would you be if I hadn't stepped in? Confused about why your data didn't make sense and probably up the creek with Dobson."

"I don't disagree with you." Andrew holds his hands out in a deferential motion. "I'm saying you should brag about that because you're absolutely right. Dobson would be all up my ass if I'd turned in that initial report with the mess the data was in before you came on the project."

"Oh. Well, we agree, then."

While I make a few notes on my outline for the presentation, Andrew checks on the food. We've been working on the outline for a while, and I'm getting hungry. It doesn't help that the whole house smells delicious as the chicken and noodles cook.

"This is almost ready. I'm just going to mash the potatoes, and then we can eat," he calls from the kitchen.

"Sounds great." I've been debating whether to ask for his help on one last thing for the presentation, and I finally decide to go for it. "Would you mind helping me pick my outfit for the interview?"

He steps back into the living room, tossing a towel over his shoulder. "Yeah, I can do that."

I go to my room and put on one of the outfits I've been thinking about wearing. I want to make sure I avoid any further skirt disasters like what happened in Dobson's office. As I come around the corner to the kitchen, Andrew stops what he's doing and looks me over. I'm wearing a pair of black slacks and a blazer over a shiny purple shirt.

"This is what I'm thinking for the day of the interview," I say.

"It's good," he says. "Professional but shows off your personality."

I beam at him, because that was exactly the look I was going for. "Awesome. Let me show you what I'm thinking about for the dinner the night before."

I go back to my room and switch to a dress that's dark navy with white polka dots. It's an A-line with a scoop neck and three-quarter length sleeves, and the skirt hits below my knees, making it longer than the one I nearly flashed the provost in. It's one of my favorites because it highlights my curves in a way that makes me feel sexy but professional.

Andrew is scooping mashed potatoes into a bowl as I

come back into the kitchen, but he nearly drops the spoon when I walk in. He recovers, then gestures for me to spin around, and I can feel his eyes on me as I do.

"What do you think?" I ask as I turn back to face him.

"Yeah," he croaks, then makes an ahem sound. "You should wear that."

"It's not too 'night on the town' for an interview?"

He shakes his head. "No, it's perfect."

"Sounds like I know what to pack, then," I say. "I'll go change back into my regular clothes."

Andrew starts to say something, but then shakes his head. I tilt my head in a question, but he says, "Never mind."

Something was definitely odd about how he reacted to my second outfit, but I'm too hungry to think about it and make quick work of changing and going back to the living room.

A few minutes later, he sets a bowl of mashed potatoes topped with chicken and noodles on the coffee table in front of me. He hands me a spoon, and I pick up the bowl. It's really too warm a dish to eat on a summer night, but it smells so good that I don't care.

I take a bite of the glorious looking concoction and practically melt in delight. I close my eyes and moan, "Oh, god. Andrew. It's so wonderful!"

The potatoes and chicken with the rosemary make the dish absolutely heavenly. I take another bite, savoring the rich sauce and perfectly cooked noodles. He stares at me as I slowly pull the spoon out of my mouth and lick the remaining sauce from the back of the spoon.

I blush at the unabashed display of pleasure that I've apparently been putting on. I nod toward him. "You're not eating."

Andrew swallows. His eyes look dark, and his breathing seems shallower than normal.

"Is something wrong?" My voice is practically a whisper.

Andrew shakes his head, then clears his throat, but his voice still comes out thick. "Nothing's wrong. Evie, I..."

I cut him off. "Do you smell something burning?"

"Shit! I must have left the stove on!" Andrew runs to the kitchen and turns off the stove. He moves the pot of chicken and noodles to a different burner, but I can tell from where I'm sitting that the rest of the chicken and noodles is probably not salvageable. I come up behind Andrew and glance around him at the pot.

"Is it ruined?"

Andrew hangs his head. "Yeah, probably. That's one thing my Gran always fusses about when I cook this. I always manage to burn it a little."

"It's ok. What I got to eat was fantastic. We'll do this again sometime." I put my hand on his upper arm, then pull him in to a hug. I don't know why I do it, except that since the flood, there's a physicality to our relationship that wasn't there before. He hugs me back and draws me closer, his hands wrapped low around my back.

"Thanks, Evie," he says as we step out of our embrace.

"For what? You cooked for me and helped me figure out what I need to do for my presentation."

"For asking me to come over and letting me cook for

you. I like cooking for the people in my life. It gives me a lot of joy to do that." He smiles at me, but it's not his usual cocky smile that makes me go weak in the knees like a 1960s teenager seeing the Beatles in person for the first time. It's a more melancholy smile—one that still makes my heart melt a little, but in a way that makes me want to make sure he always has someone to cook for.

CHAPTER 12

I haven't stopped thinking about the savory goodness of the chicken and noodles for the past three days. There's still a hint of rosemary in my kitchen, and I'm thinking about buying a counter top rosemary plant just so the scent never goes away. If it's because the smell of rosemary will now forever be associated with Andrew, I don't acknowledge it.

And if Andrew showed up on Monday with a glass container with a fresh batch to make up for the burnt mess from Saturday, I definitely did not have heart flutters about it. Because we are just friends, and bringing someone a redo batch of a food she loves is a friend move. Right?

I don't have time to think about friendly food gestures, though, because Andrew and I have work to do before we leave for the conference next week. Right now we're sifting through a set of data that is particularly in-depth and involves a lot of evidence tagging. We've been working on the tagging since Monday, and we're only halfway through. At this rate, I doubt we'll be able to finish before it's time to drive to D.C., and I still need to put the finishing touches on my presentation for my interview.

Around 3:00, I go to my office to get some notes from my desk. As I close the door on my way back downstairs, I hear Mike behind me.

"Ah, there you are. I thought you would still be out by the window."

I make a noncommittal sound and shrug. I haven't asked my boss what he thinks about me spending all this time working with Andrew in the public area of the library, but he also hasn't told me to stop.

"I'm heading out for the day, and I think you're the last one here. Kylie already left, and of course, the Access Services crew is over in the dining hall working on drying out some more of the books from the freezer. I trust you'll be ok on your own?"

"That's no problem. Andrew's here, so I won't be totally alone, anyway. Honestly, I could leave and let him run the place if I wanted to. You know someone in Admissions called here yesterday looking for him? I guess word has gotten around that this is where he's spending his all his time this summer." I mentally kick myself for rambling, but Mike laughs.

"You're right. Next time we have a coverage issue, I'll see

if he's available." He pauses, then says, "Don't get too absorbed in that gen ed work you two have been doing and forget to go home."

"We won't. Have a good afternoon!"

I lock my office, then walk through the second floor to see if any patrons are up here. When I'm the only one on duty, I like to have an idea of how many people are in the building. I don't find anyone in any of the study rooms or at the tables in the open spaces, so I go back downstairs and check the computer lab. There aren't any patrons there, either.

It's not entirely surprising that the library is empty at 3:00 on a Wednesday in June. Cooke University doesn't have any on-campus classes over the summer, although there are a lot of online classes. The slow flow of library traffic is one of the things that I hate most about summers in the Cooke Library. I'm much more at home in a busy building, rushing from meeting to meeting. It's part of why I've been enjoying Andrew's company so much this summer. His presence means that I have someone to interact with every day.

Andrew is walking back from the water bottle refilling station when I come back to the main study area.

"It's just you and me here," I say as we both walk up to the table where we've been working all day.

"Everyone else cleared out?" Andrew asks as he leans against the top of one of the chairs.

"Yeah. They all had appointments out of the building this afternoon."

"So it really is just you and me in here." Something

about the way Andrew says it makes my heart race. The air suddenly feels staticky, and I didn't realize before how close we are standing to each other. Our eyes lock for a moment, and my breathing is suddenly shallower. Andrew licks his lips, and I glance toward his mouth. As I force my gaze back up to his blue-gray eyes, I know my cheeks are turning pink.

"Yep. Just the two of us." My voice sounds wrong. I clear my throat. "I'm, um, going to go sit at the service desk, you know, in case anyone, um, calls." I still sound breathy.

"Ok. You do that." Andrew's voice sounds a little funny, too.

"Ok. I'm going now." I start to move, but he's standing between me and the table where my things are. "I need my...oops!"

I try leaning around Andrew to get my laptop from the table, but he doesn't move, so I bump into him and lose my balance. As I stumble forward, he tries to catch me but the palm of his hand slides across my breast as he tries to grab my arm. My body betrays me and goosebumps erupt all over at what feels like a caress. The wave of heat that courses through me is a combination of unwanted arousal and embarrassment.

Andrew pulls his hand back like he's touched a live wire, and the look of horror on his face looks an awful lot like rejection.

"Oh, shit. Evie. I'm so sorry. I didn't mean to..." He sputters.

My face is as red as it can possibly get.

"It's nothing!" My voice is too high.

I gather my things and practically run to the service desk.

"I'll just be over here!"

I almost miss the desk chair as I sit. I open my laptop, but I can't concentrate on what's on the screen. I don't know how long I've been sitting here when a throat clears near me. I look up to see Andrew standing by the desk.

"I think I'm going to go." He's not looking at me so much as near me, and I suspect he's as embarrassed as I am about what happened.

"Ok," I say, and my voice still sounds strangled.

"I'm sorry." He still won't make eye contact with me.

"Ok."

"I'll see you tomorrow."

"Ok," I sigh.

He starts to walk away, and the desire to clear the air between us grips me. "Andrew?"

He turns to look at me but still doesn't meet my eyes.

"I know it was an accident."

He blushes. "Ok. Good. I'll see you tomorrow."

I throw myself into work for the rest of the afternoon knowing that if I sit still I'll worry over the look on Andrew's face as he shook off whatever cooties he must think I have. When it's time to close up for the day, I take my time, fussing over little things that aren't really part of the closing procedure—dusting the reference collection, lining up chairs precisely five inches from the table, generally focusing on the minute details of making the library pristine for tomorrow.

I go to the public library and browse through the romance section until they close at 8:30. I haven't eaten dinner, and my stomach is growling by the time I leave with a tote bag full of pirate romances.

I grab a burger at a drive through and eat it in the car.

By 9:00 I have my pajamas on, and I flop on the couch, still unready to face the thoughts of the brief moment of shock and his look of disgust and my hurt from this afternoon.

As soon as I sit down, Titania comes and curls up on my chest. She always seems to know when I need comfort. I stroke her ears and sigh as she purrs.

"Oh, to be a cat whose only problem is waiting for dinner!" I exclaim. I know I'm being dramatic, but I figure the cat doesn't care.

I lie down on the couch and try to read, but it's pointless. Not even a swashbuckling pirate in tight trousers with a long sword can distract me from thinking about the way my whole body broke out in chill bumps at Andrew's touch.

After reading the same paragraph for the third time, I give up and close my eyes. I'm in that weird state between sleep and awake—the one where you can't tell if you're dreaming or not—when the doorbell rings. I answer it, and Andrew is standing on the porch, breathing hard like he's run to my house. We stare at each other for a long moment, and then I'm reaching toward him, pulling his face to me.

The beard he's been growing this summer tickles my lips when he kisses me, just like I thought it would.

I don't know which one of us moves us into the house, but suddenly we're both inside, and Andrew is closing the door behind him. He kisses me again, his tongue sweeping into my mouth, and I moan against him.

We're stumbling toward the bedroom, our kisses becoming more furious and hurried as we bump our way down the hall. I lead him to the bed, and we sit on the edge, still embracing. He reaches toward my breast, but this time, he doesn't draw his hand back like he's touched a hot stove. This time, I don't flush with embarrassment, and he moans out my name.

I make a sound of pleasure as his thumb caresses me, and he growls in response. I'm still wearing my shirt from work, a cute blouse with a low vee neckline, which is perfect because now he's kissing down my neck along the hem. When he gets to the center of the vee, he makes a hungry sound, and his teeth graze the top of my breast.

The next thing I know, we're both topless. I can't look away from his perfectly sculpted stomach. At least, I think it's perfectly sculpted, but things are a bit fuzzy, like I can't focus on Andrew the way I want to. I try blinking to clear whatever is fogging my vision. I can see that he's undoing the button and zipper on his pants, and just as he's about to pull them all the way off, I hear a crash.

I wake up with a start.

The stack of books I brought home is all over the floor, and the cat is dashing around the living room like she's possessed. It doesn't take a detective to guess what happened.

I blush at the memory of the dream, then drop my head into my hands with a frustrated sigh. I have a problem, and it's not that Andrew touched me. The problem is I want him to do it again.

I get to work at my usual time the next morning, but Andrew isn't here yet. I almost go to our table by the window, but I can't just sit there like nothing happened, so I go to my office to work on a library project until he's here.

An hour ticks by, and he hasn't shown up yet, which is odd. He's usually here by now. I pick up my phone and think about texting him.

I put the phone back down and shake my head at myself. He doesn't have any obligation to be here. We don't have a meeting scheduled, and we haven't made lunch plans. Besides, what would I even say to him when I see him?

No worries about the accidental groping and also I actually think I liked it?

NOPE.

I try to concentrate on the tutorial I'm creating for the new research methods class in the nursing program, but the minutes are running like molasses. I'm looking for a good video about how to use the library's main nursing database, but my mind keeps wandering, and I have no idea if the one

I just watched was actually useful. After another half hour of staring at my computer screen but not actually hearing the words in the videos I'm watching, I give in and text Andrew.

ME: You coming to campus today?

I stare at my phone for a few minutes, willing the three dots that indicate a reply to appear. When I realize I've been looking at the message to Andrew for a full five minutes, I sigh and put the phone back in my pocket.

I go get more coffee from the workroom to distract myself.

As I walk into the workroom, my phone pings. Not wanting Madge, the office manager, to ask me about the message, I get my coffee and try to slip out without talking to her. Unfortunately, Madge's desk is right by the door, and she has a knack for catching people when they least want to chat.

"Do you need anything from me today?" Madge asks. Madge is always very well-meaning in her offers of assistance, but sometimes I feel smothered by my overly helpful coworker.

"No, just working on a few things this morning."

"Ok!" Madge pauses for barely a breath. "I haven't seen Andrew around today. Will he be here later?"

"Oh, um, I don't know. We didn't have any plans. I don't really keep up with when he is and isn't here." I hedge. I hope the lie isn't too obvious.

"Oh, ok. I noticed that the two of you had been working together a lot lately."

I groan inwardly. I want to get out of this conversation and check my phone.

"Yeah, that's what happens when you're collaborating on a project!" I try to sound sunny, but it comes out sounding sarcastic.

Madge frowns.

"Shit. Madge, I'm sorry. I'm feeling a little off today," I apologize quickly. Madge hasn't done anything wrong, and there's no need for me to bite her head off about my weird mood.

"It's ok. I know you've had a lot going on. Just let me know if you need me to do anything!"

"Thanks, Madge." I take the opportunity to escape.

Even though I'm dying to look at my phone, I wait until I'm in my office to check the message. But it's not a text from Andrew. It's a notification for free tacos from a fast casual chain whose app I have. Ugh.

At lunch time, Andrew still hasn't replied. I've given up looking at my phone and have locked it in my desk drawer so I'm not tempted to look at it. I'm able to focus at least a little and get a few sections of the tutorial put together.

I'm about to go cash in on the free tacos, when another notification dings.

ANDREW: Hey! I won't be there today. Something came up.

I'm disappointed, but I want him to feel like things are no big deal, so I reply almost immediately.

ME: Ok. See you tomorrow, hopefully!

I sigh. My text sounds desperate, and I hate it. But

Andrew doesn't reply, and I have the feeling I won't see him tomorrow, either. I click the button on my phone to put it to sleep, then go to lunch to eat my free tacos.

Andrew doesn't show up on Friday, either. It takes all of my restraint not to call him and demand to know why he's avoiding me.

I try throwing myself into the flood project to keep my mind from lingering on images of Andrew's hands on me. The only problem is that shifting through lists of books in the library's collection to identify which ones are badly out of date and have newer editions available gets rather boring and repetitive after a while. Even under normal circumstances, it would be mind numbing work.

By the time I get home Friday night, I'm sure that Andrew was so repulsed by "The Boob Incident" that he's found another job, moved across the country, and ghosted me completely. I know it's ridiculous, of course. We're supposed to drive to D.C. together for my interview and the conference in a few days.

I groan. I haven't thought about the drive to D.C. It's going to be supremely awkward. I do what I do any time I find myself in an awkward situation. I text Kylie and Jaclyn.

ME: Sooooo, I need your advice on something.

ME: Andrew grabbed my boob

I accidentally hit send before I can type the rest of the story. Jaclyn's response is immediate.

JACLYN: YEAH GIRL GET IT

ME: Uh, that wasn't it at all. It was an accident, and I haven't seen him since. AND I had a sexy dream about him. I'm freaking out a little.

JACLYN: Oh, shit.

KYLIE: Oh no! Evie, have you tried to talk to him?

ME: I mean, we sort of talked right after it happened, but not since the dream. I have to ride with him in the car for six hours on Monday!

JACLYN: Ok, here's the thing. You're both adults. A little boob grab isn't going to ruin your friendship.

KYLIE: I'm with Jaclyn on this. Don't let something that was clearly unintentional spoil things. And the fact you haven't seen him is probably unrelated.

JACLYN: If I were in your shoes, I'd make a dirty joke about it and move on.

KYLIE: All for moving on, but I'd advise against making a dirty joke.

JACLYN: ...

KYLIE: As far as having a dream about him, don't worry about that. He doesn't know.

JACLYN: Yeah. I have sexy dreams about coworkers all the time. Doesn't have to make things awkward, especially if you don't tell him about it. One time I even had a sexy dream about Mike.

ME: Which Mike?

JACLYN: Advancement Mike. You know how he always wears that Indiana Jones hat when he walks around campus? He kept it on the whole time. Very weird.

I laugh but don't press for more details.

My friends are right. I can get past the awkwardness. Andrew doesn't know about my dream, and he doesn't need to know. Besides, he's already apologized profusely. And really, was it any different fantasizing about him now than it had been before we became friends?

But when I think more about it, I realize that it is different. Then, I had merely been ogling an incredibly attractive man, not unlike when I ogled the *People* "Sexiest Man Alive" issue every fall.

But now? Now I know that Andrew loves nerdy books and is an amazing cook and eats ice cream straight from the container. Now I know that he cares about his mom and his aunts and his grandmother and that there is something melancholy in his life that makes him want to cook for people to fill the void with joy. Now I trust him enough to tell him about one of the darkest moments of my academic career. Yes, his athletic build and scruffy beard and those damn beautiful eyes make my whole body feel like liquid, but my attraction to him is well beyond the physical at this point.

I can't tell Andrew any of that, though. I value our friendship too much to ruin it by letting my attraction get in the way. I resolve to move past worrying over the accidental groping and focus on continuing to build a friendship with Andrew. Besides, it's not like he sees me as anything more than a friend. And even if he did, there's no way we could date since I don't date colleagues.

Armed with my resolution, I am ready to be stuck in a

car with Andrew for six hours on the way to Washington, D.C.

CHAPTER 13

I'm double-checking my suitcase when the doorbell rings, announcing that Andrew is here to pick me up for the drive to D.C. I take a calming breath and go to the door.

Don't make it awkward, Evie. Don't make it awkward.

I open the door, and there he is, looking handsome as ever in his light blue t-shirt and dark jeans. He smiles at me, and the knots in my stomach relax a little.

"Hi," he says, and it's tentative, like he's not sure what our footing is like, either.

"Hi," I say back, hoping there's a warmth to my voice but feeling awkward anyway.

"Listen, about Wednesday...." he starts, but I cut him off.

"I told you, I know it was an accident. Let's just pretend

it didn't happen."

"Ok. I just...I need you to know that I would never touch anyone like that without their permission." The sincerity in his voice almost takes my breath away. Andrew is a good man, and it feels like such a rare thing.

Even so, my face flames a little. I want to tell him he has permission. That he could touch me like that—and more— any time. But he's my friend, not my boyfriend, and giving him that type of permission isn't something friends do.

I suppress a sigh as I say, "Andrew, I know you wouldn't."

Andrew lets out a breath, and I step out of the way and gesture for him to come inside.

"I was just making sure I had everything when you rang the doorbell. Come in and make yourself comfortable while I finish packing up." I smile at him, subtly trying to show him that we're ok, then I walk down the hall to my bedroom.

I check my bag one last time, but realize I've forgotten a couple items that are still hanging up in the laundry, which is adjacent to the kitchen. As I walk back into the combined kitchen-dining room-living room space, Andrew stands up from the couch.

"Got everything?"

"No, I just need to grab my bras from the laundry room." I stop abruptly as my brain catches up with my words. My jaw drops and my eyes widen, and I know without even looking at Andrew that we're both blushing and unsure of how to proceed.

I come out of the stupor we're in first and race toward the laundry room, grab the bras, and stuff them under my shirt so that he won't see them as I go back to the bedroom to put them in my suitcase.

Before I go back to the living room, I lean my head against the door. This is going to be a long trip.

Despite the awkward start, the drive to D.C. turns out to be quite pleasant. Andrew thankfully did not comment on the bra incident when I brought my things out to the car, and we only sat in uncomfortable silence for a few minutes before we started laughing about it.

We're making good time on the drive. The traffic on the interstate has been steady but not heavy. We stopped for lunch near Roanoke, and the map app Andrew is using says we'll be in D.C. around dinner time.

But right after we pass Harrisonburg, Virginia, the traffic suddenly slows, then stops. I pull out my phone to check traffic alerts, and sure enough, there's been an accident a few miles ahead of us. From what I can find online, it's a pretty bad one, and we're going to be stuck for a while.

"Since we're here...there's something that's been bugging me that I want to ask you about." I look at Andrew, but my heartbeat stutters. If this gets too awkward, I can always jump out of the car and make a run for it.

"Ok, ask away," he says confidently, although the look

on his face is more cautious than he sounds.

"So, Kylie...warned me...about you." It looks like Andrew is about to say something, but I keep going. "She said that you have a heartbreaker reputation for a reason, and that it's not just the women you date, but the women you're friends with. She said that Jaclyn used to be your best friend, but then you started hanging out with Veronica from Medieval Studies and stopped hanging out with her. So I want to know...is what we have a flash in the pan summer friendship sort of thing?"

"There's a lot to unpack there."

"Well, we have time." I gesture for him to go on.

"The Jaclyn thing was a miscommunication. We used to spend a lot of time together, and we had a very close friendship at the time. But I screwed it up because I got busy with life stuff."

He's quiet for a moment, and I think he's going to leave it at that, but then he says, "I don't think either Kylie or Jaclyn know this, but about the time Jaclyn and I stopped hanging out, Gran's illness was really ramping up, and I was spending a lot of time helping Mom and my aunts with everything."

He sounds tired as he tells me, and I wonder if this is part of that melancholy side of him that he's only started to show me.

"That makes sense why you would stop seeing each other as much, but why didn't you tell her?"

"At the time, I was trying to keep work completely separate from family stuff, but I didn't realize that you can't really separate a part of yourself from your friends like that and expect them to stick around. I'm not proud of it."

I reach out and give his hand a reassuring squeeze because he sounds so remorseful.

"Anyway, I messed up, and I probably ought to apologize to Jaclyn."

"Yeah, you should. I doubt she'd admit it, but I think it hurt her."

"You're probably right." Andrew sighs again. "As far as Veronica is concerned, we started hanging out because by the time I realized I had messed up my friendship with Jaclyn, she had met her friend Rhys and was spending all her time with him."

I've met Rhys a few times. He and Jaclyn met at some sort of local volunteering agency. That, plus the fact that every time I've met the guy he's barely said two words to anyone, is basically all I know about him. And that every time I ask Jaclyn if she and Rhys are secretly dating, she denies it.

Andrew goes on, "Veronica wasn't Jaclyn, though, and after a while, I realized the only reason she was hanging out with me was that she wanted something more from our relationship. I definitely wasn't in a place where I could pursue a romantic relationship, and even if I had been, it wouldn't have been with Veronica."

"Why not?"

"Partly because of everything with Gran, and partly because..." He hesitates, an indecisive look on his face. "Partly because there's someone I've been interested in for a while. She's funny and smart and beautiful, but I don't think she feels the same way about me. Still, it didn't feel right to pursue something with Veronica when I was holding out hope for... the other woman."

"Oh. Well, maybe you should tell her how you feel. You never know; she might feel the same way."

I don't know why I'm encouraging him to pursue this other woman, but I'm telling myself it's what a friend would do. And we're friends. Just friends.

"Maybe I will, but I really don't think she feels the same way about me." Andrew looks sad. He shakes his head a little, then smiles. "As far as you and I are concerned, no, this is not a flash in the pan summer friendship. I like you, and I like spending time with you."

"That's a relief because I like you, too." I let go of a breath I didn't realize I've been holding.

The traffic has started moving, although we're still barely inching along the interstate. The estimated time on the map app is getting longer, but we fall into a conversation about books—our go-to conversation starter— and listen to music. After another hour of interminably slow moving traffic, things start to clear, and we're on our way again.

What should have been a six-hour drive takes us closer to nine hours, so by the time we drive into D.C., it's almost 8:00, and we haven't stopped for dinner. I know we're both hungry, because I heard Andrew's stomach growl a little while ago, and we finished off the snacks that I brought almost two hours ago.

We decide to check in to the hotel before figuring out a late dinner plan because even though we're both starving, we agree we want to stretch our legs for a little while.

Fortunately, my interview isn't until Wednesday, so I don't have any obligations to McDowell University for the evening. When we were planning the trip, we decided it made the most sense to drive on Monday so that I can rest after the long drive. It was Andrew's idea.

"You don't want to show up exhausted from driving all day," he'd said. It was the first time I've felt like he was supportive of my interview.

As we enter the hotel lobby, I notice that it's rather crowded. There's a small entryway that leads to a set of escalators to the main lobby where the check in is. Across from the escalators is the hotel restaurant, and in front of the short wall that divides the restaurant from the rest of the lobby, there's a big poster that says, "Welcome International Barbershop Quartet Convention." The dates on the poster show that the kick-off for the convention is this evening, which explains why there are hundreds of men and women in matching outfits milling about.

I groan, and Andrew lifts his eyebrows.

"I don't particularly like barbershop music, and I find the overly bright expressions on the singers' faces off-putting. Being in a lobby full of barbershop groups is giving me the creeps." I whisper over the noise of the clashing harmonies happening all over the lobby.

Andrew laughs, but I give him a withering look.

There's at least one set of eight people who seem to be

engaged in some kind of epic barbershop battle near the concierge desk, which we have to squeeze past to get to the check-in counter.

"Checking in?" the woman behind the desk asks.

"Yes, my reservation should be under Evie Watson, but it might be under Katherine Miller. I have a job interview, and Ms. Miller was the one who set up the reservation."

The woman behind the desk types a few things into her computer, but gives me a customer service frown. "I don't have anything under either name. Is there another name it could be under?"

"Um, I don't think so. She sent me a confirmation email. Let me look at it." I search the name of the hotel on my email and find two emails instead of one. "That's weird. I have the confirmation, but then this morning there was a cancellation email that I must have missed. I'd better call Katherine and see what's going on."

Andrew takes care of checking in to his room while I step away to make the phone call. After a few rings, the phone connects, but it goes voicemail. I leave a message explaining the situation, but based on how late in the day it is, I don't expect to hear back until the morning. I look through the email with the interview itinerary to see if I have Katherine's cell number, but there's nothing about who to call if I have questions.

"Any luck with the folks from McDowell?" Andrew asks as he joins me.

"No, Katherine didn't answer. I doubt anyone is in the office this late, and they didn't give me contact information other than their office numbers."

I'm starting to worry, and it must show on my face because Andrew squeezes my hand.

"It's going to be ok. We'll book you a new room, and then you can ask the university to reimburse you."

We go back to the front desk, but when we ask the woman there about another room, she grimaces. "I apologize. With the barbershop convention, I'm afraid we're all full for the next two nights."

I frown. "Do you think one of the other hotels nearby would have something?"

The woman behind the desk gives me a sympathetic look. "I can't really speak for other hotels in the area, but I can tell you that finding a room at this hour in D.C. this close to July 4th is next to impossible."

I feel wobbly as Andrew and I walk away from the desk again. I'm tired and hungry, and now I have nowhere to sleep and there's too much noise in this lobby, and the fake smiles of the singers around us is going to give me nightmares. Tears prickle my eyes, and the exhaustion of the day is weighing on me. I close my eyes. What a fucking disaster.

My breathing goes shallow like it does when I'm about to have a panic attack, but Andrew must sense it because he takes both of my hands and pulls me further away from the desk and the fucking obnoxious barbershop quartets that are still singing nearby, with their clown-like cheeriness and annoying straw hats.

He looks me in the eyes and says, "Evie, it's ok. I need

you to breathe with me and then we're going to take our things up to my room. You're going to stay with me, and it will all be fine."

I take a shuddering breath, close my eyes and nod. Andrew draws me to him and counts us through a breathing exercise while he rubs soft circles on my shoulders. The pressure of having another person's arms around me and the feel of his chest rising and falling with mine brings me back to a somewhat rational state of mind.

"Ok. I'm ok. Thank you." I step back from his embrace and give him a small smile.

"Good. Now let's get up to the room and figure out which stretch of the floor I'm going to sleep on."

His words don't sink in for a minute. I'm too distracted by the fact that he's holding my hand as we walk across the lobby to the elevators. He's applying gentle pressure to the back of my hand with his thumb, and the feeling is keeping me grounded in a way I didn't know I needed.

But as the elevator doors open, I realize that he said he was going to sleep on the floor, and I blurt out, "Aren't there two beds in your room?"

Andrew shakes his head. "No, I always get a king when I travel. I like to have plenty of space to stretch out."

"Right. That makes sense." Andrew is over six feet tall, so of course he'd need a larger bed. "But what about your snack bed?"

"My what?"

"Snack bed. You get a room with two beds so you can have a sleeping bed and a snack bed."

Andrew laughs, and it's deep and rich like a decadent dessert.

"I never know what you're going to say. It's one of the things I like so much about you."

We find the room, and Andrew unlocks the door. When we step inside, my mouth drops into an "O." This is a huge and rather nice looking hotel, so I had expected a spacious room, but this room is laid out in such a way that we almost can't maneuver around the bed. The end of the mattress almost touches the TV stand, and the door to the bathroom inexplicably swings out into the main room instead of into the bathroom. There is not enough room for two people to stand comfortably between the bathroom door and the closet.

"There is no way I'm letting you sleep on the floor, Andrew. If I have to get up in the night, I'll step on you."

"It will be fine." Andrew waves his hand dismissively.

"No, it won't. Look, this is probably TMI, but I have a tiny bladder and will almost certainly need to get up in the night to use the bathroom. I do not want to step on you, and if you sleep on the floor, I will."

"Evie, I really can't ask you to share the bed with me."

"Nonsense. It's a king bed. We can make a pillow barrier down the middle. I can stay on my side of the bed. You can stay on yours."

Normally I would be mortified to be having this conversation. After the awkwardness last week, I should be feeling at least a little embarrassed about the prospect of sharing a bed with someone I have such complicated feelings about, but the exhaustion and the stress of finding out I don't have a room has given me a bizarre sense of calm about the fact that I am about to spend the night not only in the same room as Andrew Brandt but in the same bed.

For a second, he looks like he's going to keep arguing with me, but something in my expression must make him back down.

"Ok, fine. We can do that. Just one other problem."

I look at Andrew quizzically. "What's that?"

"I didn't pack anything to sleep in." Andrew looks oddly embarrassed.

My jaw drops, "Oh."

There's the mortification.

"I'm sorry. I didn't expect to be sharing a room, and I normally sleep in my boxer briefs."

I swallow. The mental image of Andrew in nothing but boxer briefs flashes before me, and I suddenly feel hot. "What were you going to do when you were planning to sleep on the floor?"

"I figured I'd wear my t-shirt but that the lower half wouldn't matter since we wouldn't be...you know...in the same space." He runs his hand through his hair. "Shit, Evie. This was a bad plan. I wasn't thinking."

I hold up a finger.

"No, no. No, we're going to figure this out because I'm absolutely exhausted and hungry and there's a fucking barbershop quartet convention and it's fine. Just going to have to sleep in a bed with my colleague slash work friend who's wearing nothing but a t-shirt and boxer briefs. I need a minute to think."

Andrew looks sheepish. But then something occurs to me, and I tilt my head at him.

"What size pants do you wear?"

Andrew frowns. "32x34. Why?"

"What? I meant, like, do you wear a 12 or 14 or something?"

Andrew looks puzzled. He glances at his waist. "Do I look like I only have a 12 inch waist?"

"What are you talking about?"

"Pants sizes. What are you talking about?"

"Pants sizes." I rub my hand down my face. "Oh right, I forgot that men have reasonable pants sizes, and women have illogical ones. Would you say you're small, medium, or large?"

Andrew smirks. "I want to say large, but probably medium since we're talking waist sizes."

"Oh my god. That is not helping!" I smack his arm. I'm not in the mood for one of his frustratingly funny jokes right now.

I rummage through my suitcase and pull out a pair of flowery pajama pants. "These might work, although they're probably too short for you. You might have to pull the drawstring, though. I have hips, after all." I toss them to him.

Andrew gapes at me, then starts to laugh. "But what will you wear?"

"I brought two pairs, obviously." I pull out a second pair

of pajama pants.

"So, wait. You almost forgot to pack your bras, but you have two pairs of pajamas?"

"Yes?" I wince.

Andrew laughs again, then steps toward me to give me a hug.

"You are the best, Evie Watson." He holds me for a moment longer than seems like a friendship hug—not that I'm complaining—then steps away to unpack his suitcase.

The rest of the evening goes without incident. We decide to splurge on food from the hotel restaurant rather than trying to find somewhere nearby that's still serving dinner. We eat and get ready for bed without any more embarrassing moments, although I have a lot of trouble concentrating on the episode of *Diners, Drive-Ins, and Dives* that I watch while Andrew showers. And I am not disappointed at the sight of Andrew in pajama pants. He kept his t-shirt on, as promised, but the flowing material of the pajama pants around his thighs and other regions makes my heart race.

I stuff my reaction as far down in my mind as it will go and busy myself with arranging the extra pillows down the middle of the bed.

Pillow barrier in place, we turn out our bedside lights to go to sleep. But my mind doesn't seem to want to shut off.

"Andrew?" I whisper after the lights have been out for a few minutes. "Are you asleep?"

"No," he whispers back.

"I'm sorry I'm such a mess."

"You're not a mess. Quirky, but not a mess. And what happened with the hotel room wasn't your fault."

I smile. We lay in silence for a few moments.

"Andrew?"

"Hmm?"

"Thanks for everything today."

"You're welcome."

I hear movement in the bed, and the next thing I know, Andrew's hand has found mine over the pillow barrier. He gives my hand a gentle squeeze, but he doesn't let go. Instead, he rubs the back of my hand with his thumb, like he did earlier on the elevator. I don't pull away. I let him hold my hand until I fall asleep.

CHAPTER 14

The first thing I notice when I wake up is that I've had a really good night's sleep. The second thing I notice is that I'm not in my own bed, which makes the good night's sleep that much more notable. I almost never sleep well away from home.

The third thing I notice is that I am not alone. Strong arms are wrapped around me, and I can feel his chest gently rising and falling against my back. For a second, I forget whose arms they are, and I scoot closer. At the exact same moment that I remember it's Andrew I'm sharing the bed with, he shifts, and I can feel something else, low where our hips meet.

Oh god.

I am suddenly wide awake, and I try to move away, but

he's holding me tightly.

"Andrew!" I hiss, tugging on his arm and trying to squirm out of his grip. He pulls me closer and mumbles something that sounds suspiciously like "Mmm, Evie."

I say his name again, louder and sharper this time, and he stirs.

"Hmm?" He sounds sleepy. And then, "Oh!"

His arms are suddenly off me, and we jump apart, which is much easier now that I don't have his massive forearm pinning me to the bed.

"Shit. Evie, I'm sorry."

"I want to say, 'It's fine,' but really, is it fine? No. Andrew, this is a huge bed. How? How did we end up...like... that?" I don't know why I'm mad. It's not like he did it on purpose.

"I was just as asleep as you were! What happened to the pillow barrier?"

"I don't know!" I look around the room. The pillows that had been so carefully placed between us are shoved to the end of the bed. "We must have moved them in our sleep."

I know I'm turning splotchy with embarrassment, but Andrew doesn't seem to be faring much better in that department because he rakes a hand through his hair and blows out a long breath.

"I promise I wasn't trying to do anything." He looks chagrined.

"I think I'm going to get dressed." I announce, grabbing my clothes and taking the two steps to the bathroom. I close the door and lean against it. Only once I'm alone do I admit to myself that I'm not actually mad at Andrew. I'm mad at myself for wanting someone I can't have and for not being able to let my silly crush go.

It's not his fault that we woke up snuggled like lovers. And it's definitely not his fault that I wish we could wake up that way every day. I know it's a me problem, especially after what he told me yesterday about the woman he's been pining for for years.

I take a quick shower, get dressed in the bathroom, and finish getting ready for the day. I'm going to have to face Andrew and try not to think about how his arms felt holding me close, how comfortable it was to wake up and feel him breathing against me.

I take a deep breath and open the bathroom door, hoping he's at least put on some real pants while I've been in here. But Andrew is gone. His things are still in the room, so he at least hasn't abandoned me in the nation's capital. I look around for a note, but can't find one. Then I check my phone.

ANDREW: Went to find us some breakfast. Be back soon.

So I do what I always do when I'm stressed. I start tidying the room and rearranging things. By the time Andrew is back with two coffees and a bag of something that smells absolutely delicious, I've made the bed and organized everything in the bathroom (twice).

"I thought this looked like something you'd like for breakfast." Andrew pulls out something that can only be described as a giant croissant-muffin crossover that seems to have sausage and cheese folded into the layers of pastry. It's still warm and smells like everything breakfast should smell like.

"Thank you." I take a bite and confirm that it is as delicious as it looks.

"Are you ok? You seemed really upset about how we woke up." There's concern in his eyes, and I feel bad for yelling at him.

"Yeah, I'm ok. Not upset. But maybe we could see if there's another hotel close by with a room for tonight? Or maybe this place will have something that's opened up?" What I don't say is that I only want another room because I don't think I could stand the heartbreak of another night of sleeping in the same bed as Andrew knowing that he's only interested in me as a friend.

"Yeah, that's probably for the best. I was just trying to solve things quickly last night so you wouldn't have a panic attack."

"I know, and I appreciate it. You're a really good friend, Andrew." I give his arm a squeeze. I think I see a twinge of sadness in his eyes, but it's gone almost as soon as I notice it.

"I'll check with the hotel later, but for now, what do you want to see in our nation's capital?"

"Hmm, I've always liked going to the National Gallery."

"Sounds good to me. Shall we?" He gestures toward the door, and we leave the room feeling back to our normal, friendly selves.

We start in the West Building of the National Gallery. I love spending time in the Impressionist rooms. The gallery features several paintings by Mary Cassat, Vincent Van Gogh, and Edgar Degas, but my favorite paintings in the collection are in the room with Renoir's *A Girl with a Watering Can* and Monet's *Woman with a Parasol.*

As we wander the gallery, Andrew keeps close to my side, and we chat occasionally about the paintings. I get the sense that Andrew isn't much of an art fan. When we get to Gallery 90, though, he snickers.

I'm walking beside him and stop, the question obvious on my face.

"What's so funny?" I whisper.

"She forgot to pack her bra," he murmurs so only I can hear him. He nods toward Renoir's painting of the Roman goddess Diana.

I have to fake a sneeze to cover the yelp of laughter that almost escapes me.

In the next room is another painting of a woman in a similar state of undress. This one, I point out to him, and he gives me a wicked grin.

It becomes a game. In each room we enter, we try to be the first person to point out a painting or sculpture with a topless woman. By the time we wander to the café and gift shop on the ground floor, we're giggling like middle school kids in a sex-ed class.

"My feet are killing me!" I fling myself into a chair. "I think I want to sit here and rest for a few minutes before we go over to the East Building, if that's ok with you."

"Yeah, that would be fine. Are you enjoying the gallery?" Andrew sits across from me.

"Yes, definitely. I might have to come back so I can see everything we've missed, though." We've seen a lot of paintings, but this place is huge, and because of our ridiculous game, I haven't had the chance to sit and study some of the paintings like I normally would at a museum.

"Just don't come without me." Andrew winks at me, and I'm not sure what to make of that statement, so I make a humming noise in reply.

We sit in awkward silence for a moment, but then Andrew abruptly stands up and asks, "Would you like anything from the café? I'm going to get some coffee."

"Nothing for me, but thanks."

While Andrew walks away to stand in line, I check my phone. I have a missed call and a voicemail from Katherine Miller. I play the voicemail, hoping for an explanation of the hotel mix-up.

"Hi, Evie. I got your message from last night, and I am so sorry about the cancellation. I looked into it this morning, and apparently when our office manager made the reservation, he accidentally made both your reservation and another candidate's reservation for the same dates. He realized the mistake when the other candidate contacted him yesterday morning to ask about the dates. Anyway, long story short, he accidentally canceled the wrong reservation. Again, I'm so sorry, and I'd like to discuss how we can make this right. I hope you were able to find reasonable accommodations last night. Please call me as soon as you can."

Andrew is back at our table with a coffee and something that looks suspiciously like a gelato with two spoons.

"I thought you were just getting coffee." I raise an eyebrow at him.

"They had gelato, and I know how much you like frozen desserts. I hope chocolate and black cherry is ok with you?"

"Yes, of course it is." I grin.

"Any great insights from the waterfall while I was gone?" Andrew sits down and hands me a spoon.

"Hmm?" I give him an inquisitive look.

"You were staring at the waterfall when I came back. Just wondering if it had given you any insights or answers to the meaning of life."

"No, nothing so deep as that. I had a voicemail from the library director at McDowell." I fill him in on the details of the message.

"Well, that explains things. I wonder if the other reservation is still active. Maybe you can have that room."

"Yeah, that might work. I'll give her a call and see."

I step away and make the call, which doesn't take long.

"Good news! They should be able to change the name on the reservation, so I'll be able to have my own room tonight. Katherine also said she would see if McDowell would reimburse you for last night since you ended up sharing a room with me."

"They don't have to do that. I would have paid for the room even if you hadn't needed somewhere to sleep."

"I'll let you take that up with them. She also invited you

to come to the dinner tonight, but I told her I wasn't sure if you'd want to. Would it be awkward since we're not...you know...together?" I'm mortified at just hinting at the possibility of "together," but the words are out before I can stop them.

He gives me a look I can't interpret.

"I don't think I should go. I'd just get in the way of your interview. This dinner is about you showing McDowell University how awesome you are, and you don't want your colleague slash work friend tagging along."

"You're right. Of course. I don't know why I was even considering it." I'm mildly embarrassed. It's obvious that Andrew shouldn't go. The fact that he's here has nothing to do with my interview and everything to do with the conference we're supposed to be attending the day after tomorrow.

"Ready to go to the East Building?" Andrew asks as he gathers the trash from our table.

"Yes! I want to see the Whistler exhibit that's over there."

Andrew offers me his arm like we're some kind of courting couple in a Regency novel. I take it, of course. But as we get on the moving sidewalk that goes between the West Building and the East Building, I hope Andrew doesn't notice how much I'm relishing our closeness.

We spend another hour wandering the National Gallery and

then go to find Chinese dumplings from a place I've heard about from a friend of mine who lives in the D.C. area. The tiny restaurant is little more than a takeout window, so we have to stand on the sidewalk and wait for the woman inside to motion for us to come get our food.

Dumplings acquired, we walk a bit to find a place to sit and eat. There's a small park about a block away, so we find a patch of grass and sit next to each other so we can eat our fill of shumai and sticky rice.

"What was your favorite painting from today?" I ask as we eat. I'm fishing a bit, to see if he actually enjoyed the art museum because I'm still suspicious Andrew made up the bra game because he was bored.

He thinks for a moment. "I really liked the one that was on the room divider panels. You know, the one that showed the street in Paris?"

"That one was lovely! I especially liked that it was a different experience viewing it up close from viewing it far away." The piece is huge, and takes up an entire wall in one of the rooms. It's not a piece that we spent much time looking at, so I'm surprised that it's his favorite. It makes me think I misjudged his boredom.

"What about your favorite from today?" he asks, and I don't hesitate to reply.

"The family portrait."

Andrew laughs. "The one where the kids are all climbing over the adults and looking like they're causing mayhem?"

"Yep, that's the one." I cheese a grin.

Andrew shakes his head, but he's smiling. "I probably

should have guessed. I know how much you love ridiculous things."

"What do you mean? I like things that make me laugh. Paintings can be funny. There's no rule that art has to be serious." I do air quotes.

"I didn't say it was bad to like ridiculous things. I like that you laugh so much. Your laugh is one of my favorite things about you."

My ears burn at the compliment. I bump him with my shoulder. "Well, you make me laugh, so we make a good pair of friends, I guess."

Andrew looks pensive. "Yeah, we do make a good pair."

He catches my eye and holds my gaze for a long moment. Our arms are touching, and his face is close to mine. The air has that same staticky feeling it did when were alone in the library last week, and the hairs on my arms stand up.

Andrew is looking at me with something like longing in his eyes, but I know that can't be right because we're friends and he's in love with someone else. I can't decide if I imagine a slight tilt of his head toward me. For a brief second I have the wild thought that he's about to kiss me, but a car horn blares nearby and we both jump.

I stuff another dumpling in my mouth and the strange moment passes. Andrew shifts slightly away from me, and our conversation moves on. But I can't help wondering what might have happened if that car hadn't startled us.

CHAPTER 15

We go back to the hotel not long after finishing our dumplings so that I can settle into my own room and get ready for the interview dinner. Fortunately, when we arrive at the hotel and check at the desk, my room is ready, and there are no panicked phone calls to make.

Andrew offers to sit with me while I wait for my ride, so we meet in the lobby and try to stay out of the way of the massive group of barbershop quartet singers who are still wandering around. The singers are less creepy today, probably because I'm not exhausted and panicky.

Tonight's dinner with the search committee has me both excited and nervous. Katherine is picking me up, and we'll join two other librarians from the Research Services department. I technically met all of them on my first interview, but that was a video call, and it's hard to make a personal connection through a screen.

A woman walks through the door of the hotel and looks around the lobby. When her eyes catch on me, she waves. "Evie?"

I reach out to shake her hand. "Yes. Katherine, right?"

The woman returns my handshake and says, "Yes. So nice to finally meet you in person."

Katherine is probably in her mid forties and is dressed meticulously in sharply pressed slacks and a flowy blouse. Her long brown hair looks like it's come straight from the "after" part of a shampoo commercial.

"I want to apologize again for the mix-up with the room. I'm frankly embarrassed that this happened, and I want to make it right," she says.

"Thank you. Fortunately, my friend Andrew was able to make space for me in his room." I gesture to Andrew, who has been hanging back, and he steps forward to shake Katherine's hand.

"Right, thank you for saving the day on that front," Katherine says, smiling at him. "We can reimburse you for the room since it was our mistake and you ended up putting up our candidate."

"It was no trouble at all. Besides, I was already paying for the room anyway." Andrew seems nonchalant, but I almost laugh out loud at his insistence that it wasn't any trouble. Between the single bed, the pajama debacle, and the accidental snuggling, it was nothing *but* trouble in my opinion.

Katherine seems to size Andrew up before saying, "Alright, I can see that this is an argument I'm not going to win." She turns to me. "I take it everything with your room for this evening is in order?"

"Yes, thank you."

"Excellent." She glances at her phone. "We'd better get on our way. The restaurant is a bit of a walk from here. Andrew, are you joining us?"

"No, I don't want to impose, and besides, I have some work that I need to do this evening."

"Very well. Evie, are you ready to go?"

"Yes, quite ready." I'm a little jittery, actually, and really wish that Andrew was coming with us.

If I get the job at McDowell, I'm going to have to get used to walking everywhere and dealing with public transit. In Sapling Grove, everything is spread out with hills and forests in between. Driving is an imperative. But here in D.C. there are sidewalks and the Metro. I'm not even sure I would need a car if I moved.

I'm grateful that the restaurant is fairly close to the hotel, but even with its proximity, my feet are aching from the sightseeing Andrew and I did this morning. I'm about to say something to Katherine when she turns to me.

"I hope despite the room situation that you've had a good trip to D.C. so far?"

"Yes, we spent the day at the National Gallery. It's one of my favorite places to visit in D.C." I suppress a smirk as I remember the ridiculous game of "She Forgot to Pack Her

Bra" that we played for most of our visit to the museum.

"Have you been to D.C. often?" Katherine asks, and I'm thankful that she's keeping the conversation moving so I don't accidentally tell her about our game.

"A few times as an adult. I came with my parents right after I graduated college, and then again a few years ago for a family vacation with some of my cousins."

We walk past important-looking buildings and at least one monument as we wind our way through the crowd that's filling the sidewalks in this busy part of D.C. It's early evening, and even though it's summer, the temperature is pleasant.

Our conversation is comfortable, and I find that talking with Katherine is giving me a sense of hope for the rest of the interview.

We finally stop in front of a busy-looking restaurant, and Katherine waves to two other people standing nearby. She introduces me to Jacob and Lisa. Jacob looks to be about my age, and Lisa is a little older, maybe around Kylie's age. They're both dressed more casually than Katherine, which makes a certain kind of sense. Katherine is the library director, after all. Jacob and Lisa would ultimately report to me. I'm glad I went with the polka dot dress, because it's a similar level of professional-looking to what Katherine is wearing.

The four of us walk into the restaurant together. Once we're inside, Katherine speaks with the host who seats us in a section of the restaurant near a small stage.

"Your server will be with you soon, and he can sign you

up for the karaoke contest when he takes your drink order," the host says as we take our seats.

"I'm sorry, did you say 'karaoke contest?'" Katherine gives the host a look that makes me think of an old woman clutching her pearls.

"That's right. We host one every Tuesday. Do you sing karaoke?"

"I most certainly do not," Katherine says. "We're here for an interview dinner. Is there somewhere else we could sit?"

The host shakes their head. "I'm afraid not unless you want to join the list of walk-ups and forgo your reservation."

"How long is the walk-up wait?"

"At least an hour."

Katherine looks irritated. I understand. I don't love karaoke, but surely it won't be that bad. Maybe we can eat quickly and avoid most of the singing.

"I don't mind if we stay. I'm sure it will be fine," I say, trying to salvage the dinner before it goes completely off the rails.

Katherine turns to me. "Are you sure you're ok with staying? I don't want you to feel like you've had a horrifying interview dinner experience."

"It's really fine. If nothing else, I'm sure it will make a good story later."

"Katherine, we'll make it work," Jacob says.

"Yeah, I'm with Jacob on this," Lisa adds. "Let's get our food and then worry about the karaoke. They haven't started yet. The whole evening isn't a loss."

Katherine gives her assent, and the host finally leaves the table. A few minutes later a server comes to take our drink orders, and then the four of us settle into our conversation.

On the whole, I enjoy the evening. Jacob and I connect really well, partly because of our closeness in age, but also because we seem to be on the same page about things like which is the best Star Wars film (*Return of the Jedi*) and the frustration of book-to-film adaptations that strip out important character development.

Lisa reminds me a bit of Kylie. If I end up at McDowell, I wonder if I would be able to forge some kind of friendship with Lisa similar to my relationship with Kylie, even though I would be Lisa's boss.

Even the karaoke turns out not to be all bad. There are a few excruciating performances, but generally, the singers are decent. Thankfully, this place has a permanent sound system instead of one of those temporary set ups, and we're far enough from the speakers that we've been able to carry on our conversation during most of the performances.

As the dinner comes to a close, Katherine orders a ride-share to take me back to the hotel. A little while later, I walk into the lobby and find Andrew waiting for me near the door. He hugs me, but it's awkward because I'm not expecting it. I'm still not used to this new dynamic we have of hugging whenever we see each other. As I stand there wrapped in his arms, my mind snags on the memory of how we woke up this morning, which sends a wave of heat through my belly.

I start to step away from the hug, trying to put some distance between us, but before I can, Andrew says in my ear, "How did it go?"

The sound of his voice so close to my ear sends goosebumps all over me, and when he releases me from the hug, his beard brushes along my cheek. I expected it to be coarse, but it's surprisingly soft. I swallow and hope Andrew can't see the want in my eyes.

"It was fine. Fun, actually. Even with the karaoke." I give a little laugh.

Andrew's eyes widen. "They took you to karaoke?"

"Not on purpose. It seems like maybe they didn't check to see if the restaurant had anything else going on when they made the reservation."

Andrew's brow furrows.

"What?" I put my hand on his arm. "You look like you want to say something."

"It's just..." Andrew trails off. "I don't want to color your perception of the people at McDowell, but..."

"But what?" I'm getting concerned because Andrew seems surprisingly angry about this.

"But don't you find it odd that they messed up your room reservation and then accidentally took you to karaoke?"

"I mean, mistakes happen." I try to wave it off.

"They do, but it seems disorganized to me."

I frown. "I don't see how pointing that out is helpful to me when I'm going to have my full interview tomorrow."

"It's just that I think if a place was interested in hiring you, they'd want to bend over backwards to make sure your interview experience is excellent."

"Are you saying you don't think they want to hire me?" I sound angry. A few people walking by give us a concerned look.

"No, I didn't mean it like that."

"Then what did you mean it like?" I cross my arms, stepping back a little from him.

"I meant that it doesn't seem like they're putting their best foot forward for you. You should be able to have an interview that doesn't include a panic attack and karaoke." Andrew winces as the words leave him. I know he regrets them based on the look on his face, but I dig my heels in anyway.

"Well, I'm sorry my mental health got in the way of my interview, but it's my problem, not yours. I'm going to bed." I stomp toward the elevators.

Who does Andrew think he is to question whether this interview was going well? Didn't I enjoy the evening? It's not like he has any right to try to get me to stay at Cooke. We're just friends, and not even particularly close ones at that.

As the elevator door opens, I hear Andrew call out across the lobby, "Wait!"

But I rush inside and press the button for my floor, hitting the "door close" button as he comes into view. A few minutes later, I enter my room and put the "Do Not Disturb" hanger on the outside handle. I get ready for bed and don't even check to see what's playing on FoodNetwork.

Unlike yesterday when I woke up relaxed and well-rested in Andrew's arms, this morning is not going so well. For starters, I was so mad at Andrew last night that I had trouble falling asleep. When I finally did get to sleep, I had a vivid dream about Andrew singing a karaoke song about how McDowell University isn't going to hire me. I wake up with a headache and a sinking feeling that today is not going to be a good day.

I check my phone to see what time it is, and there are a bunch of missed messages from Kylie and Jaclyn asking about how the interview dinner went. There's also a string of messages from Andrew. I don't want to look at those before I have my coffee, though, so I send a reply to my friends.

ME: Interview dinner was ok. They had karaoke at the restaurant, which was weird.

I don't expect either of them to reply since it's so early in the morning, but a few moments later, a series of notifications blasts my phone.

KYLIE: Karaoke?!?!?!

JACLYN: That is super weird. Between that and the room mix-up, are you sure you want to go through with the interview today?

KYLIE: Yeah, Jaclyn's right. Seems like they're not doing a good job of courting you.

JACLYN: I'm ok with that. I want Evie to stay at Cooke with us!

ME: Not you, too. Andrew got all huffy about the room and karaoke stuff. The jerk actually said I should be able to have an interview that didn't include a panic attack.

KYLIE: Whoa whoa whoa. Surely he didn't mean that?

ME: IDK, but that's what he said. He texted me a bunch last night after I went to bed, but I haven't looked at what he said. I'm too mad.

JACLYN: What the hell?

KYLIE: Evie, you need to look at his messages. Maybe he misspoke?

JACLYN: Yeah. That kind of statement doesn't sound like Andrew.

I grumble, but I know I can't avoid reading his messages forever. If nothing else, we're going to have to drive back to Tennessee together in a few days, so it's probably better to hear him out now rather than ride back in silence because we're not talking to each other. With a frustrated huff, I open his messages.

ANDREW: Evie, I am so sorry.

ANDREW: I didn't mean things to come out the way they did.

ANDREW: I can't blame you for being upset.

ANDREW: I wasn't trying to make light of your anxiety.

ANDREW: I just meant that you deserve an interview process that doesn't trigger a panic attack because you're worth hiring, and they'd be so lucky to have you.

ANDREW: It looks bad on them that you had a panic

attack, not on you.

ANDREW: I'm worried they don't see how great you are.

ANDREW: You're so good at what you do, and you should work somewhere that appreciates that.

ANDREW: Evie, please text me back. I fucked this up, and I'm really sorry.

I take a screenshot of Andrew's messages and send it to Kylie and Jaclyn.

ME: Well, shit

JACLYN: You can say that again

KYLIE: Are you going to text him back?

EVIE: I think I'd better

This is a conversation best had in person, so I text Andrew and ask him to meet me at the hotel restaurant for breakfast. Besides, we're switching to the conference hotel this afternoon, and I need to give him my suitcase.

A little while later, we're sitting across from each other, neither of us actually eating the food we have in front of us.

"Evie, I'm really sorry," he says for at least the fifth time.

"You don't need to apologize anymore. I saw your texts. I'm sorry I got so defensive."

"You had every right. I shouldn't have phrased things the way I did. I made it sound like it was your fault you almost had a panic attack." Andrew takes a sip of his coffee.

"I just wanted you to be happy for me. Friends are supposed to be happy for each other when things are going well." I look away from him. If I'm honest with myself, I'm still hurting from his reaction last night.

I don't see him reach out, but Andrew's hand is suddenly

on mine, rubbing small circles along the back of it with his thumb like he did before. "I am happy for you. I want you to be where you'll be happy, and I meant what I said about you working somewhere that appreciates how good you are at your job. I just...I want that place to be Cooke."

I turn slowly to look back at him, my heart thumping, because it almost sounds like...I can't even let myself finish the thought of what it sounds like. Instead, I ask him, "What do you mean by that?"

He's blushing, and suddenly lets go of my hand. He sounds flustered when he says, "Just because we're friends. I mean, I want to keep being friends with you and hanging out, and we can't do that if you move."

"Oh, ok." I'm disappointed. For a second I thought he was going to confess that he had feelings for me, but that was clearly wishful thinking. He's already told me he's in love with someone else. "Even if I move, we can still be friends. Just long-distance ones."

"Yeah, of course. I know that."

My phone chimes to let me know it's time to meet Katherine in the lobby. I eat a few more bites of my food, then ask Andrew to check my teeth for anything stuck in them. He laughs at the request, and it seems to clear the air.

He gives me a quick hug goodbye and wishes me good luck. He even sounds like he means it.

CHAPTER 16

The rest of my interview is free of location mix-ups and bad singing, and I'm thankful that it seems like the search committee did a better job of preparing for the day on campus than they did in the lead-up to the interview.

The only thing odd is that they put me up in a hotel so far away from campus. This morning as Katherine and I drove to the McDowell campus, which is outside the Beltway on the Virginia side, I was amazed to see how many hotels we passed, including a few within walking distance of the campus.

McDowell University has one of those lush, green campuses that look like it's straight from a movie. The library is in a beautiful old building with the front entrance flanked by trees, but it's clear that the interior has been meticulously maintained and even updated within the past decade. Whoever designed the renovations did an excellent job of keeping the cozy, old-world feel balanced with modern conveniences like a coffee bar and a series of nap pods.

My presentation went well, which is a relief. During the course of the day, I met several people from different departments on campus, which is surprising since in my experience, everyone in academia disappears for the summer as soon as the spring commencement ceremony ends. I leave the interview with a feeling of possibility and more excitement than ever at the prospect of making McDowell my new place of work.

I am practically buzzing with that sense of possibility as I walk into the conference hotel and find Andrew waiting for me. He crosses the lobby toward me, and my face lights up as he approaches. He returns my smile with a grin that could stop hearts.

As we get closer to each other, though, my smile falters a little. He's not wrong that it would be easier to maintain our friendship if I stay at Cooke, even if it means staying in my current job. I haven't heard anything yet about the Director of the Teaching and Learning Center position, even though I submitted my application more than a month ago. I tell myself it's the job prospect and not the potential for losing Andrew's friendship that causes my stomach to drop.

When he's close enough, he opens his arms to hug me. His hugs feel like a luxury that I can't get enough of. I savor the warmth of his arms around me and whatever it is that makes him smell so good. One thing is certain. Something between us has shifted on this trip, but I'm not sure what, exactly.

"Tell me about the interview over dinner?" Andrew asks as we step out of the hug, his hand still on my arm.

"Sounds good, but let's go somewhere close by. I'm exhausted." I give him a tired smile. All-day academic interviews are draining, even when they go well—or maybe especially when they go well. It makes me extra grateful that he's on this trip with me since that meant he could handle switching our things over to the conference hotel.

"I take it check in went smoothly?" I ask as we walk out onto the sidewalk.

"Perfectly. No canceled reservations and no more emergency bed sharing."

I laugh, but after the other hotel mess, it does make me thankful that Amber, Dobson's assistant, is so efficient and competent at her job.

We find a deli not far from the hotel that's only moderately busy, and after we order at the counter and find a booth tucked in the corner, I tell him about the interview. He listens attentively as I talk about how the Provost started her career as a librarian, so the conversation she and I had centered around the role of libraries in the larger university context. He nods and smiles as I tell him about how I immediately clicked with Devin, one of the Access Services librarians, when we talked about best approaches to promote borrowing library materials in an age of streaming and downloading. He doesn't interrupt, even when I tell him that I almost exchanged phone numbers with several people so that we could keep our conversations going.

"I can see from the way you're talking about this that you're really interested in the job," he says when I'm finished, although there's a slight downward curve to his mouth as he speaks.

"Yeah, I really am." I smile tentatively. "But I've not been offered anything yet, and even if I am, I might not take it." Despite my excitement about the job at McDowell, I still love working at Cooke, and I'm holding out hope for the Teaching and Learning position.

Andrew is quiet for a while. He seems to be mulling over my last statement. Finally, he says, "If they make you a good offer and Cooke doesn't fight to keep you, you should take the McDowell job."

His statement catches me off guard. It's the first time he's expressed something like excitement about my potential move. I'm not even sure I should call it excitement. More like acceptance. Does this mean I've misinterpreted the shift in our friendship? Maybe instead of shifting to a deeper friendship, we're shifting away from each other.

"I guess the good news is that I don't have to decide anything tonight except which pajamas to wear." I cover a yawn, and the corner of Andrew's mouth twitches.

"Not the flowery ones. Those are mine now." The way he says it, all deep and gravelly, sends shivers down my spine. "But I can tell you're tired. Let's get you back to the hotel so you can rest up."

Andrew walks me to my room and gives me another hug before wishing me goodnight. I change into my pajamas—not the flowery ones—and barely make it into bed before I fall asleep.

The next two days of conferencing are a blur of presentations and networking. I try to have an open mind when I go to academic conferences, and I legitimately love assessment, but there is no getting around the fact that the content of a general education assessment conference is a bit dry. Andrew and I spend our free moments talking through some of the things we're learning in the sessions we're attending, and we have a few ideas for things to incorporate into our plans for the committee's fall initiatives.

The conference lasts through Saturday morning, so we leave right after lunch, hoping to get home before it's too dark outside. We drive for hours, talking mostly about the conference. The sun is setting, and we are about an hour from Sapling Grove, when Andrew turns to me and says, "I don't want to think about measures and outcomes any more. New topic: first celebrity crush."

I laugh as he glances over at me. I was ready for a subject change, too.

"I'll start. Mine was Julia Roberts in the movie *Hook*." He gives me a wink and a grin.

"Doesn't she have a terrible haircut in that movie?"

"No. I mean, yes, except right at the end. That's the part I fell in love with."

"Ah, ok. Makes sense." I nod, then sit quietly as we pass a clump of trees.

"Don't try to get out of sharing your first celebrity crush by dumping on Julia Roberts' Tinkerbell hairdo." He nudges me with his elbow. "Spill it. I want to know yours."

I don't have to think too hard because the answer is obvious. "Chris Pine."

"From *Princess Diaries 2: A Royal Engagement*?" Andrew asks, his voice teasing.

He's smirking at me as he leans casually back in the driver's seat, one hand resting on the top of the steering wheel and the other resting against his chin as he tries to hide the smirk. I give him a mock incredulous look.

"What's wrong with Chris Pine?"

"I didn't say anything."

"No, but you were judging me. I can see it in the evil look in your eye."

"What? What evil look?"

"The evil look you have stroking your beard like I won't notice your face."

Andrew laughs at that. "Ok, how's this? Current celebrity crush? You go first this time, and please don't say it's one of the Chrises of Marvel."

I make a hmph sound. The Chrises of Marvel certainly are quite the set of crush-worthy celebrities, but none of them is my favorite. "Paul Rudd. The man doesn't age, and he's been sexy since 1995 when he was in *Clueless*."

"Good choice, good choice," he says, clearly more approving of Paul Rudd than Chris Pine. "And sneaky of you to pick someone not named 'Chris' but still in the Marvel movies."

"And yours?" I ask with laughter in my voice.

"Carey Mulligan," he says without hesitation. It makes sense somehow that she's who he'd pick. She's not one of those twiggy stick figures of a celebrity, and with how much he loves a good story, I can see why he'd develop a crush on a woman who makes such story-rich films.

"First kiss?" I ask before I can think too hard about the question. I feel bold and a little crazed at moving the conversation so close to something like flirting.

"Samantha Dwyer, freshman year of high school. It was sloppy and awkward, but I was totally in love with that girl. She was a junior, and I didn't know how I'd managed to catch her eye."

I smirk and think to myself, "I know exactly how you managed to catch Samantha's eye."

"What was that?" Andrew asks.

Oh, shit.

"Uhhhhh, nothing." I blush. The exhaustion of the week must be really getting to me if I'm making side comments like that out loud.

"I'm pretty sure you said something." Andrew reaches over and pokes me in the side. I yelp and start to laugh.

"I didn't say anything," I lie.

"I'll let it go as long as you tell me about your first kiss."

I playfully roll my eyes. "Fine. I was not as early to the

dating scene as you were. My first kiss wasn't until college. Taylor Haynes, a history major. We were in sophomore composition together, and he was my first boyfriend."

"Oh, a thing for history majors, hmm?" Andrew laughs. I roll my eyes again.

"He asked me out one day after class. We dated for the rest of the year, and then he broke my heart." My voice cracks a little at the memory. Even though now I'm glad that he ended things, the way he ended them still stings a little. I thought we were going to stay together forever, and at the end of the spring semester it seemed like we had a solid plan for staying in touch over the summer. But once we were both home, he stopped calling and texting, and when I got back to campus for the fall semester, I found out that he had transferred without telling me.

I don't know why, but I tell Andrew the whole story.

"I hate him," Andrew says with conviction when I'm finished.

I laugh at his assertion, in spite of the painful memory. "Why?"

"Because he hurt you, and I care about you." Something in Andrew's voice shifts as he speaks. It's turned warm and... intimate.

I shake off the flicker of heat that blooms from my stomach. "It's ok. He was a terrible kisser, actually. At the time, I didn't know any better, and... well, let's just say 'sloppy and awkward' would also be a fitting description for my first kiss."

"I hope you've had the chance to be kissed the way you

deserve since then," Andrew practically whispers.

"And how do I deserve to be kissed?" The words are out before I can stop them, and my heart pounds as the question seems to take physical form between us. It lingers, weighing down the air like just before a thunderstorm and making the small space in the front seat of the car feel even smaller. We're still driving, but time seems to stop, and I'm silently cursing myself for my brashness.

Andrew makes a coughing sound but then is quiet for so long that I think he's going to ignore my question, which is probably for the best. But then, in a voice that's reminiscent of the way he mumbled my name when we woke up together in that hotel bed, he says, "You deserve to be kissed like it means something. Like the man kissing you can't keep his hands off of you, can't believe he's tasting your mouth."

I shift in my seat because the rush of dampness between my thighs is immediate, and my chest is heaving a little.

"I sometimes wonder what it would feel like to have your hands on me. To taste your mouth."

"You want that?" Andrew's voice is husky.

"I, um, I mean...shit." I didn't mean to say it out loud. There is no coming back from that statement. I want to try to explain it away, but I know that I need to keep my mouth shut. Any further talk about this and my friendship with Andrew will be over.

I can't look at him. My words are hanging there between us like an electrical current—they're dangerous, something not to be touched.

We keep driving, but minutes that feel like hours pass as we sit in this sizzling silence and watch the trees on the side of the interstate fly by.

Then Andrew is signaling to pull off at a rest stop. It's dark, and there aren't many other cars parked here. He pulls into a space by the street light and cuts off the engine, unbuckles his seatbelt.

"Evie?" His voice is soft, a little tentative.

I still can't look at him, and I bury my face in my hands. "Forget I said that. I didn't mean it…I'm so embarrassed, and I've…I've ruined our friendship."

He gently pulls my hands away from my face. "You haven't ruined anything."

I stare at him, not sure I believe my ears. He rubs the backs of my hands with his thumbs, and understanding hits me with a shock.

"I've wondered the same thing about you," he says, confirming what I already know.

"Oh. You…Oh. Wait. You said there was someone you were interested in. That was why you and Veronica didn't…"

"It's you."

The only sound in the dimly lit car is our twin breaths and the thumping of my heart. It's beating out a refrain. *It's you. It's you. It's you.*

Heat and adrenaline rush through my veins, and my world feels upside down. I should be thinking about why any forward motion with what Andrew has revealed would be a mistake. But the golden glow of the street light is illuminating his face in such a way that I can see he's every bit as nervous about the outcome of this conversation as I am.

The next thing Andrew says is barely above a whisper. "Since your faculty workshop two years ago. You wore that blue and white sleeveless dress with the little tie at the waist. I haven't been able to get the image of you in that dress out of my mind."

I stare at him with my mouth hanging open. *He's been thinking about me like that this whole time?*

"It wasn't even the dress that did me in. It was the way you handled all those inane questions from the business faculty. You just...eviscerated them without them even knowing. I thought it was so funny and... hot."

I blink at him. I remember the questions the business faculty members asked during my presentation. I had been talking about strategies for collaboration among university departments, but the business faculty must have been confused about the purpose of the workshop because they kept asking weird questions about the timeline for when they had to "get the collaboration done." I kept trying to explain it wasn't something with a deadline, just a set of strategies they could use, but after a few tries, I ended up pasting a fake smile on my face and saying, "You know, I'll have to have administration get back to you on that, but I think they wanted everyone to engage in a collaboration by the end of the semester."

Andrew reaches for my cheek with a question in his eyes. My heart pounds in my ears, and it's exactly like in the dream I had last week. I lean my face into his hand, which is soft and warm. He runs his thumb along my cheek and tilts my face toward his.

"Is this ok?"

I nod because I don't know how to make words anymore.

"Do you know how many times I've wanted to do this?" he asks as he brings his face close enough that our noses are touching.

I shake my head slightly, not wanting to lose contact with him.

"Every time I've seen you this summer." His lips graze mine as he speaks. It's torture to have him so close—close enough that all I have to do is tilt my head a little and I'll be kissing Andrew Brandt.

So I do it. I tilt my head and close the distance between us, and the moment our mouths touch, that staticky, electrical feeling in the air releases.

Andrew *does* kiss like a pirate. Like he's been lost at sea, searching for something. He said I should be kissed like it means something, and that is exactly how this kiss feels. Like we've found this treasure together.

His tongue sweeps into my mouth, and I nearly melt at the sensation. I reach around his neck and pull him closer to me. He takes the action as the invitation it is to deepen our kiss. I unbuckle my seatbelt because I can't get close enough to him with this ridiculous strap pulling me back.

His hands are on my back now, moving down toward the curve of my hips. His lips leave mine, and I make a little sound of displeasure, but then his beard is tickling my neck and he starts kissing me lower and lower. His lips find the hollow in my collarbone, and I gasp as he nibbles at that sensitive spot. I pull his face back to mine and kiss him hard on the mouth again.

I never want to stop kissing this man.

He nips at me and tastes my mouth, turning to change angles. He shifts again, but a sudden "HONNNNNNNK" erupts as his elbow hits the car horn, startling us apart.

We're both breathing hard, and Andrew's lips look swollen. I'm sure mine are the same. He rests his forehead against mine, our breath mingling, and the urge to keep kissing is overwhelming.

"We should probably get back to Sapling Grove," I say, even though it's not really what I want to do.

"I'd rather stay right here." His breath is ragged.

"I would, too, but we have to work on Monday, and I really want to get home. Besides, I'm sure Kylie is ready to be done cat sitting for me." I don't know why I am suddenly approaching this so rationally, and I mentally kick myself because the other option is to stay here and make out with Andrew until the sun comes up.

"Ok, fine. But not before I kiss you one more time."

This kiss isn't as desperate as the first one. It's soft and tender and full of the promise that there will be more of this to come.

As we pull away from each other and refasten our seatbelts, I fight the urge to reach up and touch my lips. It's hard, though, when the phantom feeling of his kiss is still there.

I barely notice the rest of the drive. We don't talk, but Andrew drives with one hand on the steering wheel and one hand holding mine.

It's fully dark as we pull into the driveway. We get out of the car, and Andrew pops the trunk to get my bags for me. He walks me to the door, and waits while I open it. He puts my suitcase inside, and then we stand on the porch, both of us a little unsure of what to do next.

"Thanks for the great trip," I say a little awkwardly. "I had a great time. It was really great...And thanks for driving. That was really great of you. Oh my god, I need to stop saying 'great!'"

Andrew chuckles. "No, you're right. It was great." He grins at me, then checks his watch. "It's late. I'm sure you're tired after a long week of interviewing and conferencing."

I look at my phone and gasp at the time. We must have stayed at that rest stop longer than I realized. "Goodnight, Andrew."

He steps closer to me and puts his hand on my elbow. I don't say anything, just reach for him and draw him to me. My whole body warms as his lips part mine. It's another sweet kiss, nothing so rushed as the first one in the car.

He steps away from me, a contented smile playing on his lips. He brushes my hair behind my ear, then trails his hand down my arm and interlaces our fingers. He brings my hand to his mouth and kisses my knuckles. Then he drops my hand and turns to walk back to his car. I catch his hand before he takes two steps.

"Stay."

He studies me, his eyes shining. He gives me a small nod, then whispers, "I'll go get my bag."

CHAPTER 17

You know how your bed feels extra comfortable after you've traveled? That's the first thing I think as I wake up Sunday morning. My limbs are heavy, and it's clear I've slept like a rock. It's a little surprising, since it was so late when I went to bed last night. Usually, I'm in bed by 10:00, even on the weekend. Later than that, and I don't rest well.

But this morning, snuggled under the covers with the light barely shining through the windows, I'm content and relaxed. Snippets of a dream I had in the night play across my mind—Andrew's mouth on mine in the car. His hands on my body. Then walking to the door together, kissing on the porch.

I hear a deep sigh from the living room, and my eyes

snap open, all the relaxation of a moment ago gone.

It wasn't a dream. Not only that, but I'm pretty sure I invited Andrew to stay the night. But he is definitely not in my bed. There's a body next to mine, but when I reach over, it's the cat. In fact, I'm still fully clothed. I close my eyes again and try to remember what happened after he closed the door behind us.

There was more kissing, but we were both tired. I remember sitting on the couch for a while, just being close to each other, but then the details get fuzzy. And clearly we must not have made it past kissing because I'm in here, and he's in my living room.

I stretch and change out of yesterday's clothes into my sweatpants and a clean t-shirt. I brush my teeth—just in case—then walk down the hall toward the living room. The cat follows me, probably looking for her breakfast. As I round the corner, I find Andrew stretched out on my couch with his feet hanging off one end. He looks simultaneously peaceful and uncomfortable.

He must sense my presence in the room, because he opens an eye and looks up at me.

"Good morning, beautiful," he says, giving me a sleepy smile.

I flush at the endearment.

"Good morning, yourself." I bite my lip, unsure if I should go to him.

He sees the indecision in my expression and reaches a hand toward me. "Come join me on the couch."

"Are you sure? Doesn't look like there's enough room."

He pats a tiny space next to him. "Plenty of room right here."

I step closer to the couch, and he takes my hand and tugs me toward him. There's not much space for me to curl up next to him, but he scoots further into the couch cushions and angles himself so that he's almost lying on his back. I lie with my chest against his, my head tucked under his chin and hand resting lightly on his shoulder.

All that hugging we've been doing hasn't prepared me for the way he feels beneath me. I knew he had strong arms, but lying together, I can feel how toned his stomach is in a way I couldn't when we've stood this close.

"There, now this couch situation is perfect," Andrew says into my hair.

And I have to admit it *is* pretty perfect. I'm surrounded by his warmth. It's like the morning in the hotel room, except this time we're not jumping apart, pretending that neither of us wants to be wrapped up in each other's arms.

We stay like this for a while, holding each other, our chests rising and falling in sync, the sound of Andrew's heartbeat against my ear. It feels so much like a dream, and yet, he's here, lying with me on my couch in my flowery pajama pants.

Wait, when did he put those on?

I sit up, causing Andrew to shift and give me more space on the couch.

"Why was I in my bed in all my clothes from yesterday, but you're out here wearing my pajamas?"

"You don't remember?"

I shake my head. "I was dead tired when we got back."

"Well, you asked me to stay." He gives me a suggestive smile.

"I remember that part."

We had come inside, and as soon as the door closed, I'd practically jumped him. Or may he'd practically jumped me. Either way, the kissing was intense once we were inside the house. I vaguely remember moving to the couch at some point, and him leaning over me, the muscles in his shoulders flexing, the desire in his eyes. My stomach flutters as I remember the way his body pressed against mine, the way we kissed until my eyes started to feel heavy.

"I remember everything up to when we stopped kissing," I say.

"You fell asleep pretty soon after that. I carried you to your bed and tucked you in, then I came back here. I didn't want you to wake up and think I'd kissed you and then bailed. And I'm sorry I got into your suitcase, but I wasn't sure how you'd feel about finding me on your couch in nothing but my boxer briefs this morning. Plus those flowery pajamas are so comfortable."

My tongue feels thick in my mouth at the thought of Andrew in my house in nothing but boxer briefs. I swallow and in a wispy voice say, "That would have been ok."

The look he gives me in return has my stomach dropping and heat flaring through my body. I don't know how I'm going to survive if he keeps looking at me like that.

My eyes dart to his mouth as he licks his lips. He leans closer to me, resting his cheek against mine, his beard tickling my jaw. In my ear he whispers, "Next time. I promise."

He trails his nose along my cheek, then down my jaw where he nips a little kiss that makes my body tingle all the way to my toes. Then he does the same thing on the other side in reverse—a kiss, his nose along my jaw.

"But for now, I'm starving," he whispers against my other ear.

I'm so shocked at the incongruity of his actions and his words that I let out a laugh so loud it startles the cat, who's been sitting on the arm of the couch staring at us.

"I'm hungry, too," I admit.

A little while later, we sit across from each other at my favorite coffee shop. It's a cute place that features everything from homemade Pop Tarts to fancy croissants to bagel sandwiches. Our table is tucked in a corner with a bookshelf and a fireplace. Since it's summer, the fireplace isn't lit, but there's still a cozy vibe to the space.

We're waiting on our breakfast sandwiches to arrive as we sip our coffee. I take a sip, then look up at Andrew across my mug.

"So, since my faculty workshop two years ago, huh?"

"Yeah." Andrew blushes a little, and it's nice to know that I can make him blush just as much as he makes me.

"But you never talked to me. How long were you planning on pining away for me?"

"You intimidate me! I thought there was no way you'd be interested in me." Andrew gives a shrug.

"Have you seen you? How could I not be interested in

you? And I don't buy for a second that I'm that intimidating." I preen a little, though.

Andrew rubs his hand behind his head as he talks. "Evie, trust me, you are an intimidating woman, at least to me. You've got this savvy, confident air about you that somehow both turns me on and scares the shit out of me."

I shiver because something about the way he says it makes me want to kiss him.

"I'm not sure I've ever had such a...compliment? And I'm not sure I'm as confident as you think."

Andrew chuckles. "Well, you do a good job of faking it then. I like smart, confident women. Like I said in the car, the way you handled those business faculty during the workshop was incredibly hot."

I take another sip of my coffee to hide my reaction to the way he says "incredibly hot."

"Anyway, when you came over to chat that day in the library, I decided there was no way I'd ever get up enough nerve to ask you out, so I went for the next best thing."

"Getting me to fix all your spreadsheets?"

Andrew lets out a loud laugh. A few other people in the bakery turn to look at us.

"See, there's that wit of yours that makes me both want to do something completely inappropriate in a coffee shop and terrifies the hell out of me. Remind me never to get on your bad side."

I briefly imagine Andrew sweeping our coffee cups off the table and doing something very, very inappropriate with me in our little corner of the bakery, and it is not an unpleasant mental image.

"I figured working closely with you would demystify you a bit, make you seem more human. Surely the fantasy I'd built up about you in my head would burst once we were working together, right? But mostly getting to know you better had the opposite effect."

I don't know how much more of this I can take. Just listening to Andrew talk about how much he's attracted to me is making my heart race, and I am this close to abandoning our breakfast and taking him back to my place to have my way with him.

"I could say the same about you," I say, thinking how surreal it is to be having this conversation. "You intimidate me, too."

"Why?" Andrew looks genuinely flummoxed, and I almost laugh.

But as I start to answer, I think about it for a moment. Why had I been so intimidated by him? Because he's good looking? Ok, yes, that was why at first, but I'm nearly 30. Getting flustered talking to an attractive man seems so juvenile now, especially since we've spent all summer being not just friendly, but friends.

"I don't honestly know anymore." It's a moment of clarity that I didn't expect of myself. But things have been changing for me this summer, between getting the interview at McDowell and taking on managing the flood clean up efforts. Maybe I am more confident and savvy than I realized. Andrew certainly seems to think so.

It occurs to me that maybe it should have been more

obvious to me that Andrew was interested in something more than friendship. Looking back, there were definitely some signs, particularly from early in the summer. One thing in particular.

"So when you asked me to go to that LeVar Burton thing, had someone really canceled on you?" I ask.

"Yes and no. I was supposed to take my mom, but..."

"You gave me your mom's ticket?!" I give Andrew a horrified look.

"Yes, but she knows about you. And when she found out that I'd asked you to be on the committee and that you were as much of a book nerd as I am, she refused to take it. She said it was my chance."

He told his mom about me?

"Your chance?"

"To finally ask you out."

"I see. Well, good for you mom, because that talk was pretty much the highlight of my summer because I finally got to meet LeVar Burton." I tease him.

"I'm sure that's the only reason." He smirks.

"Yes, definitely the only reason."

"And not because I was doing everything I could to touch you while we were there?"

Another wave of heat passes through me. However intimidated by me Andrew was before he knew I wanted to kiss him, it seems all that is gone. He's not holding back when it comes to making sure I know he's attracted to me now.

"No, definitely not because of that."

Andrew licks his lips and gives me a wicked grin, which makes my fantasy of him doing naughty things in the coffee shop zip through my mind again.

Oh the things I want him to do with that mouth.

I have a feeling he's thinking exactly the same thing.

Fortunately (or unfortunately?), a bakery employee arrives with our sandwiches, bringing me out of my steamy fantasy and bursting the sexually charged bubble around us. For the rest of breakfast, it's like we're back to how we were before we kissed.

No, not quite like that, I think. It's comfortable, like kissing is the next logical step in our friendship.

The next morning, I wake up with a goofy smile on my face. I get ready for work, humming a song, and sighing happily as I remember the way Andrew kissed me in the driveway before he went back to his place.

He walked me home from the coffee shop, but we didn't make it all the way to my door because once we were in the driveway, he took my hand, pulled me to him, and kissed me, right there in broad daylight where anyone could see us. I was almost dizzy from the kiss and stumbled backwards until I bumped into his car. He followed me, framing me in with his arms and kissing me softly. It was the best "see you later" kiss I've ever had.

We made plans to see each other at work today, and then he left. He wanted to visit his mom and see how his grandmother was doing. I had some errands to run anyway, so even though all I really wanted to do was take him back to my bedroom and confirm my suspicion about what's under those tight t-shirts he's always wearing, I said I'd see him later.

I haven't texted Kylie and Jaclyn to let them know about Andrew and me yet, because I'm not sure I'm ready to share that piece of news. They'll want to know, though, so I'm mulling over how to tell them as I start catching up on my emails from last week.

I did a little email maintenance while we were in D.C., but there are at least twenty-five more emails from library vendors waiting in my inbox since the last time I looked. I'm idly clicking through the pile of unimportant-looking messages cluttering my inbox when one of them catches my eye.

It's from the human resources office about an upcoming Title IX training. It's not the email itself that I'm concerned about, though. The training will probably cover the usual Title IX topics—how not to sexually harass people on campus, what to do if you witness harassment, what the university's policies are about reporting sexual harassment. I could probably quote the entire training video from memory.

No, as I'm reading the email, reality sinks in, and I second guess everything that happened after D.C. I'm suddenly glad we did nothing beyond kissing, because I swore I would never date another coworker. Not after John Vance.

We only went on a few dates, but it was clear that we weren't right for each other. At least, it was clear to me. At the end of the third date, we went to his place, and he lunged into a kiss, jamming his tongue in my mouth and squeezing my breast uncomfortably. I was able to stop things from going any further, but when I did he laughed derisively.

"I thought you would be into this. You're always wearing those tight dresses that show off your tits," he'd said as I'd fled toward my car, too embarrassed to say anything.

Over the next few months, he'd texted me increasingly rude messages, until I finally blocked his number. After that, he mostly left me alone. But every now and then I'd hear from someone that he'd badmouthed me at the lunch table. Once I made a proposal for an interdisciplinary course assignment to a group of faculty, and he immediately dumped on what I'd said only to suggest an almost identical proposal later in the meeting.

Fortunately, because of the way courses are assigned, he didn't teach composition for two years after the bad date, and I was able to avoid him for the most part. That is, until last year when a change in staffing in the English department put him back in the rotation. That's what sparked the infamous screaming incident outside the dining hall and started my panic attacks.

Even though nothing in Andrew's personality has indicated that he would act the same way John did, I don't want to risk the fallout of a relationship gone sour.

I'm deliberating over how to end things with Andrew

without destroying our friendship when Kylie knocks lightly on my door frame.

"Well, how was it?" she asks.

"How was what?" I start to sweat because I think for a second that she already knows somehow.

"The conference, of course. What else would I be talking about?"

"Oh, right, yes, the conference. Definitely that's what you would be asking about." I know I sound nervous, but I can't help it. "The conference was fine. Lots of assessment ideas from it."

"Evie? Are you ok? You sound...discombobulated."

"Yep. Definitely fine and not freaking out about anything." Shit. I have to stop rambling when I'm nervous.

"Evelyn Watson. What is going on?" Kylie demands.

Damn. She used my full name.

"I kissed Andrew this weekend and now I'm freaking out because I don't date colleagues!" I say in a rush of words that blur together.

"Evie, slow down!" Kylie lowers her voice, "Did you say you kissed Andrew?"

I consider denying it, but there's no point. "Yes. This weekend. Several times, in fact. And he stayed the night."

"He stayed the night! What?"

"Not so loud! And nothing happened. I mean, we kissed a lot, but not... you know." I wince.

Kylie takes a deep breath and says, "Ok. tell me the whole story."

I fill her in on the details—the flirty conversation at the

National Gallery, the electrical storm of conversation in the car, the rest stop. Everything right up to breakfast yesterday.

"So anyway, that's what happened, and now I'm trying to figure out how to tell him it was all a mistake."

"Oh my goodness! Evie, I don't know what to say." Kylie frowns a little.

"Please say I'm not going to lose his friendship when I tell him we can't do this."

"Oh honey, you'll most definitely lose his friendship if you tell him kissing him was a mistake."

Her words feel like a slap, and I stare at her speechless.

"I will say this, because I care about you and want what's best for you. You don't have to stick to your 'no dating colleagues' rule."

It's not at all what I thought Kylie would say. She's always been the friend who plays it safe and follows the rules.

"I know you made that rule to protect yourself, and I think that's wise. But John Vance is grade-A asshole, and while Andrew is a flake and a flirt, he's not mean or conniving like John."

I still haven't found my voice and continue to stare at her, wondering if I know Kylie as well as I thought.

"But," she says, and I brace myself for whatever truth bomb she's about to drop. "Don't compromise your career for a man, even one as good looking as Andrew. Be careful. I don't want you to get hurt."

She gives my arm a squeeze, then leaves my office. I lean

back in my chair and fling my arm over my eyes. I don't know what to do, but knowing Kylie will support me whatever I decide helps calm my nerves.

She's right that Andrew is not John, and that if I break my own rule it probably won't end in disaster like everything did before. But she's also right that I can't sacrifice advancing my career just because a man with stormy blue-gray eyes thinks I'm kissable.

CHAPTER 18

A week later, I'm still debating with myself about whether everything with Andrew was a mistake, but it hasn't stopped me from continuing to kiss him. We've been hanging out in the library during the day, and in the evenings, we've been at either my place or his for dinner almost every night since we came home from D.C. He's surprised me with home cooked meals twice, and I almost can't remember what I used to do after work.

As I fill up my coffee in the workroom, I smile to myself at the memory of the homemade pizza we had last night. I almost drop my mug when a throat clears behind me, and I turn to see Mike Dobson standing in the doorway.

"Ah, Evie. I was coming to see if you were here yet. Do you have a few minutes? I have something I'd like to talk with you about," Dobson says.

"Sure, I'll just be a second." I point toward my half-full coffee cup.

Dobson nods, then stands awkwardly in the doorway while I fill the coffee the rest of the way. I take my time, sneaking in an extra moment to calm my nerves. If Dobson shows up unannounced to talk with you, it means one of three things: 1. You've done something really good and he wants to personally congratulate you. 2. You've done something really bad and he's there to reprimand you. 3. He has a new initiative on his mind and you're about to get voluntold to do something.

I can't think of anything that fits in the first two categories that I've done lately, so it must be the last one, which does not make me feel good. It's hard to say no to the provost.

As I turn back to where Dobson is messing with the knickknacks on Madge's desk, I mentally file through all the university initiatives I've heard rumors about, wondering which one he could want me working on. We make eye contact, and it hits me.

Oh god. He's not here to ask me to do something! He's here to tell me I didn't get the Teaching and Learning job.

With a full coffee cup and a heavy heart, I follow Dobson to the big study room past the stairs. The study room is large enough to host up to ten people. The tables are on wheels so that students can reconfigure the space to meet their study needs. Right now, there are four tables pushed together in the center of the room. Dobson sits on one side then gestures to a chair across from him as though I'm in his territory instead of my own.

My hand shakes as place my coffee on the table, sloshing hot liquid over the rim. I watch as a bead of dark coffee runs down the side of the mug. It's the mug Andrew usually uses. The one that says "Library School Didn't Prepare Me for This."

You got that right, mug.

"Thanks for taking the time to chat with me. I wanted to talk to you sooner rather than later about this."

For a second, I worry that somehow Dobson's found out about Andrew and me and that's why I'm disqualified for the job because there's probably a policy about dating other faculty members and I didn't even need my personal rule and maybe he's about to fire me after all and...

Dobson clears his throat, snapping me out of my catastrophizing spiral. I realize I've been intensely staring at the coffee mug for too long.

"What can I help you with?" I force my voice to sound normal.

Dobson looks temporarily worried, probably because that was the least normal I've ever sounded, but his expression clears, and he beams at me.

"I have some very good news. I'd like to invite you to interview for the Teaching and Learning Center position."

"That's great news!" My relief is instant, and my shoulders relax as he continues.

"I know it's a little unconventional for me to come talk to you before officially inviting you to the interview, but I'm really excited about your candidacy. There's just one thing I want you to know going in."

My heart drops. I have a feeling I know what he's going to say, and I'm not going to like it.

"If we hire you, we won't be able to fill the position you're currently in. I wanted you to know because I want you to have the full picture of what this change could mean for you and the university."

As expected, his words hit me in the gut. The library has already been understaffed for the past two years, and losing another librarian position would be devastating. I almost ask if the same would be true if I take the job at McDowell, but I stop myself. I haven't heard from them in the two weeks since my interview, and I am definitely not at the point of letting the provost know about that possibility.

"I understand. It gives me a lot to think about."

"I'm sure it does. You're good with moving forward with the interview?"

"Yep! Peachy!" I give him an overly bright grin. Internally, I'm reminding myself that I don't have to take the job if they offer it to me. My loyalty to the library is warring with my desire to move my career forward. But Dobson doesn't need to know that right now.

He stands to leave and reaches to shake my hand.

"Good talking with you. Amber will be in touch with details about the interview. Talk soon."

I barely nod in response as he leaves. My mind swirls with this new information. As much as I want the Teaching and Learning position, could I stay here and watch my colleagues suffer the consequences of my departure? Not that taking the McDowell job would be any better. They would still suffer, but I wouldn't be here to see it.

And speaking of the McDowell job, even though I haven't heard from them yet, I still have a good feeling about how the interview went. Or at least, how most of the interview went. The mix-up with the hotel room and the karaoke were both annoying, but the people seemed pretty great.

Now that I'm a few weeks removed from the interview, though, I'm not excited about the prospect of moving. Staying at Cooke would be easier in some ways, and I could get the managerial experience I want if I get the Teaching and Learning job. Plus, I really like working at Cooke.

There are other reasons to stay, of course. Kylie and Jaclyn are becoming like sisters to me, and leaving them would be hard. I also genuinely like everyone here—well, almost everyone. I could certainly do without John Vance.

And then there's Andrew. He's become such a good friend to me this summer. And I never would have guessed that he'd be too afraid to ask me out. But now? Now I know how his mouth feels against mine and how his beard tickles when he kisses me. Not only that, but I know what books he loves and how much he loves to cook for other people. Leaving Cooke would be difficult even without considering the direction things are going with Andrew, but our new dynamic complicates things even more.

He hasn't stayed the night again. We agreed to take things slowly since things are so up in the air with Andrew's

Gran and he sometimes has to help out his mom and aunts. I'm not in a rush to move things too quickly either. Besides, I'm still not one hundred percent sure that this isn't a mistake.

It's certainly not for lack of wanting. The way he kisses, like he's parched and I'm his oasis in the desert, leaves me breathless. But every time we start to move beyond kissing, I put the brakes on. I'm worried that once we cross that line, there will be no going back for me, and the thought terrifies me a little.

Regardless of the kissing, I know Andrew will be excited to hear about my conversation with Dobson, and I can't wait to tell him tonight.

I practically yank Andrew into the house when he arrives for dinner. He spent the day helping one of his aunts move some furniture, so he wasn't in the library today, and I want to tell him in person about my conversation with Dobson.

"I take it from your grin that you had a good day at work?" he asks as wraps his arms around me to give me a hello kiss.

"Yes, a very good day, in fact. Dobson asked me to interview for the Teaching and Learning job!"

Andrew's face lights up. "Evie! That's wonderful news! You're gonna do it, right?"

"Of course! There's a catch, though."

Andrew frowns as I fill him in on the rest of my

conversation with Dobson.

"I don't know what will happen if I get the job at McDowell instead. I could see them filling the librarian position if I'm not at Cooke anymore, though. After all, if I'm still working at Cooke, I could theoretically help out when the library needs something."

His expression shutters, and I realize that we haven't discussed the McDowell job since we got back. We've both been so focused on other projects since the trip that the interview just hasn't come up. Or at least that's what I'm telling myself.

In truth, as I think back over the things that happened between Andrew and me during the trip to D.C., it's obvious now that the things he said about McDowell's mistakes with the interview process came from his feelings for me.

"I haven't gotten an offer from them, though. It's been two weeks. I might not get one."

Andrew doesn't look as cheered up by that as I hoped he would. "Yeah, I guess that's true."

I'm not sure how to respond to Andrew's obvious disappointment that I'm still considering the McDowell position. We've only been aware of our feelings for each other for two weeks, so it's not like we're in a long-term relationship. I know he doesn't want me to leave, and not talking about it means I don't have to face the choice between the job of my dreams and my new relationship.

Bringing up the McDowell position has thrown our entire evening into awkwardness. Neither of us seems to know how to move past the weird tension that happens every time it comes up in conversation. We're quiet for so long that I almost suggest we take a rain check on dinner.

Andrew's phone rings, finally breaking the silence. He checks to see who's calling, then steps out onto the porch to take the call.

I start tidying the shoes by the door because I don't know what else to do while I wait for him to come back inside.

A few minutes later, he walks back through the door, his face grim. "I need to go take care of something. I'll see you tomorrow."

I nod and barely say goodbye as he pecks a kiss on my cheek. As he leaves, I have the distinct feeling that the phone call is an excuse to avoid talking about McDowell, and the worry that I've somehow messed things up with Andrew settles in the pit of my stomach.

CHAPTER 19

Andrew doesn't show up at work the next day. He doesn't text me, either. I know there's an explanation, but I can't help the feeling that the explanation is that he doesn't want to see me anymore after our conversation about my potential move.

After work, though, I'm fully in worry mode because he still hasn't texted me. I know it seems extreme to be so worried, but anxiety is rarely rational.

I pace around my living room, my mind churning with all the possible reasons I haven't heard from him.

Maybe I imagined all the things he said about wanting me for the past two years. Maybe I've done something to put him off. Maybe he's realized that I'm not that great of a kisser after all and that kissing me on the way home from D.C. was a mistake. Maybe his heartbreaker reputation is really the truth, and the way he ends things is by ghosting women.

Maybe he talked to John Vance and found out that the real reason John and I hate each other is that I wouldn't sleep with John and he harassed me for months afterward.

Maybe he realized that he couldn't be with someone who can't get her shit together enough to stop having panic attacks.

Maybe it would be better if I go ahead and break things off so Andrew can't hurt me first.

The spiral of my thoughts pushes me toward a panic attack. My hands shake, my ears ring, and I'm dizzy.

They're just thoughts. Thoughts lie. I tell myself over and over again, but no matter what I do, I can't seem to get myself out of the loop.

I find my way to the couch and curl up there.

I can't breathe.

I'm gasping for air, but my lungs can't get full.

My heart rate is skyrocketing, and my pulse beats in my ears.

I still can't breathe. *Have to breathe. Need to breathe.*

I try to take myself through my breathing exercises, but this attack has come on strong and sudden. I'm lightheaded, and my arms tense with pain.

Somehow, through the fog of my panic, I remember what Andrew said when I had the panic attack after the library flooded. "Call or text me anytime you need someone to help you through one."

With a gasping breath and trembling hands, I pick up

my phone and press the call button next to Andrew's name.

Even if he's decided we're through, he's still my friend... right?

He answers on the second ring.

"Evie? I'm in the middle of something, can I call you back?"

"Andrew, I..." My voice is barely audible and so shaky I don't know if he can understand me. "I...can't...breathe.... I'm...having...an...attack."

"An attack?" He drops his voice. "I'm here. Just give me one second."

I hear him cover the phone and say something to someone, but I can't make out the muffled words.

My ears are still ringing, and my heart feels like it's going to burst out of my chest.

"Evie?" His voice is so, so gentle. "Evie, it's going to be ok. I need you to breathe with me, ok?"

He talks me through a couple rounds of box breathing, and as I listen to his voice tell me to breathe in and out, the panic begins to subside.

It takes a few minutes, but my breaths return to normal. I am completely drained, though.

"All better?" Andrew asks tenderly.

"Better," I say, but I can still hear the shakiness in my voice. "Thank you."

"Do you want to tell me what happened? What triggered the attack?"

"No, not right now." I sound a little stronger now.

Not strong enough, though, because there is concern in

Andrew's voice as he says, "I'm worried about you. I can't leave right now, but I'm coming over as soon as I can, ok?"

I suck in a breath—a real, deep one. If he comes over we'll have to talk about McDowell, and I already know where that discussion will lead. But there's no getting around it, and I know what I need to do.

"Yes, please come over when you can. I..." I swallow. "I need to talk to you about something anyway."

We end the call, and I lay my head on the couch pillow. I feel stretched thin from the panic attack and the impending conversation with Andrew.

I close my eyes and take some more deep breaths. Before long, I'm asleep.

Bang. Bang. Bang.

I don't know who is hammering, but the sound startles me out of a fitful sleep.

I press my eyes together more firmly, but the hammering isn't letting up. And then suddenly it stops, and I hear someone call, "Evie? Are you there?"

I open my eyes, realizing it's not hammering. It's knocking, and it's coming from my front door. I unwind myself from the curled position I'm in, stretching out my legs as I stand, and walk to the door.

I know without looking in the mirror that my hair is a mess, and I probably look like Bozo the Clown did my make up. My stomach rumbles, reminding me that instead of having dinner tonight, I had one of the worst panic attacks I've had in months.

I open the door, and Andrew is standing there, concern lining his face. His arms open for me, and I go to him without thinking. It's fine. I'll take this last opportunity to enjoy the way my head fits just below his chin when his arms are around me. But god, I'm going to miss it.

He steps back slightly so we can look at each other, but he keeps his arms around me. "Are you ok? I was worried sick about you."

I look at his chest where my face was buried just moments ago. His shirt is wet. I must be crying because my face is wet, too.

"I don't know if I'm ok. I...I can't do this," I croak out. I try to step out of his arms, but he holds me fast.

"Can't do what? Evie, what happened?" His brows pinch together, and there's a fearful look in his eyes.

"This." I motion between the two of us. "I can't. I can't risk my career for whatever this is. And if you're going to ghost me, then please let's just end this now. It's too much."

"What do you mean?" Andrew looks stricken. "Who's ghosting you?"

"You, Andrew. Just like..." I trail off.

"Just like who, Evie?"

I let out a shuddering breath, trying unsuccessfully to keep my tears at bay. Andrew finally lets me go, and I move further into the living room, stopping behind the recliner and wiping the tears from my eyes. "In college. My first boyfriend."

"Taylor of the sloppy kisses who broke your heart?"

"Yes, the one who just stopped calling. Stopped texting. I didn't hear from him for two months. I know I was young and hadn't figured out my life yet, so I probably did something to push him away, too, but it still hurt. I thought I was smarter than that now. Anyway, when you didn't text..."

"You thought I was doing the same thing. Dammit." He reaches for me again, but I step away and shake my head.

"It's not just that. I can't date you, Andrew. I promised myself I wouldn't date another colleague after..." I trail off, realizing he doesn't know about the real reason John Vance and I don't get along.

"After what?"

I hesitate. I don't want him to think less of me for dating John, even if I didn't know what he was like before we started going out.

Andrew takes my hands in his, and the look he gives me is so tender, I almost start crying again.

"Whatever it is, no judgment."

"Promise?" My voice is weak, the evidence of my exhaustion clear.

"Promise."

I shift my glance from his face to his shoulder. I can't look him in the eyes while I tell him about the hurt and embarrassment of the way things ended with John.

Andrew is still as I lay out the entire history. The first time I taught a class for John and he complimented my teaching. The two reasonable dates before he showed his true character. The last one that left me feeling gross and vulnerable. The belittling behavior in the months that followed.

When I finish, I raise my eyes toward Andrew's, and what I see in his face nearly knocks the breath out of me. His normally boyish smirk has been replaced by a firm line. There's a glint of steel in his eyes, and his nostrils flare as he breathes.

But then we make eye contact, and the simmering rage dissipates. He cups my jaw with his hand and tilts my chin toward his.

"I'm sorry that happened. I'm sorry you've been carrying that, and that I put you in a position to interact with him more regularly with the general education committee. If I had known, I wouldn't have asked you to join us."

A tear that I've been holding back escapes and runs down my cheek.

"If you hadn't asked me to join the committee, we wouldn't have gone to D.C. together. We wouldn't have found each other."

Andrew chuckles. "You're right. But it shouldn't have come at the cost of your mental health."

He pulls me to him, and we stand in my living room for a long time, his hand rubbing gentle circles on my back, my breaths matching the rise and fall of his chest. The moment is perfect, and I don't want to ruin it, but there's something else that contributed to this particular panic attack that I can't ignore any longer.

"I think we should break up. My job situation is too messy for this, and if I get the job at McDowell, it will just complicate things between us." I say it fast, not letting him interrupt me.

I risk a glance at Andrew's face. He looks hurt, which doesn't surprise me, but makes me feel awful all the same. But he narrows his eyes at me and sighs.

"You're right. It will complicate things, but that doesn't mean I don't want to be with you," he says evenly.

"But what if I get that job and leave? Are we just going to ignore the fact that I'll be six hours away from you?"

"No, we're not going to ignore it," he says. "We're going to figure it out together if you get the offer. Will it suck to live six hours apart? Absolutely. But I'm willing to make it work if you are."

His words hit me square in the chest like a punch. He wants to be with me. It's not just words. I can hear it in his voice; I can see it in his eyes.

And the truth is, I want him, too, and now here he is, offering himself to me. I just don't know if I can accept it.

He sits on the couch and pats the spot next to him, inviting me to join him. He turns to me as I sit and takes my hand.

"Evie, do you want to be with me?" He looks at once hopeful and fearful.

I hitch a breath. "I do, but..."

"Then let's be together. The fact is, I like you. A lot. And until a few weeks ago, I thought I would never have a chance with you. I felt like I'd won the fucking lottery when you told me you wanted to kiss me after D.C.”

I search his gaze. He looks vulnerable, like what I say next could potentially break him. I want so badly to say yes to being with Andrew, to dive head-first into what this could be.

Instead, I close my eyes and ask the thing that's been bothering me since this morning.

“Where were you today?”

Andrew frowns, and I know he knows I'm avoiding his question, but he doesn't push it.

“I'm sorry I didn't tell you. I'm not used to sharing when something bad happens, and I forgot to tell you.”

“Forgot to tell me what?”

Andrew looks sad as he says, “The call I got last night. It was about my Gran. She had a fall at her care facility, and I was helping my mom and her sisters with the paperwork at the hospital all day today.”

“Oh. Andrew, I'm so sorry. You shouldn't have answered my call. I would have been ok eventually.” I feel awful that I let my fears about our relationship trigger a panic attack when he had such an important reason for not calling.

“You don't need to apologize. I'm not sure I was as much help as I could have been, actually. The poor hospital staff had enough on their plates with the Brandt Biddies—that's what my mom and her sisters call themselves—swooping in and causing a fuss over Gran. They didn't need an extra person taking up space in the lobby.”

I give Andrew a puzzled look. “The Brandt Biddies? Wasn't Brandt your dad's last name?”

Andrew shakes his head. "No, my mom kept her name when she married my dad. Brandt is actually my middle name, but I use it professionally because dad's last name invites too many jokes."

I narrow my eyes at him. "What's your real last name?"

Andrew sighs. "I don't tell very many people because it's so embarrassing. But I trust you."

"I can't imagine a last name that's so embarrassing you'd not tell anyone, but I'm honored."

"Trust me, it's embarrassing."

He doesn't keep going, and I know he's stalling so I give him a pointed look. He lets out a deep sigh, like he can't believe he's about to say it out loud, then he mumbles something that I can't quite make out.

"Andrew. Tell me," I implore him.

"Aycock. My real name is Andrew Brandt Aycock." He looks chagrined.

I burst into laughter, and it is exactly what I needed after the emotional drain of the last few days. Through my laughs, I wheeze out, "Wait, you're telling me your actual name is Andrew, A Cock?"

He frowns so deeply I'm worried his smile will never reappear. "It's not that funny."

"Oh yes it is." I double over in laughter.

He pokes me in the side to try to get me to stop, but it just makes me laugh harder.

"I said it wasn't funny." His tone is gruff, but there's humor in his eyes.

I lean against him. "And I said it was." I smirk and lift an eyebrow, challenging him to disagree with me.

The light in his eyes shifts, turning dark with heat, and I suddenly remember that he told me he likes it when I'm confident. He dips his head so his lips graze my ear as he whispers, "A cock is no laughing matter."

I let out another yelp of laughter. I think he meant it to be sexy, but I'm too giddy to think about that.

Andrew rolls his eyes, but I know I've won because he finally relents and laughs with me. "Ok, fine. It's funny."

We laugh until we can't anymore.

When we've finally regained our composure, my stomach lets out the loudest, most embarrassing growl possible. Instead of trying to ignore it, I say, "What time is it? I missed dinner because of the panic attack, and I'm starving."

"Right," Andrew practically growls. He stands abruptly and leads me to the kitchen where he starts opening cabinets.

"What are you looking for?" I ask as he opens another cabinet.

"Something that I can fix you to eat."

I'm hit by a sudden wave of warmth from the look in Andrew's eyes. He's taking care of me, and it's almost too much to bear. I like to think of myself as fiercely independent, and I don't know what to do with the swell of emotion that overtakes me.

"I'm afraid all I have is boxed macaroni and cheese." I grab a box from a cabinet that he hasn't opened yet.

"Do you have real butter?"

"Yes."

"That will work, then." Andrew takes the box from me and goes to the fridge, pulling out butter and milk. "I'm going to make you the best boxed macaroni and cheese you've ever had."

He's not wrong about the macaroni and cheese. He browns the butter before mixing in the powdered cheese and milk. After he stirs everything together, he sprinkles some shredded sharp cheddar cheese that he found in my fridge over the top.

We eat standing in the kitchen, leaning against the counter hip to hip, playfully bumping elbows and continuing to giggle about Andrew's unfortunate last name.

When we finish, I take both our bowls and place them in the dishwasher. As I turn around, I take a moment to enjoy the sight of him in my kitchen. He's still leaning casually against the counter, giving off a relaxed, sexy vibe. I've been seeing him in tight t-shirts and jeans all summer, but something about the way the light from my kitchen fixture washes over him makes my breath hitch. He's all smooth planes and hard muscles, and the fabric of his shirt is doing little to hide it.

I take a step toward him and put my hands on his shoulders, going up on my toes to brush my lips against his.

"Thank you for dinner," I say against his mouth.

"You're welcome." His voice is low and gravelly. His hands cup my ass, and he tugs me forward so we're standing chest to chest. He murmurs my name against my ear, sending a shiver down my spine and turning my insides to liquid.

My heart is hammering in my chest, but this is not like during my panic attack.

"Kiss me," I say, trying to give my voice that confident tone I know he likes so much.

"Does this mean you're willing to try to make this work?"

I look into his blue-gray eyes with a mixture of desire and trepidation. I know I'm taking a risk with my heart, but that doesn't stop me. "Yes."

My "Yes" hangs in the air between us.

Andrew's eyes turn dark with desire as he searches my face. The next thing I know, he's letting out a low, hungry sound as he finds my mouth with his. He kisses me hard, like that first time in the car.

His tongue plays with my lower lip, each taste sending shocks of heat through me. I let him part my lips with his tongue, relishing the sensation as he sweeps into my mouth.

His hands are still on my ass, pulling me closer and closer, and I know he's just as aroused as I am because I can feel the evidence of it against me.

His hair has gotten longer this summer, and I wonder for a moment if he's not been cutting it because of the stress of dealing with his grandmother's care or the fact that he doesn't have to keep it as trim when we're out of the regular academic term, but I don't have time to dwell on the thought because I'm running my hands through the unruly waves and he's groaning my name.

One of his hands is under my shirt, and it's soft and

warm against my back. He reaches the clasp of my bra, and I let out a little gasp as he deftly unhooks it. I shiver as he grazes a thumb on the underside of my breast, and I am so glad it's not an accident this time because *god, yes.*

The pleasure he's unleashing with his hands is making me want to grind against him, so I run my hands down his back and pull myself as close to him as I can, savoring the feel of his increasing arousal against me as I do.

"Fuck, Evie," he growls, taking his hands out of my shirt and tugging at the hem. In one swift movement, he yanks my shirt over my head. I ease the straps of my bra off my arms and let it fall to the floor. My chest is heaving, and Andrew's eyes widen with lust as he takes in the sight of me topless.

I nod to him, because it doesn't seem fair that he's getting an eyeful when I've been fantasizing about what's underneath all that cotton all summer. "Shirt. Off."

He winks at me with an almost maniacal grin, but he holds my gaze as he peels his shirt up and over his head.

Now it's my turn to stare. His chest is broad and muscular, just as I had imagined. A layer of golden hair dusts his torso, and my fingers itch to tangle in it.

I don't deny myself the urge. I reach forward and place a hand on his chest, and the hair there is so soft. I let my fingers glide over his stomach. His muscles are hard, strong, and it's a delectable contrast to the velvety hair covering them. I look up at his face again, and take a moment to just enjoy the look of him reacting to my touch—his eyes half closed, lips swollen.

He shivers, then moves toward me with a swiftness that makes the space between my legs pulse. He finds my nipple with his mouth, and I arch my back to give him better access.

He kisses up my breast to my neck, and his voice rumbles in my ear, "Bedroom?"

Ignoring the little voice in my head that warns against what taking Andrew to my bed will mean for my heart, I nod and say, "Yes, please."

I yelp as he lifts me off the ground and carries me down the hallway.

CHAPTER 20

My bedroom has always been my favorite room in this house. The house is old, built in the 1940s, and it has little details of cozy character throughout. The bedroom is no exception. It's off the main hallway and faces a small porch on the back of the house. Three of the walls have windows, which means the lighting in here is amazing on a midsummer evening. It's filtering through the blinds, giving the room a soft, sensual glow— the perfect amount of light to see by as Andrew lays me down on the bed.

I can't decide where to look. His broad chest heaving as he stares at me? The line of hair leading into the waistband of his pants? His eyes, which are full of lust and longing?

I meet his eyes, and he gives me a slow, seductive smile.

"I've dreamed about this," he says, his words making my heart stutter.

He takes a slow step forward, then drops beside me on the bed. His hand comes up to cup my cheek, and I lean into his touch. He runs his thumb along my bottom lip, and I shiver at the contact.

That spicy, clean scent he has envelopes me as our mouths meet again, and I am hit with the exquisite realization that my sheets are going to smell like Andrew in the morning.

Our kisses are growing furious, and the urge to grind against him overwhelms me, but it feels like he's holding back, waiting for something. I reach for his belt, and he stops me.

"You're sure?" he asks.

I nod, but he shakes his head.

"I need you to say it."

I've never been someone who is good at saying what I want, but I don't hesitate this time. "Yes, I'm sure."

He nips another kiss on my collar bone, then stands and undoes the button on his jeans. He discards his clothes on the floor, and my mouth goes dry at the sight of Andrew Brandt standing naked in my bedroom.

"Your turn," he says, voice gruff in a way that makes me nearly perish on the spot.

I stand up from the bed, managing to undo the little hook and eye closure on my pants as I stand, and kick them to the corner of the room.

What happens next is that I find out exactly what

Andrew meant in the car when he said I deserved to be kissed like it meant something. Everything he does—every touch, every soft murmur and deep moan—it means something.

Afterwards, we lay on my bed curled around each other, and we stay like that until morning. The way we wake up is so much like back in D.C. that I forget for a minute that we're not there. But that morning seemed mortifying at the time, and this morning... this morning is nowhere close to mortifying.

Andrew's arm is wrapped around me, holding me close. We never put clothes back on, and the warmth of his skin seeps into mine. There's a luxuriousness to it that makes me never want to leave this bed again.

I ease myself out of Andrew's hold and roll onto my other side so I can watch him sleep. I lay my hand on his chest, stroking my fingers through his luscious hair.

He stirs and places his hand on top of mine, giving me a drowsy grin. "Good morning, beautiful."

It's the same thing he said the morning after he slept on my couch.

"Good morning, yourself," I say, just like before.

He squeezes my hand, then brings it to his mouth. He kisses my fingertips, then my palm, and my wrist. I sigh contentedly.

"What time is it?" Andrew whispers against my wrist.

I shift to look at the clock, my hand still in his. "Almost 6:30."

"What time do you have to be at work?" He's started

kissing his way up my arm, slowly.

"Hmm? I can't hear you when you're kissing me like that," I say, only half joking.

"It wasn't an important question anyway," he says against my neck. He tugs at my ear with his teeth, and I let out a little moan.

He kisses every inch of my neck and shoulders, and the thought strikes me that there is no way I'm going to be able to function at work if Andrew is there, giving me lusty looks and making flirty jokes. It was fine when I thought we were just friends. Some of our conversations were flirty then, but I assumed it was because Andrew is a flirty person.

Obviously, I misread that situation.

He's still kissing me, having moved on to my other arm now, but I can't let the thought of work go, and for my own sake, I'm going to need some ground rules.

"No kissing at work," I blurt out as his mouth makes its way toward my chest again.

Andrew looks up at me with a raised eyebrow from where he's just kissed the top of my breast. "Excuse me?"

"No kissing at work." I repeat. "I won't do it. It's not appropriate."

He straightens up, his face serious, but I almost laugh because the juxtaposition of his seriousness and our nakedness is farcical.

"Ok. I can deal with no kissing at work," he says. Then his eyes take on a wicked gleam. "Although I will admit, I have a very specific fantasy that involves you and me and bookshelves."

My mouth falls into a perfect "O" because now I think I have that fantasy, too. I shake myself to recover and say in what I hope is my most intimidating voice, "No. Kissing. At. Work."

Andrew holds up a hand. "I won't try to make that fantasy happen at work. I promise."

"Good. Thank you."

"But I can't promise I won't try it here," he mutters as he kisses my neck again.

I'm about to let myself melt into his kisses, but something else is tugging at my mind.

"Another thing." I put my hands on Andrew's face so he'll stop kissing me and listen. "Communication. The thing that drives me most crazy in romance novels is when the characters don't communicate with each other."

"This isn't a romance novel, Evie."

"No, but the concept still applies. Especially after how your friendship with Jaclyn ended."

Andrew winces. "Harsh, but fair. I promise I will communicate with you. I know it's important to you, and it's important to me, too."

He looks at me in a way that I know he's sincere. I smile and drop my hands from his face, then start running a hand along his back.

Andrew murmurs with pleasure. "Is it bad that you laying down the rules like this is turning me on a little?"

I laugh. It doesn't surprise me that he'd say that, given everything I've learned about Andrew over the summer.

"Are there any more rules you wish to lay out?" he asks

with a sly grin.

"No, I think that's all. Thank you for listening."

"Of course." He kisses me on the nose. Then he gives me another serious look. "If we're done with the rules for now, I have some very important business that I need to take care of this morning."

I scrunch my eyes at him. "What business?"

"This." He gives me a wicked grin as he dives below the sheets.

I hum with pleasure as he nips my inner thigh. I could definitely get used to this.

A little while later, we are breathless in my bed, and the alarm clock is beeping. I lean over Andrew to turn it off, then flop back on the bed.

"Maybe I should call in sick," I say in a breathy voice.

"Yes, definitely. I'm too sick to work today, too." Andrew's voice is deep and gravelly. "If you're too sick to work, and I'm too sick to work, maybe we should just stay here in bed."

"Hmm, I like that plan. Just one problem." I sit up.

"What's that?"

"We have a committee meeting, and I think they would notice if we both missed it."

"Ugh, fine," Andrew grunts.

He stands up from the bed, and I bite my lip as I watch him find his clothes. I almost pinch myself because it feels like a dream. I'm not sure how I'm going to make it through the day without pulling Andrew down one of the aisles of bookshelves and enacting that fantasy of his.

The meeting isn't until 11:00, so Andrew goes home to finish getting ready for the day after we shower. I've never seen the appeal of showering with someone else before, but now I realize I've been severely limiting my imagination in that regard.

I get to the room for the meeting ten minutes early. I want to have enough time to mentally prepare myself for working with John. The last meeting was better than the first one, even if John was openly hostile about my going to the conference in D.C. But I didn't have a panic attack, which I'm counting as a win. Still, I want to be in the room before anyone else so there won't be a repeat of my late arrival from last time.

Andrew and Katie arrive at the same time—their offices are next to each other, so they probably walked here together. Lauren is right behind them, and Mike Radford and Chris appear a few minutes later. There's no sign of John.

Andrew glances at his watch.

"John's late, but we can go ahead and start. Evie, why don't you start us off with some of the things we learned at the ReGENerate conference?"

I give Andrew a meaningful look as I think about what I

learned at the conference, or rather on the way home from the conference. I know he must be thinking the same thing because he winks at me. And that is the moment that John saunters into the room.

"Hi, John. Evie was about to tell everyone about the sessions from the conference she and I attended."

John makes a grunting noise, but takes a seat on the other side of the room away from me. Andrew gives me a nod to start.

"Andrew and I both have some ideas that we'd like to implement after seeing what other universities are doing with their general education outcomes. For starters, I attended an excellent session on using faculty peer-reviewers for developing new approaches to teaching familiar content."

John rolls his eyes and sighs loudly. I grimace a little at his sigh but keep going.

"Basically what the presenters talked about was developing an internal peer-review system to provide support for faculty within each department. So Arts and Sciences would have a peer-reviewer, Health Sciences would have one, and on down the line. The idea is that someone would receive training on new approaches to pedagogy and then be the point person for the school when faculty want to try something new in the classroom."

I look around the room. Everyone seems to be nodding their heads and taking notes. But when I look at John, I'm met with a deep frown and crossed arms.

"So what you're saying is that not only are librarians

going to try to come into our classrooms and take over, but now the university is going to have a group of people who don't know anything about my curriculum coming in and telling me how to teach? Hell no. It's a violation of my academic freedom." John practically spits the words at me.

Through gritted teeth, I say, "No, that's not at all what I'm saying. I'm saying we would develop a system of mutual support among the faculty to give us room to try new things."

"Right, so that the administration can keep tabs on us and bring down the hammer when we get out of line, I suppose?"

"Do you have a problem, John?" Andrew has been watching the exchange between John and me with a tight look on his face. I suspect he's worried that going head to head with John would trigger another panic attack, but I am feeling surprisingly calm and ready to spar with my nemesis.

"Yeah, I've got a problem. My problem is her." He jabs a finger in my direction. "Always trying to horn her way into everything. The ReGENerate conference for starters, and my classroom so she can 'teach' about library services." He uses air quotes around "teach."

"I've had enough of it. What the students need to know about the library is that they need to go in there and find some damn books for their papers. End of story. You don't need a whole class period to teach that." John is yelling at this point.

"That's not what I teach," I grind out.

"Then what the hell are you doing being a librarian?" John stands up.

"You are out of line," Andrew stands up, too, crossing his arms as he glares at John. Andrew has at least four inches in height on him, so he's towering over the other man.

"Not surprised to see you defending her. It's obvious to anyone with eyes that you're fucking her."

It feels like all the air has been sucked out of the room. A vein pulses on Andrew's neck, and the other four committee members all have slightly varied versions of the same expression of shock. My entire body flames with embarrassment.

"What? Isn't that why you asked her to be in this group? So you could ogle her all day? It certainly wasn't because she brings anything else to the table."

Andrew's jaw looks so tight I'm afraid it might snap.

"Get. Out." Andrew says through gritted teeth.

John holds up his hands. "I'm just saying. I know she's ambitious. She probably weaseled her way in to the committee so she could get in good with Dobson."

I flinch.

John fixes his eyes on me with a glare. "I know what you did. I know you went and told on me. Just came from Dobson's office."

"I told you to GET OUT." Andrew looks like he's about to pick up a desk and fling it across the room.

My anxiety starts to ramp up, but I take deep breaths and try to focus on my senses like my therapist taught me to do.

"Fine. I'm quitting this sham of a committee, by the way." With that, John stomps out of the room and slams the door.

No one moves or says anything for what feels like an age. Andrew is still standing, looking grim. My hands are shaking, but other than that, I'm breathing normally. Maybe my visits with my therapist have been more helpful than I realized.

"What in the actual fuck was that?" Katie asks.

"Pretty typical John. Dude's always been an asshole," Chris says. He's worked at Cooke the longest out of anyone on the committee, even John.

Andrew rubs a hand down his face. "I think we'd better reschedule this meeting."

Everyone nods their assent and starts to pack up their things and file out of the room.

Katie comes over to me before she goes and puts a hand on my arm.

"Are you ok?"

I nod. "Yeah, just shocked, and somehow not shocked, I think."

"Let me know if you want to talk about it." She gives my arm a squeeze.

"Thanks, I appreciate it."

Katie leaves, and now it's just Andrew and me. He crosses the room and pulls me into a hug. I want to protest —this is definitely somewhere close to the no kissing at work rule—but once his arms are around me, I sink into them, leaning my weight against him.

"Was that what it was like when he yelled at you before?" Andrew asks against my hair.

"Exactly what it was like," I say into his chest. He's rubbing slow circles on my back, the movement soothing.

I look up at him. "What do you think he was talking about when he brought up going to Dobson's office? I never said anything to Dobson."

"I talked to Dobson this morning and told him what John did to you."

"You? You told Dobson?"

"Yeah. I have a very low tolerance for men who treat women like that. Especially women I lo...like."

I furrow my brow. "But I didn't want to report him. I was handling it myself." I don't miss Andrew's skipped syllable that sounded suspiciously like the word "love," but now isn't the time to examine that particular issue.

"The man was spreading lies about you, and it was giving you panic attacks! Do you call that handling it? He deserves to be called in to Dobson's office and reprimanded, if not fired."

I push away from him. "Maybe he does, but that's not the point. It wasn't your place to report him, and I don't need you swooping in and rescuing me every time I have to deal with an asshole at work."

"I was just trying to help." Andrew steps toward me, but I move away, closer to the door.

"I didn't ask for your help."

"Are you going to report what happened today?" He asks.

"I don't know. I need some time to think."

He looks incredulous. "If you don't, someone's going to."

"Fine. But it had better not be you. I'm asking you not to. Please." I give him a pleading look, but he doesn't say anything. He turns and lifts his eyes toward the ceiling, letting out an exasperated breath.

I leave quickly, hoping Andrew doesn't hear my whimper as the tears fall from my eyes.

CHAPTER 21

I sleep on the couch because my bed still smells like Andrew, and I'm still mad at him. Unsurprisingly, my sleep is terrible.

When I get to the library in the morning, I'm already nursing a throbbing in my temples that explodes into a terrible headache when I check my email. I have a message in my inbox from Dobson asking me to come to his office for a meeting this afternoon with him and Bert Billings, the head of security. Even without any context in the email, I know that someone must have reported John. Andrew was right, but I still hope he's respected my wishes and wasn't the one to do it.

I don't know why it bothers me so much that he reported the first incident. John does deserve to be disciplined for treating me that way. But I've heard so many stories of women's workplace complaints about male colleagues being dismissed as hysteria and the women being ostracized, or worse, that I'm worried it will happen to me.

I spend the whole morning on edge. Andrew is sitting at his usual table when I come downstairs for lunch, but I avoid him.

I hardly eat the leftover lasagna I brought because it tastes like ash on my tongue. I go to the workroom freezer and find a tub of salted caramel truffle ice cream that's left over from someone's birthday and scoop myself a huge bowl.

After lunch, I sit in my office, barely registering what's on the computer screen. I have things I need to do, but I'm so distracted with the anticipation of my meeting with Dobson and Bert that I can't focus.

When it's finally time to go to Dobson's office, I grab a notepad and pen—mostly so I have something in my hands to keep me from fidgeting. Andrew is gone, and I sigh with relief that I don't have to interact with him. I arrive in the lobby of the office suite, and Amber greets me with a warm smile.

"Dr. Dobson will be with you in a minute. Have a seat."

I sit in one of the chairs across from Amber's desk. A few minutes later, Dobson's door opens, and out walks Andrew. I give him an incredulous look, and he smiles uncertainly at me but doesn't say anything. Does that mean he's completely ignored my wishes and reported John's behavior from yesterday?

"Evie, come on back," Dobson says as he appears behind Andrew. "Brandt, thanks for talking with us about this." The men shake hands.

I feel sick. Andrew has definitely reported yesterday's incident.

Bert is already in the room, so I sit in the same chair I used the last time I was here. I have the absurd urge to laugh as I remember my skirt riding up, and it makes me wish that was the extent of things to worry about now.

"I suppose you know why we asked you to come in this afternoon?" Dobson asks.

"I have an idea, yes."

"Mainly, we want to get your side of things on the incidents with John Vance. I'm meeting with everyone who was involved yesterday, including John, to get their perspectives."

"That makes sense." My voice doesn't sound like my own, but it's good in a way because my emotions are roiling.

"Do I understand correctly that yesterday was not the first time you and John have had a disagreement?" This question comes from Bert, and I nearly scoff.

A "disagreement." Seriously?

"That's right. John and I have not been on good terms for most of the time I've been at Cooke, and yesterday was not the first time he's yelled at me."

"Tell us about the first time, if you would," Bert prompts.

I look between him and Dobson. Bert gives me a sort of grimace that I think is supposed to be an encouraging smile.

I take a deep breath and explain what happened last year.

I thought I would have trouble talking about it with someone I don't know well, but it turns out that finally saying something to someone in a position of power is easier than I expected. Almost like a weight I've been carrying has been released.

Dobson scribbles some notes on a pad of paper as I talk, but mostly he and Bert listen.

"And a few weeks ago, he got really angry during a meeting when Andrew announced that we were going to the ReGENerate conference," I say. "I don't want to make assumptions, but it seemed like he wanted to go to the conference and was upset that I was going."

Bert gives Dobson a look that seems to be part of a silent conversation between the two of them.

"Now, about yesterday's incident. Tell us what happened, but take your time. I don't want to rush you to relive it." Dobson's pen is poised to begin taking notes again.

Just like a moment ago when I told them about the first incident, sharing the details of yesterday's meeting is much easier than I expected it would be. As I finish outlining the details, I realize I am calmer than I was at the beginning of the meeting. Even though things haven't been resolved yet, just the act of sharing the story seems to make a difference.

There's one thing, though, that I'm not sure I should include in what I tell Bert and Dobson. Andrew and I haven't talked about whether we're telling anyone about our...whatever this thing is we're doing is.

"Is there anything else you want to tell us about?"

Is Dobson reading my thoughts?

I decide I should wait to say anything until I talk to Andrew. Besides, after our argument yesterday and the fact that he probably betrayed my trust and reported things with John, there might not even be anything to report.

"No, nothing else." I start to leave, but then I stop and ask, "Do you mind if I ask what the next steps are, though?"

"Of course. We'll finish meeting with everyone who was involved yesterday as well as anyone else you think we should talk to, especially regarding that first incident. Then we'll reach out again for a follow up with you."

I nod. "Ok. You might want to talk with Kylie Conner and Jaclyn Beckett. They know as much as anyone about the first incident."

"Thank you for sharing today. I know it was hard to do," Bert says.

Dobson escorts me out of his office, shakes my hand, and thanks me for coming. Amber smiles at me as I leave the office suite.

Even though having the problems with John out in the open has made me feel a bit lighter, I still have a knot in my stomach. I pull out my phone and send a text. I'm going to confront Andrew, but first I need to talk to my friends.

"He said WHAT?" Jaclyn looks horrified as I fill her in on what happened at the last committee meeting. "The next time I see that asshole, he'd better watch himself."

"I appreciate the sentiment, but I have a feeling you might have to get in line. I thought Andrew was going to fling a desk across the room at him. Even Bert and Dobson looked like they were gearing up to have a not so fun conversation with John."

I take a sip of my wine. Jaclyn and I are waiting for Kylie at the bar. It's midweek, so there aren't many other people here. We've still picked a table that's a little secluded so we can have some privacy.

The door opens, and Kylie waves at us as she enters. She stops to order a drink, then joins us. I already filled her in on the committee meeting and a little about what had happened in Dobson's office.

She leans over and clasps my hand. "I'm so sorry you're having to deal with this."

I give her a sad smile. "I know. But I'm really glad I have you two to talk to about it."

"You said you had more to tell me than what we'd already talked about. What else is going on?" Kylie looks concerned.

I look between my friends and sigh. "Well, you know that Andrew and I made out after the D.C. trip."

"WHAT?!" Jaclyn's mouth drops open, and I realize that in the chaos of the past few weeks, I haven't talked to Jaclyn about the biggest news of my summer.

Jaclyn recovers from her shock and says, "Good for you! I've always thought you two would be a cute couple."

Jaclyn is beaming at me, and I feel a surge of happiness that is almost immediately doused with regret.

"We might not be a couple. There's more." I fill Jaclyn in on everything that's happened since the ReGENerate Conference—the kisses in the car, Andrew staying the night the first time, my worries over dating another colleague. "Anyway, the night before the meeting, Andrew came over after my panic attack and made me the best boxed mac and cheese I've ever had."

Jaclyn snorts, and Kylie and I raise our eyebrows at her. Jaclyn shrugs. "Sorry, I thought that was a euphemism."

I hang my head. "Oh my god. No. Or well, rather, yes, that did happen. After the mac and cheese."

Kylie's eyes go wide. "You slept with him?"

I grimace. "Y-yeah."

"Oh."

I look at Jaclyn, who's giving me a thumbs up, then back at Kylie, who isn't exactly frowning but still making a face that doesn't seem entirely pleased with the news. This is not going as smoothly as I had hoped.

"Anyway, after John screamed at me—at us, really—during the meeting, Andrew told me he had told Dobson about the incident in front of the dining hall, which I wasn't super happy about. I asked him not to report what happened during the meeting, but when I got to Dobson's office, Andrew was coming out. I think he reported it even though I asked him not to."

By now, tears have started to pool in my eyes. I wipe a hand at them. "I should have listened to you, Kylie. You warned me that he was a heartbreaker, and I didn't listen. I just didn't think he'd break my heart by betraying my trust."

"Oh, Evie." Kylie puts her arm around me. "Have you talked to him about whether he reported it?"

"No. I don't know what to do."

"I think the first thing you need to do is talk to him," Jaclyn says. "Find out whether or not he actually made the report. There were other people at that meeting who could have gone to Dobson."

Kylie nods as Jaclyn speaks. Then she adds, "I agree with Jaclyn. You're borrowing sorrow by worrying about whether it was Andrew."

"Right, and the second thing you need to do is have hot make-up sex after you find out that it wasn't him." Jaclyn's eyes gleam with humor.

Kylie shoots Jaclyn a look, but Jaclyn says, "What? Reporting things after she asked him not to doesn't sound like the Andrew I know. He's sometimes flaky and never shows up when you expect him to, but he doesn't go back on his word on stuff like this."

I turn to Jaclyn. "Are you talking about when he ghosted you for a month and you stopped hanging out?"

Jaclyn makes a face. "What do you mean?"

"Kylie told me about how he ghosted you and then started hanging out with Veronica from Medieval Studies and that you were really hurt by him."

Jaclyn looks at Kylie. "That's not what happened at all."

"You seemed really hurt at the time. Maybe I misinterpreted things?" Kylie asks.

Jaclyn looks back at me. "Here's what happened. He and I had been hanging out a lot, but I knew he was having some family issues. He never talked to me about it, but you all know how good I am at reading people, especially people who leave their phones unlocked on the table." Jaclyn grins.

"Remind me never to leave my phone on the table when Jaclyn's around," Kylie says.

"It was only minor spying. I could tell something was up, and I was worried about him." She pauses to take a sip of her drink. "Anyway, around a year and half ago, I happened to sit with Veronica one day in the dining hall, and she asked me if Andrew and I were dating. I was really confused by that because I've never seen Andrew as anything but a friend, even though he is a straight hottie. I told her no, obviously, and she confessed she was interested in him. So I told her to go for it. It was before you and I had started hanging out regularly, so I didn't think your thing for him was serious, or I wouldn't have encouraged her."

Jaclyn winces at me, but I can't fault her for encouraging Veronica. At the time, my interest in Andrew was purely based on appreciation of his remarkable good looks.

"So he didn't ghost you and dump you for a new friend?" I ask.

"Well, he did ghost me, but I wasn't hurt about it. Like I said, I knew there was something going on with his family, and I figured he was just absorbed in whatever it was."

I'm stunned. Everything Jaclyn has said lines up with how Andrew described the situation.

"And you weren't hurt by his new friendship with Veronica?"

"Not in the slightest. Besides, I had just met Rhys, and I

can really only handle having one hot, platonic friend at a time." Jaclyn smirks.

"I do not understand you." Kylie shakes her head.

Jaclyn shrugs. "I don't know why you thought I was bent out of shape about it. You and I never talked about it."

"I thought you didn't want to talk about it because you were sad. I know you don't like talking about your feelings," Kylie says.

"Oh, well, now you know." Jaclyn shrugs again. She turns to me. "I hope knowing what really happened between Andrew and me helps."

I nod resignedly. "I guess I should talk to him. I hope you're right about him, Jaclyn."

"I still think you should be careful," Kylie says. "I don't want you to get your heart broken, especially now that you and he have taken things to a more intimate level."

"Of course. I know that." I give her a half smile.

After that, the conversation veers toward other things until Jaclyn's phone starts buzzing on the table like it's possessed. Jaclyn glances at the screen and grimaces.

"Everything ok?" I ask.

"It's just my mom." Jaclyn scrunches her nose.

"Is she still trying to set you up with that banker guy?" Kylie asks.

"Yes," Jaclyn sighs. "She's convinced he's the one."

Jaclyn and her mom have been trapped in a battle of wits over her dating life for as long as I've known her. Mrs. Beckett has made no secret of the fact that she wants grandchildren. But even if Jaclyn were in a serious relationship, I don't think Mrs. Beckett would get her wish.

As I make my way home later in the evening, I think about the conversation from tonight. I'm relieved to know that Andrew didn't hurt Jaclyn's feelings when he started hanging out with Veronica. But I still have a sense of trepidation when it comes to talking to him about what happened with John. I hope he didn't report the incident, but thinking about confronting him makes my stomach turn.

I know what I have to do, though, and as I walk into my house, I pull out my phone and text Andrew.

ME: Can we talk?

ANDREW: Yes. Now?

ME: No. Meet me at the coffee shop tomorrow morning. 9:00

ANDREW: I'll be there.

CHAPTER 22

I'm trying—and failing—to keep my knee still below the table. Andrew is supposed to arrive any minute now, and I'm nervous about how this conversation is going to go. I hope I haven't made a mistake by asking him to meet me here, at the same coffee shop where we had breakfast the morning after he spent the night on my couch. I don't want to taint that memory, although I suppose it doesn't matter. If Andrew reported the incident with John, the memory will be tainted anyway.

The bell above the door rings as someone enters the coffee shop. I look up to see Andrew walking toward me. The moment we make eye contact, I shift in my seat and bang my knee on the table leg. So much for playing this cool.

"Hi," I say awkwardly, rubbing my knee to take the sting out.

"Hi," Andrew replies with equal wariness.

"Do you want to sit?" I gesture to the seat across from me.

"This is about the meetings we had with Dobson yesterday." It's not a question, but I nod anyway.

I want to ask him directly if he reported John's blow up, but my throat is tight, and I can't seem to muster the words. Instead, neither of us speaks, and I absentmindedly stir my coffee with a spoon.

Andrew lets out a deep sigh and closes his eyes. When he opens them, I have the sinking feeling that he's about to tell me he made the report. That thought starts to grind its way through my mind. I know I need to approach this conversation with an open heart, though.

I take a deep breath and brace my hands on the table. I look Andrew in the eye and in a rush say, "I need to know if you reported John the second time." My voice is shaky, but I hold his gaze.

He doesn't appear surprised by what I've said, but he does hesitate for a moment. It feels like a lifetime before he finally shakes his head and says, "No. You asked me not to, so I didn't. Even though I wanted to. That man deserves to be fired for the way he treats you."

A wave of relief washes over me. He didn't report it. He listened to me.

My shoulders relax as the tension of the past several days finally dissipates. A tear rolls down my cheek, but I'm smiling at Andrew. He lifts his hand and wipes the tear away with his thumb.

"Sorry, I don't know why I'm crying." I sniff as another tear falls.

Andrew gives me a warm, comforting smile. "It's ok to cry. I'm sure the past few days have been hard. And I need to apologize to you. I should have called you after I saw you in Dobson's office, but I didn't think you wanted to hear from me after the way we left things."

I let out a long breath. He's right. I didn't want to talk to him. But at the same time, I *did* want to talk to him. It's confusing and frustrating that he has been both a source of stress over the past few days and the person I most wanted to talk to about everything that's happened.

"Yeah, I didn't really want to have this conversation," I finally say. "I was convinced that you had reported things, and I didn't want to face the consequences if that had been true."

Andrew reaches across the table and takes my hand. "I promise if you ask me not to do something, I won't do it."

I search his blue-gray eyes, looking for any indication that he's just telling me what I want to hear, but there's nothing but seriousness there. I nod at him and give him a tiny smile.

"How about I get a coffee to go, and we blow off work and go do something?"

My smile broadens. "I'd like that. I already called in a personal day." I wince. "I was sort of anticipating that this would be an upsetting conversation, and I'd need Ben and

Jerry to keep me company for the rest of the day."

Andrew nods his head. "I hope you don't need them now. You're not upset, right?"

I smile again. "No, the opposite."

We get Andrew's to-go coffee and leave the coffee shop. I heave a sigh of relief as we walk through the door. Things have gone much better than I anticipated, with no memories tarnished.

Outside the coffee shop, Andrew takes my hand. I turn to face him, and he tentatively steps closer to me. I look up to see his eyes are stormy with questions. I wrap my arms around him, and he lets out a breath as he folds me into his arms. I give myself over to the hug. His hugs are becoming like home for me. A place I always want to come back to.

I could stay wrapped in Andrew's arms like this forever.

When we finally step apart, Andrew finds my hand and intertwines our fingers. It feels right to be holding hands and enjoying the mid-July sunshine. My heart warms as we walk to his car.

We decide to spend the morning wandering through Under the Covers, the bookstore that hosted the LeVar Burton event. We agree to each find a book we think the other should read and then meet in one of the little reading nooks in the store. I know exactly what to pick for Andrew. I find a beautiful copy almost immediately and go look for him. He's already waiting for me at the reading nook with a stack of books.

"I thought you'd like this series," he says.

I look at the back of the first one. It's a series about a

band of space pirates.

"They're secretly romance novels disguised as sci-fi," Andrew says with a wink.

My heart warms at his thoughtful choice. I hand him the book I found for him.

"Pride and Prejudice?"

"I thought you'd want to read the book that made me fall in love with romance, especially since you haven't read it before." I blush a little. Maybe I made the wrong choice.

"I absolutely want to read it." His hand wraps around mine, and he pulls me close. We kiss, a little scandalously, but stop ourselves before things go too far. The bookstore is definitely not the place to enact that bookshelf fantasy of his.

Our books purchased, we leave the store and spend the rest of the day enjoying the sunshine and each other's company. As we drive back to my house late in the afternoon, I take my phone out of my purse. It's been on airplane mode since we got to the bookstore. I didn't want the distraction while we were together. But there's a phone call I've been waiting for that I don't want to miss.

As soon as I tap the button to switch off airplane mode, a notification pings. I have a missed call from a Washington, D.C. phone number. Excitement rises in my chest.

"I got a voicemail while we were at the bookstore."

"Yeah? Who's it from?"

I hedge, suddenly less excited than I had been a moment ago.

"Oh, um, I'm not sure."

Andrew glances at me and smiles, then turns back to keep his eyes on the road.

"Are you going to listen to it?"

I start to open the voicemail, but I look at Andrew. The day started off tense and stressful, but it's ended up being a fantastic day. I don't want to listen to the voicemail in the car in case it's bad news. I'm not totally sure what bad news means in this case, though—an offer or no offer.

"I'm sure it will keep until later."

———

Jaclyn was right. Having hot make-up sex was a very good idea. When we arrived at my house, I invited him in for an early dinner. We didn't make it to the kitchen, though. As soon as the door closed behind Andrew, we moved toward each other like magnets. Now, we lie tangled together, late afternoon sunlight filtering through the windows.

I still haven't listened to the voicemail that is almost certainly from someone at McDowell. Andrew is snoozing, so I gently unwind myself from the sheets and his arms. I put on my bathrobe and dig my phone out of the pocket of my shorts, which are lying on the floor. I quietly close the bedroom door, tiptoeing down the hall toward the living room. Once I'm sure I'm out of earshot, I pull up the voicemail and hit play.

"Hi, Evie. It's Katherine Miller at McDowell University. I'm calling in regards to your application for the Research Services Team Lead position. If you could give me a call back as soon as possible, I would appreciate it. I'll be in the office until 5:00 tonight."

I check the time. It's only 4:45, so I should be able to catch Katherine. I glance at what I'm wearing, though. It would be weird to call about a job opportunity while I'm wearing nothing but my bathrobe. I go to the laundry room and find some clean clothes. By the time I'm dressed, it's 4:50. Not much time to call, but I cross my fingers that Katherine will pick up.

She answers on the second ring. "McDowell University Library. Katherine speaking."

"Hi, it's Evie."

"Evie! Hello! How are you?"

"I'm doing well. I got your message." A sudden wave of nerves makes my stomach drop.

"Wonderful! I was hoping to hear back from you today so that I could officially offer you the position. What do you say? Will you come work for McDowell?"

I'm caught off guard by the direct question. I don't know what the pay will be or any information about the benefits and paid time off yet. I clear my throat and say, in the most professional sounding voice I can muster, "I'd like to think about it? If that's alright?"

Oh great. It came out as a question. I literally facepalm.

Katherine must be thrown by my hesitance, because she sounds mildly flustered as she says, "Oh, of course."

"It's just that I'd like to know what the pay will be and a few other things about the position before I make a final decision."

"Yes, yes, of course." Katherine seems to have recovered. "Someone in HR will send you an email with that information first thing Monday."

"Ok, sounds good. I'll take a look at that and get back to you. When do you need to know my answer?"

Katherine seems to be clicking on something, probably bringing up a calendar on her computer. "Ideally, I'd like an answer on Monday."

I frown. "I'm not sure I can give you an answer that quickly. I'd like a little more time to look at the information from your HR person first. Could I have until Tuesday at least?"

Katherine sounds mildly disappointed as she says, "That will be fine. I look forward to hearing from you."

I end the call and turn around. I jump because Andrew is unexpectedly standing in the doorway leading from the hall into the living room in nothing but his underwear.

"Those aren't the clothes you were wearing before." He raises an eyebrow.

"I had to make a phone call, and I didn't think it was a good idea to do that naked." My face heats. I still can't quite believe that being naked with Andrew is a thing I get to do now.

"Is everything ok?"

I hesitate. I'm not sure I'm ready to tell Andrew about the offer from McDowell. That's part of why I asked to think about it, too. The fact that Andrew was sleeping in my bed while I heard the offer complicates my answer.

It's not just Andrew who complicates things, of course.

It's Jaclyn and Kylie and the possibility of the Teaching and Learning job that stopped me from immediately answering Katherine's question.

"Just a work thing. Nothing to worry about." It isn't a lie, exactly. But I can't tell Andrew yet. I need a little time to think about the offer and what I'd be leaving if I take it. Plus, I have my interview with Dobson on Monday afternoon.

CHAPTER 23

The first thing I do when I get to work on Monday is go to Mike Pearce's office. His door is open, so I rap my knuckles on the door frame.

"Do you have a few minutes?"

Mike looks up from where he's been typing.

"Yes. What can I do for you?"

He gestures to the chair on the opposite side of his desk as I enter his office. I've always liked coming to Mike's office. It has a cozy but cluttered vibe. There are floor to ceiling built-in bookshelves along one wall, and Mike has filled them with pictures of his husband and kids, some of his favorite books, and a collection of decorative coffee mugs, most of which have pictures or quotes with obscure pop culture references and dad jokes.

I have a lot of respect for Mike, and I hope he has some insights on what I should do about the offer from McDowell. Not about the complications the offer presents for my relationship with Andrew, of course. I'm not ready to waltz into work and announce that I've been sleeping with the history professor. No, I figure Mike might have some perspective on why I should stay at Cooke instead of moving six hours away and starting over.

"Is this about the Teaching and Learning position?" Mike looks hopeful.

"How did you guess?" I smile.

"Just a hunch," Mike says. "I was wondering when you'd tell me."

I start to apologize, but Mike shakes his head. "It's alright. I knew when they posted it that there was a chance we'd lose you. Besides, you don't have to tell me every time you try to stretch yourself professionally. I'm just glad that you're looking at something here at Cooke, because we'd be worse off without you."

Mike's words send a shot of happy warmth through me, like a little ray of sunshine found its way inside and burst. He's always been complimentary of my work, but this feels like more than a "Great job!" or "Keep it up!"

"Thank you. I'm not sure if I should take the job if they offer it to me, though."

"Why's that?"

"Dobson said they wouldn't hire another librarian to replace me. I wouldn't want to leave you all down another person."

"Evie, you don't need to worry about that. It's my job to make sure that we're adequately staffed, and I have a few tricks up my sleeve to get Dobson to see reason." He says it with such kindness that I almost don't want to tell him the other reason I wanted to talk to him this morning.

"There's something else." I inhale deeply before continuing. "The reason I went to D.C. early was because I had an interview at McDowell University."

Mike frowns. "Oh, I see."

"I applied a few months ago because it looked interesting, not because I was particularly looking for a new job."

Mike looks relieved.

"But the interview went very well, and I received an offer from them on Friday."

Mike frowns again. "So, you want to know why you should stay here instead of leaving?"

"Basically, yes."

Mike considers for a moment. "Well, without knowing anything about McDowell and what their position is like, I can't necessarily speak to that. But what I can say is this: you are a great employee, and a fantastic librarian. I want to do what I can to keep you, but I know that sometimes the right thing for a manager to do is let the good ones go. I think the question you need to answer for yourself is which position is going to give you the best room to keep growing."

That's not what I expected to hear. I thought he would throw out a list of reasons Cooke was a great place to work that sounded like it belonged on the employment opportunities page of the website. But instead, he's not only given me a huge compliment, he's also acknowledged that I need space to grow professionally. I should have known, of course. Mike really is a fabulous boss and is incredibly perceptive about these kinds of things.

We talk for a while longer, and Mike listens as I tell him about the kinds of things I want to do if I stay at Cooke—things like implementing the faculty peer-mentor program I proposed to the General Education Committee and ideas I have about better integration of library instruction within academic programs.

Mike suggests reaching out to Dobson once I've seen the particulars of the McDowell offer. He says Dobson might be willing to negotiate a bit if he knows that I have another opportunity.

I leave his office without a decision, but with the feeling that the pieces for making one are falling into place. As I open my email back in my office that another piece of the puzzle pops up on my computer screen.

There is a message from the McDowell HR department in my inbox. With trembling fingers, I open it and look through the information.

The pay is quite a bit higher than what I'm making at Cooke. Even with the cost of living in D.C., my take-home pay would be higher than it is on my current salary. The benefits are almost identical to what I have at Cooke. They have the same number of holidays and vacation days that we do at Cooke, and the health insurance looks like it's even the same plan I'm currently on.

I'm weighing the advantages and disadvantages of each job when another email pings my inbox. It's from Katherine with the subject line "Job Offer." There's an attached spreadsheet called "Position Analysis." Without looking at the text of the email, I open the spreadsheet thinking it must be something Katherine wanted to share with me to help in my decision-making.

At first, I'm not sure what I'm looking at. My name is at the top of the page, and there is a column with different statements next to some rows of numbers. As I look at the statements in the first column, the phrasing seems familiar, but I can't put my finger on why. The numbers in the rows range from one to five, with most of the columns having fours or fives for each statement and a few with ones or twos.

I notice a button at the bottom of the screen to open another sheet. The one I've been looking at is labeled "Watson." The second sheet is labeled "Felix." I click on it and gasp.

The second sheet is almost identical to the first one, but at the top of the page, instead of my name it says "Penelope Felix." The columns of numbers are similar to what was on the first page, but with slightly fewer fives than on the other page. I rush to close the spreadsheet.

The reason those statements in the first column seemed familiar is that they are qualifications from the job ad for the position at McDowell. This isn't an analysis of the position to help me understand the role. This is an analysis of the candidates who interviewed in person, and it is completely inappropriate for me to be looking at it.

I reopen the email and mutter, "Oh shit," as I look at the "To" line and read the body of the email. It clearly was not meant for me.

From: katherine.miller@mcdowell.edu
To: jacob.reed@mcdowell.edu;
lisa.jenkins@mcdowell.edu; devin.phillips@mcdowell.edu;
hilary.crews@mcdowell.edu;
jennifer.morris@mcdowell.edu; emwatson@cooke.edu;
p.e.felix@ku.edu
Subject: Job Offer
Hi all,
Please see the attached spreadsheet with the feedback on the candidates from last week's interviews. Let me know if you have any questions. I will call Evie this afternoon to make the offer based on our conversation this morning.
Best,
Katherine

I don't know what to think. Something has obviously gone very wrong if I'm receiving this email. It reminds me of what happened with receiving the wrong link for my video call. Is this a sign that a job at McDowell will be an exercise in frustration?

On paper, the McDowell position and the Cooke promotion are so similar that I can see myself in either role. The people I met at McDowell during my interview all seemed like they would be good to work with, but learning a new work culture and a new type of position at the same time could present its challenges. Even though I like a challenge, I'm not sure this is the type of challenge I want to take on. Plus I already have a great network of friends at Cooke.

It isn't just the problem of getting to know new people, though. The hotel room issue and the karaoke at my interview dinner are red flags. I understand that now, even though at the time I thought Andrew was overreacting to the whole thing. Thinking back on his reaction to my panic attack at the hotel and the bizarre interview dinner, I realize that he was conflicted because of his feelings for me and his desire for me to succeed in my career.

Now there's this email with not only my ranking by the committee, but also the other candidate's ranking. I'm pretty sure the other candidate was copied on the email, too. One of the email addresses was from a different university, and the last name was the same. A wave of nausea crashes over me. I feel awful for Penelope, who is probably finding out in a most unfortunate way that she wasn't the committee's top choice.

I know I need to do something about this email, but I'm not sure what. I consider calling Kylie. But as I'm about to pick up my phone and press the call button, I stop myself. I have two universities who want me to work in a leadership role. I can figure this out without Kylie.

I reply only to Katherine and let her know that I've seen the email.

From: emwatson@cooke.edu
To: katherine.miller@mcdowell.edu
Subject: RE: Job Offer
Hi Katherine,
I thought you should know that I was somehow copied on
this email. I opened the spreadsheet before I realized
what was going on.
Thank you,
Evie

I hit send and sit back in my chair to wait. I know I should get to work on other things, but I'm antsy waiting for Katherine's response. Fortunately I don't have to wait long. Another email notification pings on my computer. With my heart thumping, I open the reply from Katherine.

From: katherine.miller@mcdowell.edu
To: emwatson@cooke.edu
Subject: RE: Job Offer
Evie,
I am so sorry. This was not meant to come to you. I'm not
sure what happened since I sent this email to the
committee on Friday. I hope it will not influence your
decision. I still want to hear from you by Tuesday.
Best,
Katherine

I'm weirdly dissatisfied with Katherine's response. Sure, Katherine apologized. But the tone of the email is abrupt and a little off-putting.

I'm still trying to figure out what, exactly, has put me off when the calendar notification for my interview with Dr. Dobson chimes. I set aside the off-kilter feeling about McDowell and make my way to Dobson's office.

When I arrive at his office suite, Dobson is standing by Amber's desk, apparently already waiting for me.

"Evie! Glad you're here! I'm looking forward to our conversation."

He ushers me into his office, and we take our seats. I can't help but think of our conversation the last time I was here, and he must be thinking about it, too, because he says, "First of all, the business with John. We've had all our meetings, and you don't need to worry about any further issues with him. I can't really say more than that."

"Ok, thanks for letting me know." I wonder if that means John has been disciplined in some way, but I don't press the matter. I know administrators can't go around telling people about personnel issues.

"Now, about the Teaching and Learning position. What about the job made you want to apply?"

"I love the collaborative work that it would involve," I say without hesitation. "When I read the ad, it ticked all the boxes for the kind of work I want to do."

He doesn't ask anything else, so I keep going, explaining the same things I told Mike Pearce earlier. As I talk, he nods, but doesn't look at me. Instead, he just shuffles some papers on his desk like he's looking for something. I have no idea what to make of his apparent distraction, but then he finds whatever it was and looks back at me.

"I talked to Mike Pearce, and I want to talk about how we can keep you here at Cooke. I know this is technically your formal interview for the position, but I'm hoping our conversation this afternoon can be more of a brainstorming session."

"I'm sorry. You what?"

I see now that what he has in front of him is a file folder with my resume and cover letter. From where I'm sitting, I can tell that he's underlined parts of the cover letter and written notes in the margins. I don't want to snoop, but the word "excellent" is written in big letters next to one of the underlined sections.

"I think you're the right person for the job based on the things I've seen from you this summer with the General Education work and the way you've managed the library flood. Your application was the strongest we received, and I'm ready to move forward. I think we've been under-utilizing your talents in your current role."

My mouth drops open, but I recover enough to ask, "But don't you have other candidates to interview?"

I know it's probably not the best idea to question Dobson's surprise job offer, but it wouldn't sit right with me if I thought I got the job without actually being the best candidate.

"Already done, and while they were decent candidates, none of them had your background and skills."

I have no idea how to respond, and I sit in silence until Dobson clears his throat.

"Now, I understand you've got an offer from another university. McDowell, is it? What did they offer you?"

I tell him the pay rate McDowell offered me. Dobson is quiet for a moment—a rare occasion with him.

"I don't think I can match that, but let me run some numbers. Let's get a meeting on the calendar—you, me, and Mike Pearce—to talk details of how we could transition you over to the Teaching and Learning job. Then we'll give you a couple days to think it over."

"Ok, sounds good. Thank you, Dr. Dobson."

"Thank you. Talk soon!"

"Actually, Dr. Dobson." An idea is taking shape as I'm processing this conversation, and I don't want to miss my opportunity to negotiate.

"Yes?"

"What would you say to changing the position a little?"

———

As I return to my office twenty minutes later, I bask in the feeling of accomplishment. Dobson was surprisingly receptive to my request, and if he can make the budget work then I'll essentially have created my own dream job. One that sounds like it will have a good mix of challenge and stability. Even if they can't match the salary from McDowell, this is an excellent opportunity for my career.

I lean back in my chair. Things are looking promising on the job front. I have options, and it feels good to have options.

I pull up the last email from Katherine again and write her back.

From: emwatson@cooke.edu
To: katherine.miller@mcdowell.edu
Subject: RE: Job Offer
Hi Katherine,
I haven't decided yet, but I'm going to need a few more days. My current employer is making a counter offer.
Thank you,
Evie

Katherine's response comes almost immediately.

From: katherine.miller@mcdowell.edu
To: emwatson@cooke.edu
Subject: RE: Job Offer
Thanks for letting me know. You have until Friday.

I'm irritated at Katherine's tone in her last email, and it gives me pause about having her as my supervisor. But Friday is good. Friday gives me time to figure out which job would give me the room to grow like Mike Pearce said. And it means I have time to figure out where I want to take things with Andrew.

CHAPTER 24

I meet Andrew for dinner at the Indian restaurant. I still haven't told him about the offer from McDowell, but I'm glad because it means I can tell him about the counter offer from Dobson at the same time. Like a good-news-bad-news sandwich.

The restaurant isn't too far from campus, so even though I'd normally drive, I decide to walk because the evening is so pleasant. It's late July, and the days have been hot, but there was a little thunderstorm this afternoon that cooled everything down.

As I enter the restaurant, the smell of delicious spices floods my senses, and I'm immediately transported back to that first time we had lunch here at the beginning of the summer. I'm smiling to myself as I find Andrew, who's already sitting at a table with a plate of samosas. He stands up to hug me in greeting, then we sit across from each other.

"How was your day?" he asks, and I'm suddenly nervous.

I should have told him about the McDowell offer the moment I got it, but I was so worried it would lead to another fight, and we had just made up.

I don't have to answer him immediately, though, because Priya comes over to take my drink order and chat with us, buying me another minute. I smooth my napkin in my lap as she leaves, then smile anxiously at Andrew. My foot bounces below the table.

"Is everything ok?" Andrew asks, looking a little worried.

"Everything's fine," I lie, knowing my smile is probably more like a cringe because he looks skeptical.

Priya comes back with my drink, and I think she's going to take our food orders since they only have the buffet at lunch, but Andrew says, "I went ahead and ordered our usual."

"Oh, that's good," I say. We've been here several times since our first visit, and Andrew knows exactly what I like.

I pick up my drink to take a sip, but my hand is shaky with nerves, so I spill a little.

"Are you sure you're ok?" Andrew asks.

"Yep. Totally fine." I try to sound nonchalant, but I'm pretty sure I don't.

"Ok...It's just you've been acting kind of weird since

Friday."

Well, shit.

I thought I'd been mostly normal over the weekend—I certainly hope he didn't notice anything off with the way I acted in bed—but the stress of keeping the news of the job offer from him must have been more obvious than I realized.

He'll be glad to hear about the offer from McDowell and the counter offer from Cooke, but I realize now what a huge mistake I've made in not telling him. Time to rip off the proverbial bandage.

"I got an offer from McDowell on Friday," I say in a rush.

I can tell he's trying to look more excited than he feels because he takes a little too long to say, "That's great."

"I asked them to give me a few days to think about it, of course."

Andrew's phone starts buzzing in his pocket. He takes it out, glances at it, and ignores the call. He sets the phone on the table and looks back at me.

"It's significantly better pay than what I'm making now." I'm trying to sound excited, but the look on Andrew's face makes the end of my sentence feel like a question.

His phone buzzes again, and again he ignores the call.

"More pay is nice." His tone is a little flat.

"There's more. I have a meeting with the Mikes to talk about job transitions..." I trail off as Andrew's phone buzzes a third time.

He frowns and picks up the phone. "Sorry, I think maybe I'd better take this. My mom doesn't usually call three times in a row like this."

"No, that's fine. Go ahead and answer."

"So sorry. I want to hear more about the job offer. This should just take a second."

He answers the phone and steps away from the table toward the lobby of the restaurant. I try not to eavesdrop on his conversation, but it's hard not to notice the transformation on his face. He starts out looking mildly concerned, but as the call continues, his frown deepens. I hear him say, "I'll be there as soon as I can," as he hangs up and walks back toward our table.

"What's wrong?" I ask.

"I...have to go."

"Why? What's going on?"

"Gran's in the hospital. They...they think she had a stroke." His face has gone pale, and I'm worried because I've never seen him like this before. He looks like he's going to be sick, but he just stands in front of me even though he said he needs to leave.

I stand up and touch his arm.

"Are you ok to drive?"

He looks at me as though he doesn't recognize me, and I almost gasp at the wild look in his eyes.

"Give me your keys. I'm driving you." I hold out my hand.

Andrew barely nods as he reaches into his pocket and gives them to me. I motion to Priya to come back to our table.

"Could we package these up? We got a call that we need

to get to the hospital for a family emergency."

Priya nods. "I'll get a bag for you."

When she comes back, she's carrying not just a box for the samosas, but also our meals already packaged. I try to pay for the food, but Priya says, "This one's on the house. Tell Ruth to let me know how I can help."

I thank her, and Andrew and I rush to his car.

The drive to the hospital is silent. I try to strike the balance between getting there quickly and obeying traffic laws because I can tell that Andrew is anxious to be there. Despite my best efforts, it seems like the drive takes forever, but we finally pull into the hospital parking lot. I drop Andrew off at the door then find a parking space.

After I park, I'm not sure what to do. I'm not part of Andrew's family, and I've never met his mom and aunts before. It would be weird for me to be with them, right?

Thankfully, I don't have to deliberate over what to do for long because Andrew texts me.

ANDREW: Gran is in a room in the E.R. We're in Family Waiting Room 2 on the second floor.

He doesn't say if I should join them, but I figure if he's sending me the room number, it means he wants me there. Besides, I need to return his car keys. I can always text Kylie or Jaclyn to come get me if things get too awkward.

I walk in the front door and ask at the visitor desk for directions, then navigate my way through the busy hospital. Soon enough, I'm outside the door of Family Waiting Room 2. I stand still for a moment, wary of interrupting what I imagine is a very painful, personal experience for Andrew's family. I'm still debating whether to knock on the door frame or just walk right in when a voice beside me says, "You must be Evie."

I jump a little. I didn't hear the woman approach as I stood here deliberating. She's about my height and has the same blue-gray eyes as Andrew. Her hair is a little gray, but I can tell it was once the color of Andrew's. She's holding a tray of coffees from the chain coffee shop that has a kiosk in the hospital. She smiles at me, although I can see worry in her eyes—worry that things for Andrew's Gran, her mother, aren't looking good.

"Yes, I'm Evie," I say, starting to extend my hand to shake and then realizing a moment too late that the woman has both hands on the coffee tray. I try to cover myself at the last second. "Here, let me carry those for you."

"Oh, you're too kind. I knew you would be, of course. Andy's told me all about you."

"You must be Andrew's mother."

"I am. Ruth Brandt." Ruth hands me the tray of coffee, which I awkwardly balance in one hand along with the bag of Indian food so that I can shake her hand. "It's so lovely to meet the woman who's made my son stop worrying about things so much. He's been trying to be the adult in our lives since his dad died and I had all those anxiety issues while he was in high school."

I flush at the compliment.

"Now come on in. The rest of the Brandt Biddies have been dying to meet you."

I follow Ruth into the waiting room. I'm not sure what I

was expecting, but it certainly wasn't the scene before me. Andrew is sitting between two older women who are arguing over top of him about whether it's ethical to watch the security camera channel on the hospital TV. The slightly younger-looking one is saying something about people's privacy, and the older one shouts back, "They wouldn't put the channel on there if they didn't want us to watch it!"

Andrew looks up as Ruth and I enter, and he mutters, "Oh thank god" as he stands up to take the coffee from me.

Ruth claps her hands loudly to get the attention of her two arguing sisters. "Ladies, we have a guest. Let's try to make her feel welcome."

The women abruptly stop shouting and both turn and smile sweetly at me. "Oh, you must be Evie! We're so glad Andy has finally brought you to meet us!" The older sister hops up from her chair and comes over and wraps me in a hug. "I'm Phoebe, and this is Tabitha."

The younger sister waves, then nudges Phoebe out of the way so she can hug me, too. "Evie, what do you think about whether we should watch the security channel?"

"Oh, I don't..." I look at Andrew who is shaking his head and waving his hands in a "Don't answer that" gesture. I try to hide my smirk at the look on his face.

"Tabitha, leave her out of this. Let's just leave the TV off for now. I'm sure mom is almost out of her scan by now, and the doctor will probably come in soon with an update," Ruth says, giving me a kind smile. "Besides, your coffee is getting cold." She hands her sisters each a cup from the coffee tray.

"I'm sorry we're meeting under such unfortunate circumstances," I say to Andrew's mom and aunts.

Ruth sighs and says, "I am, too, but I really am glad to meet you," then she gives Andrew a stern look. "It's certainly taken Andy long enough to introduce us."

I stifle a laugh and catch Andrew's eye. "Andy?" I mouth at him. He grimaces.

He looks a bit disheveled. Not surprising given his reaction to the call at the restaurant. Although now that I'm watching him interact with his mom and her sisters, I wonder if half his reaction was because of having to manage the chaos that seems to be part of these women's routine.

Phoebe is muttering something about wanting to watch the security channel, and I swear I see Tabitha stick her tongue out at her older sister. It's a little jarring, seeing a pair of grown women bickering like teenagers. But then Tabitha reaches an arm around Phoebe and gives her a side hug. I watch as Phoebe's shoulders droop, and the sisters lean in to each other.

I glance away, not wanting to intrude on a private moment of grief. I imagine the stress of sitting in a hospital waiting room while your mom undergoes a scan to determine if she's had a stroke would drive even the most even-keeled person to bicker with a sibling.

Andrew has been talking to Ruth while I've been observing Phoebe and Tabitha, but now he comes over to me and motions to a corner away from the other women. I follow, and lean in to hear him whisper, "You don't have to stay. I know Phoebe and Tabitha are a bit much, and I don't want you to feel obligated to be here."

"It's ok," I whisper back. "I can stay if you want me to. I don't mind doing coffee runs or getting food for you all."

"You really don't have to do that."

"I know I don't have to, but I want to. I know the circumstances aren't great, but I'd like to get to know your mom and aunts." I realize as I'm saying it that I mean it.

I want to know more about the women who raised Andrew and shaped who he is. I've never wanted to get to know any of my boyfriends' families like this before. I try not to think about what that might mean for how I'm really feeling about Andrew.

Andrew's eyebrows furrow. "I don't know...What I mean is, I'm not sure it's a good idea."

I tilt my head to the side. "What do you mean it's not a good idea?"

"I'm sorry. It's not..." Andrew sighs deeply. "The doctor will be here soon, and then we're probably going to have to make some decisions about how to proceed with Gran's care. I don't want you to have to sit around and wait for me all night. It will be boring."

"It's really ok. I don't mind..."

"No." Andrew cuts me off. He looks almost angry, although not in the same way he was during the committee meeting when John verbally abused me. There's hurt in his eyes. "I just think it would be better if you left."

"Ok? I'll go then. I just need to call Kylie to come get me." I step into the hallway to make the call then go back into the waiting room to say goodbye to Andrew's family.

"Oh, but you just got here!" Tabitha says.

"I'm sure Evie has better things to do than sit around with us in a hospital, Tab," Phoebe chimes in.

"I don't want to intrude on you all while you're dealing with everything. But hopefully soon Andrew and I can have dinner with you all." I'm trying to remain bright and optimistic, but the way Andrew told me to leave is bothering me. It's not like him to cut me off like he did.

He doesn't kiss me goodbye, which I figure is because we're standing in front of his family. But he doesn't hug me, either, which is unusual. In fact, he barely looks at me as I say goodbye to him and ask him to update me on his Gran's situation. As I make my way back to the hospital entrance, I have the distinct feeling that I've said or done something wrong.

I don't say anything about Andrew's strange behavior when Kylie picks me up. I don't want to add fuel to her warnings about Andrew breaking my heart. I went into this evening thinking Andrew would be excited for me, but now I'm doubting the solidity of our relationship. Thankfully, Kylie doesn't pepper me with questions as we drive back to campus to get my car.

Before I go to bed, I check my phone one last time to see if Andrew has sent any updates about his Gran. There aren't any.

I send him a text to let him know I'm thinking about him and ask him to tell me when he has any news. But as I get into bed, I can't help feeling that something has changed between us.

CHAPTER 25

On Tuesday morning, I check my phone, but Andrew hasn't sent an update. I figure he's busy with whatever care decisions he and his family are making, so I don't think anything of it. I don't even send a follow up message because I don't want to add to the noise of dealing with a major health crisis.

I don't hear anything from him on Wednesday, either, and I chalk it up to the fact that he is probably home resting or still running errands for his mom.

By Thursday afternoon, I'm worried. I finally text him, and right after I send the message, the three dots indicating that he's typing pop up, but they disappear and reappear three times before the screen goes quiet.

When there's still no message from him by Friday

morning, I feel sick to my stomach. I know he's not always the fastest responder when it comes to text messages, but it's been three days. He hasn't been in the library all week, either, so it's not like I can just talk to him in person.

Something is definitely wrong.

I think back over the days leading up to the ride to the hospital, but I can't think of anything that I did that would upset Andrew so much that he'd ghost me, especially because he knows communication is important to me. Was Kylie right about his heartbreaker reputation after all? Has he just gotten tired of me and moved on? The thought makes my heart race, and I feel the familiar swoop of adrenaline that comes with the start of a panic attack.

I focus on my breathing and regain control of my senses. I look around my office and silently name five things I can see—whiteboard, laptop, computer mouse, coffee cup, notepad.

Then I think about the things I can feel—the fabric of my cardigan, the floor beneath my feet, the arms of my chair, the hair that's fallen into my face, the breeze from the air conditioner.

By now, my breathing is almost back to normal, but I inhale deeply anyway, and identify things I can smell—the orange peel in my trash can from breakfast, the faint scent of coffee from my mid-morning cup, the particular smell of the library that I can never quite quantify.

My panic subsides, but the ache of not knowing what's going on with Andrew is still there. I need to talk to someone and figure out what's gone wrong, so I call in reinforcements.

ME: I haven't heard from Andrew since his Gran went to the hospital on Monday. He was acting weird when I left, and now I'm worried I've done something to upset him. I need your help.

KYLIE: You've got it.

JACLYN: Lunch in 20 minutes?

ME: Yes, that's perfect.

KYLIE: We'll be there.

True to their word, Kylie and Jaclyn are already waiting for me when I get to the restaurant. Kylie jumps up to hug me, and Jaclyn raises her glass—as good as a hug from my friend who hates showing emotions.

I settle into the booth with them and tell them everything—the job offer, the interview with Dobson, the Indian restaurant, and Andrew's weird behavior at the hospital. I even fill them in on my conversation with Andrew after we slept together, when I made him promise to communicate with me.

"I keep going back over everything that happened that night at the hospital, and I can't figure it out. What did I do that made him cut me off like this?" I slump a little in the booth.

"Did you ever actually tell him about your conversation with Dobson?" Jaclyn asks.

"Of course I..." I trail off. I play back our conversation at the restaurant. I told him about the McDowell offer and started to tell him about the job at Cooke, but then his phone rang and rang. "Oh my god. He thinks I made the decision without him."

I sag and lay my head on the table in exasperation.

"I've totally screwed this up, haven't I?"

"I don't think it's so screwed up that it can't be fixed," Kylie says in a gentle voice.

"Yeah, just call him and tell him you're taking the promotion at Cooke, and he'll be fine."

I lift my head and stare at my friends.

"What? No. Maybe? I haven't decided yet."

"You have totally decided, you just don't know it. You'd be a fool to pass up the opportunity the Mikes are giving you. You realize they're basically giving you the chance to do whatever the hell you want, right? Plus a raise. If I were you, I'd find that man and declare your intentions as soon as possible."

Jaclyn's words make the hairs on my arm stand up.

"What do you mean 'declare my intentions'?"

She shrugs. "You know. Tell him you love him and want to marry him and have his babies."

"I don't love him. Do I?"

I certainly like Andrew. He makes me laugh, for starters. And he shares my love of reading. He's also thoughtful and kind, and he's always bringing me food, usually something delicious that he's made himself. And seeing the way he does so much for his mom, his aunts, and his Gran, I know that he cares deeply for the people in his life. But am I in love with him?

"Yes, you do. You've been obsessed with him since you met him, and watching the two of you 'work' in the library this summer has honestly been a little gross. The two of you are like walking heart-eye emojis when you're in the same space." Jaclyn shudders and makes a barfing sound.

"Jaclyn has a point," Kylie chimes in. "I know I was skeptical, but seeing the two of you together lately, I don't think there's much chance Andrew's going to break your heart. But you'll break his if you move to D.C."

I'm speechless. Jaclyn and Kylie rarely agreed on anything, and for them to agree on this. Well. It's rarer than a snowstorm in Florida.

Jaclyn waves a hand in front of my face. "You ok?"

She turns to Kylie, "I think you broke her."

"She's just processing." Kylie squeezes my hand.

I blink at my friends. I'm still thinking about what they've just said, and the more I think about it, the more I realize that I *am* in love with Andrew.

"I'm in love with Andrew." Saying the words out loud makes it more real.

"Yes, it's been established." Jaclyn smirks.

"But he won't respond to my messages, so what does it matter? I'm in love with him, but after the way things went at the hospital, he's clearly not in love with me."

Jaclyn snorts. "If that man isn't in love with you, then I'll let Kylie pick the next five places we go for lunch."

I gape at my friend. Jaclyn usually haaaaates the restaurants Kylie picks.

Kylie gives me an empathetic look. "I think Jaclyn's right. He's in love with you, but he probably hasn't realized it's mutual because you haven't communicated that to him."

"For sure. And we'll help win him back for you." Jaclyn smiles at me, but it's the kind of smile one expects from an evil villain.

We spend the rest of lunch strategizing. As I listen to my friends make wild suggestions about everything I should do to win back my boyfriend, my heart warms. I know in my very core that Jaclyn is right. Not only am I in love with Andrew, but taking the job at Cooke is absolutely the right choice. I wouldn't trade my friendship with Jaclyn and Kylie for anything—even the extra take-home pay that McDowell is offering.

It turns out that Jaclyn's "minor spying" back when she and Andrew were spending all their time together included copying phone numbers for a variety of people in his contact list.

"I just did it in case he had an emergency, and winning him back for Evie seems like a justifiable emergency to me," she says.

I ignore the ethics of how Jaclyn got Ruth Brandt's phone number and thank my friend for sharing it with me.

When I call her to explain the situation, Andrew's mother just asks what I need her to do, which is how I've ended up spending Saturday afternoon with Ruth and her sisters. The afternoon has been fun, despite the butterflies in my stomach as I anticipate Andrew's arrival at his mother's house.

I'm in the kitchen with Ruth, Phoebe, and Tabitha when we hear the front door open. The Brandt women erupt into a frenzy of excitement, tossing pots and pans into the sink and generally causing a ruckus.

"Mom?" Andrew calls from the front of the house.

I turn to see Ruth ushering Phoebe and Tabitha out the back door, although I can tell they want to stay and watch what's about to happen. Finally pushing her giggling sisters out of the house, Ruth comes to stand by me and gives me a reassuring look just as the kitchen door opens and Andrew walks in, looking at his phone.

"What was it that you needed..." Andrew trails off as he looks up and notices me standing in the kitchen with his mother.

My breath catches at the sight of him. He's gotten even scruffier in the past few days. His beard looks wild and unruly, and he has dark circles under his eyes. I resist the urge to run to him and hold him. I can't read his expression, but there's a certain melancholy about him, like the way it feels to listen to Taylor Swift's *folklore* on repeat.

"I think you two have some things to discuss," Ruth says with all the authority of a mother of an adult son. As she leaves the room, she squeezes her son's arm and smiles at him.

We stare at each other, neither one of us moving. The air in the kitchen feels thick, suffocating almost, and it's not from the cooking steam that the Brandt women and I have generated.

Finally, Andrew clears his throat. "What are you doing

here?"

I can hear the hurt in his voice, but I know that what I have to say to him will ease the hurt. Or at least I hope it will. If it's not too late.

"Making chicken and noodles."

"Making chicken and noodles?"

"Your mom and aunts helped me." I take a halting step closer to Andrew.

"But what are you doing here?"

I take a step back because that's not hurt in his voice anymore. He sounds angry.

"Trying to win you back," I say with a slight wobble to my voice.

"Trying to win me back? Look, Evie." Andrew steps further away from me. He pinches the bridge of his nose and closes his eyes, sighing. "I don't think this relationship is going to work out."

His words hit me with a force that almost makes me stumble. I knew this reaction was a possibility, but I didn't anticipate the sting of hearing Andrew actually suggest we break up.

I stand up straighter and take two steps closer to Andrew. "No."

"No?" He's clearly taken aback by my response.

"No, I think you're wrong."

"Evie, don't make this harder than it has to be. You already broke my heart."

Something inside me crumples at the look on Andrew's face. I start to speak, but the words catch in my throat.

"Dammit!" Andrew slams his hand against the side of the refrigerator. "This is why I haven't been in the library since the hospital. I knew seeing you would make me lose my resolve."

"Wha-what do you mean?"

"You said we'd make the decision together. That if you got the offer from McDowell, we'd figure it out. But then you turned around and talked to the Mikes without talking to me first. I don't want to be with someone who goes behind my back like that."

"Oh." I start to say more, but Andrew cuts me off.

"No, please wait. I have to say this. I can't keep pretending I'm ok with you taking that job, Evie. I tried really hard not to fall in love with you, but I think by the time you kissed me on the way home from D.C. it was already too late. And the fact that I love you is why I can't keep seeing you. Because you hurt me by making that decision without me, and I know it's not fair to you because you've got the chance at a fantastic career move." Andrew hangs his head.

"You love me?" Hope blooms in my heart.

"Yes. Of course I do."

I take another cautious step closer to him and smile.

"What?" Andrew looks like he wants to take another step back, but he stays where he is, close enough that I could put my arms around him if I wanted to. And I want to, but I need to tell him first, need to see his reaction.

"I love you, too, Andrew." I reach a tentative hand toward him.

"But you're leaving," he breathes out.

I shake my head. "No."

"No?"

"No."

"But the McDowell offer…"

"I turned them down."

"But it was such a good opportunity for you. You didn't turn it down because of me, did you?"

I shake my head and smile again. "The Mikes made me a better offer. You're looking at the new Teaching and Learning Librarian. Dobson agreed with me that it made sense for the Center for Teaching and Learning to be a sub-department of the library to help with our staffing problems. I was going to tell you at the restaurant, but then you got the call about your grandmother, and there wasn't a good chance."

"But you were so excited about McDowell."

"I was, but then I got the weirdest email from them." I pull out my phone and show him the email string.

He looks horrified. "That's completely inappropriate for them to send that to you."

"You were right. You tried to warn me in D.C. about all the red flags with McDowell. I should have listened." I look straight into Andrew's eyes. He's studying me, searching my face.

We stand that way—breathing, staring, questioning—until Andrew finally takes a step back, but this time it doesn't feel like he's putting distance between us. He leans against the counter, takes a deep breath, and closes his eyes.

When he opens them, I can see a mixture of hope and trepidation in them.

"So you're not leaving?"

"No."

Andrew reaches for my hand. "And you don't mind that I fell in love with you?"

"No, I don't mind." I'm standing fully in front of him now, and he takes my other hand. "I don't mind at all because I fell in love with you, too."

He pulls me to him and wraps his arms around me. His lips touch mine, and my shoulders relax as the sensation of the kiss washes over me.

Andrew ends the kiss, pulling away slightly with a question on his face.

"You never told me why you were here, at my mom's house."

"Oh." I grin. "I came here to set up a grand gesture for you."

Andrew raises an eyebrow. "I should have known my romance-loving girlfriend would have to have a grand gesture."

I stick my tongue out at him, but I'm glad we're back to him teasing me.

"So what was the grand gesture?"

I indicate the pot of chicken and noodles on the stove. "I learned how to spatchcock a chicken for you."

Andrew lets out a choked laugh. He's still laughing when I stand up on my tiptoes and kiss him the way he deserves to be kissed. With love.

EPILOGUE

One Year Later

"I'm pleased to introduce for the first time Andrew and Evie Watson-Brandt. Everyone raise your glasses to the happy couple!" The crowd under the reception tent erupts into applause as we enter from beside the stage. The green space in the center of campus has been transformed for the evening into a wedding venue, complete with a makeshift dance floor and twinkle lights.

We invited the entire campus—faculty, staff, and students—and although it's summer, a lot of people showed up to celebrate with us. It's a little disorienting to see all my coworkers mingling with the gaggle of Watson cousins who have come to Sapling Grove for the wedding. All of the Mikes (Dobson, Pearce, Mike Stewart from Advancement AND Mike Radford from Student Success) showed up. Even the new English professor, Sebastian Thacker, is here.

After the inquiry into John's behavior last summer, John left Cooke. The rumor is that he was fired, although I suspect he probably saw the writing on the wall and left out of anger. Either way, he is out of my life. Sebastian was hired a few months later and is already one of my favorite people on campus, although I can't say the same for Kylie. She won't say why, but his presence makes her bristle.

I look around the reception tent and take everything in. I laugh as I notice that Andrew's Gran is shamelessly flirting with Jaclyn's friend Rhys at the bar. I catch sight of Jaclyn sitting at a table glaring at her mother.

Jaclyn looks stunning in her bridesmaid outfit. I wanted all my bridesmaids to be comfortable, so I picked a color scheme and had them pick their own outfits. Jaclyn's is a flowing blue shirt that she's paired with satiny black pants. When she told me about them, she grinned mischievously and said, "They're actually stretchy pants."

I wave at her, and she waves back. She makes a face behind her mom when she turns to see who Jaclyn's waving to. I try to signal to her to see if she needs an escape, but she just rolls her eyes and shrugs. Jaclyn's not the type who likes to be rescued.

I turn back to watch Gran flirt with Rhys some more. The past year has been difficult for Andrew's family after Gran's stroke last summer, but Gran has slowly improved. It turns out that Gran and I have the same taste in Regency romance novels, so I've started spending a lot of time reading with Gran, much to Andrew's mock horror and his aunts' great amusement.

Andrew's family has welcomed me into their lives with open arms and lots of love. It's almost like being back home with my bevy of cousins. But the Brandt Biddies are a force to be reckoned with. Planning the wedding has been a bit of a comedy of errors, thanks in no small part to Andrew's well-meaning aunts. Thankfully, I haven't let them mess with the spreadsheet I made to keep the wedding planning on track. Andrew didn't even want to touch it, for fear he'd break one of my formulas.

Planning a wedding and starting a new job in the same year has been an undertaking, but I'm glad I had Kylie and Jaclyn to help me with both things. Even though John left, I continued having panic attacks for a few months after his departure. I asked about medication after I had one during a presentation I was giving at a faculty meeting. It's taken a few tries to get the dosage right, but at this point I haven't had an attack in months.

I hit the ground running with my new position, and I've already made a lot of headway with the faculty peer-reviewer program I've started. Enough faculty signed up in the first call for participants that we needed a waitlist. Now things are going well enough that some of the faculty who joined the program at the beginning are starting to mentor new participants.

On the library side of my job, things are going fantastically, as well. The insurance company ended up paying for the repairs to the building after the flood last summer, and there was enough to cover the cost of replacing most of the books. June and I presented a workshop for other librarians in the area about our response to the flood, and we've had a request from the state library association for a larger presentation at their conference next spring.

I'm admiring the way my husband's suit clings to him in all the right places when I hear a glass tinkling over the microphone by the musicians. Andrew opted for a dark blue suit that somehow makes him look even more like Chris Evans than usual. It is the perfect contrast to the off-white summer A-line dress that I'm wearing.

I turn to see Kylie calling for everyone's attention.

"Thank you all for coming tonight," Kylie says. "I'm so excited for Evie and Andrew and their new life together."

She pauses while the crowd cheers and claps. When they finish, she continues, "I have to admit, when Evie first told me that she and Andrew had started seeing each other, I was skeptical. I'm very protective of Evie. She's like a sister to me. But seeing these two together, I know I don't have to worry about Evie. Andrew adores her. I can see it in the way he looks at her and the way he treats her. I'm so glad I was wrong about him."

"And if he ever hurts her, Kylie and I will come for him!" Jaclyn shouts from the crowd.

Kylie rolls her eyes. "Anyway. Evie, I'm so happy for you. May you and Andrew have a long and happy life together! To Evie and Andrew!" Kylie raises her glass, and the rest of the crowd lifts their glasses in a toast.

I wipe the tears from my eyes that pooled during Kylie's

toast. Andrew leans over and kisses me gently. "You ok?"

I smile. "Yeah. Just really happy."

Andrew smiles and kisses me again. A few more people get up to make toasts. Phoebe and Tabitha even attempt a duet, which is more funny than sweet. I love every minute of it.

After the toasts, the Cooke jazz band plays, and Andrew leads me to the dance floor. He puts one hand on my waist and takes my hand in his other one. I slide my free hand onto Andrew's shoulder. I lean my face against his chest. I can feel his heartbeat. I breathe deeply, taking in that spicy, clean scent I've come to associate with Andrew.

"Is that Jaclyn?" Andrew nudges me.

I look up to see him squinting at a spot beyond the glow from the tent. He points toward a tree just outside the tent.

I peer in the direction he's pointed. "I think so? Is she kissing someone?"

"Yep, definitely. I think it's her friend Rhys."

I laugh. "Oh, that makes sense. She brought him as her date to keep her mom from trying to set her up with someone. I didn't think their agreement involved making out, though."

Andrew snickers. "I can't wait to hear how that ended up happening, then."

The two of us devolve into giggles, both slightly tipsy from the champagne we've been drinking but also from the joy of the evening.

Andrew gazes at me with warmth in his eyes. "You do realize we've been breaking the rules tonight?" he asks with a sly grin.

"What rules?" I'm puzzled.

"Rule number one: no kissing at work."

I laugh. "I don't care about the rules anymore."

"No? Too bad. I like your rules." He pulls me against him, and I feel a thrill at his implication.

"I propose a new rule, then." I flash him a wicked grin, which he returns with an equally wicked grin of his own. I stand on my tiptoes and whisper into Andrew's ear, "The new rule is this: I will tell you I love you every day if you'll do the same for me."

I ease myself back down and look up at Andrew, suddenly nervous at what his response will be. Andrew's eyes search mine, and my face flames at how corny the rule sounds.

"I think I can handle that," he says. Then he takes my face in his hands and looks me straight in the eye. "I love you."

"I love you, too."

He leans down and brushes his lips against mine. I tilt my head and kiss him back. Neither of us acknowledge the cheer from the crowd of wedding-goers around us. As our kiss ends, Andrew pulls me closer into his arms. I sigh and lean into his embrace.

Acknowledgments

I've always felt that the best way for humans to do anything is in the context of a community, and writing this book has showed me that this is true no matter what we're doing. I certainly couldn't have written, edited, formatted, or marketed this book without my community both here at home and online.

Thanks to BJ for not laughing when I said I wanted to write a romance novel and for making space in our lives to make sure I could. And for not getting mad when the hero wasn't a dashing Occupational Therapist.

Thanks to S. and A. for not reading what your mom was writing. You can read what you want. Except this book.

Thanks to Alexander, Jennifer, and Keri-Lynn for being the best part of working at the same place. This book is a love letter to all the laughter and tears we've shared. I am so glad to have you all.

Thanks to Hilary for helping shape this story and telling me I needed a plot, not just a bunch of scenes. For all the weekend text conversations and copy editing. For reading the whole thing twice. This book would not exist without you.

Thanks to the Bravo Bunch for all the support and the memes and the friendship. I don't know what I would do without you. You are the best friends the internet has ever given me.

Thanks to some really great beta readers: Ashley S., Natalie, Lindsay, Hannah, Kristi, Lauren, Steph, Sadie, and Sher. And to Marisa for hopping on the phone with me and commiserating about publishing and the world in general.

Thanks to Anna, Ashley E., Shelley, Ashley C., and Bailey for your support and friendship.

Thanks to the writing community on Threads for all the advice and encouragement.

And thank YOU, dear readers, for picking up this book. I hope you have enjoyed your time in Sapling Grove!

About the Author

Dawn Banks is an academic librarian and romance author. When she is not writing, she is reading, although she still hasn't found the pirate romance of her dreams. She believes cats should be named after classic literary characters. Dawn lives in Tennessee with her husband, kids, and two cats (Eowyn and Peaseblossom).

Find out about upcoming books:
Website: www.dawnbankswriter.com
Instagram & Threads: @dawnbankswriter